SUN BOY

Center Point
Large Print

Also by Robert J. Steelman and available from Center Point Large Print:

The Great Yellowstone Steamboat Race
The Fox Dancer

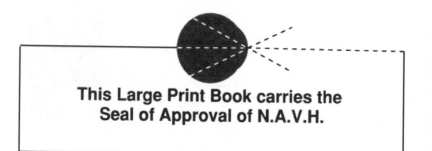

This Large Print Book carries the Seal of Approval of N.A.V.H.

SUN BOY

Robert J. Steelman

CENTER POINT LARGE PRINT
THORNDIKE, MAINE

The text of this Large Print edition is unabridged.
In other aspects, this book may vary
from the original edition.
Printed in the United States of America
on permanent paper.
Set in 16-point Times New Roman type.

ISBN: 978-1-68324-355-7 (hardcover)
ISBN: 978-1-68324-359-5 (paperback)

Library of Congress Cataloging-in-Publication Data

Names: Steelman, Robert J., author.
Title: Sun boy / Robert J. Steelman.
Description: Center Point Large Print edition. | Thorndike, Maine :
Center Point Large Print, 2017.
Identifiers: LCCN 2017000418| ISBN 9781683243557 (hardcover :
alk. paper) | ISBN 9781683243595 (pbk. : alk. paper)
Subjects: LCSH: Large type books. | GSAFD: Western stories.
Classification: LCC PS3569.T33847 S86 2017 | DDC 813/.54—dc23
LC record available at https://lccn.loc.gov/2017000418

"The trails were thick with travelers, and white contacts were increasing. The Kiowas turned their fury on those who tried to cross the southern Plains, and earned their reputation as being the most predatory and bloodthirsty of all the prairie tribes. It was said they killed more white men in proportion to their numbers than any other tribe."

MILDRED P. MAYHALL
The Kiowas
UNIVERSITY OF OKLAHOMA PRESS
NORMAN, OKLAHOMA, 1962

"I partook of the rude cheer of a hostile [Kiowa] chief, rendered propitious by his ideas of the sacred rites of hospitality. After breakfast in White Wolf's lodge, I was soon *en route* for the camp of my destination, accompanied by the wife and daughter of 'mine host', who went with me for several miles, in order to answer the challenges of the several Comanche pony herders whom I would have to pass. Afterwards they pointed out Kicking Bird's camp to me, and left me to pursue my journey alone.

"What a challenge is here for civilized man! A rude chief of an unfriendly tribe of savages, whose hand is skilled in the shedding of blood, manifesting such a sense of the sacredness of the rites of hospitality, as not only to receive and entertain one whom he regarded as an enemy, but, after having done this, set him on his right road in peace!"

THOMAS C. BATTEY
The Life and Adventures of a Quaker Among the Indians
BOSTON, MASS., 1876

SUN BOY

CHAPTER ONE

It was raining on Fort Sill. Sporadic June drizzle soaked the aimless collection of raw-wood sheds, condemned tentage, adobe shacks, and brush huts that lately had been called Camp Wichita. Now, supplied over a new corduroy road from Fort Arbuckle, the post was beginning to take on form and meaning, a hopeful bulwark against the Kiowas, who were raiding the Red River settlers.

Looking calculatingly at Rainbolt, the *comanchero* took out a deck of greasy cards and dealt two hands on the issue blanket covering his straw pallet. In the mill only until his Jacksboro lawyer could get him out on a writ, old Coogan gestured to his guardhouse companion.

"How about a little coon-can?"

Philip Rainbolt was tall and lean, almost lanky, with pale blue eyes and a sweeping and untrimmed blond mustache of the type favored by Eighth Cavalry troopers.

"I said," Coogan insisted, "how about a little game of coon-can, if you ain't too ree-fined to associate with a raggle-tail old bastard like me?"

There was about Rainbolt a shabby aristocracy strange in a millbird, a way of keeping himself private and apart, a manner of pausing long before

9

speaking, then talking like a schoolmaster. It annoyed Ike Coogan.

"Ain't you interested in nothin'?" Ike demanded.

Rainbolt turned his head and looked at the comanchero, a flat and passionless gaze that made Ike shift uneasily and scratch at a crust of dirt encircling an unwashed wrist. Finally, with an air of decision made, Rainbolt sat down cross-legged opposite Coogan and picked up his cards.

"I am," he admitted. "I'm interested in getting out of here." Ike hooted cheerfully. "Then you better stop assaulting sergeants!"

The blond man thoughtfully arranged his cards. "That's a sight better than trading guns and liquor to Indians for stolen horses and cattle, you smelly old goat."

"Why, sonny"—Ike grinned—"you're just a busted-ass yellow-leg private goin' to get six months on the rockpile! Me—I'm a prominent local businessman!" Leering at Rainbolt, he snatched up a trick. "You make thirteen dollars a month, when you ain't forfeited it for striking your betters, but I got ten thousand dollars put away in an iron box! *Now* who's the pot that's callin' the kettle black!"

"You're a dirty crook," Rainbolt said evenly, "and ought to be hanged."

"Hee, hee!" Coogan snickered. Sly, peering over his cards with small malevolent eyes, he looked at Rainbolt. "Though if I was you, bucko, I wouldn't fret too much. A handsome young stud ain't goin' to stay in the mill too long, not with Major Cameron's wife prinkin' round to bring him books and sugar-bits and yaller posies in a pickle-jar!"

For a big man, the cavalryman moved quickly. The loose-jointed frame snapped together in purposeful movement. One red-knuckled hand caught Coogan's jacket in a grasp that pinned the old man against the adobe wall, the greasy buckskin so taut it made the comanchero's eyes pop.

"Don't speak of her!" Rainbolt blurted. "Don't say her name!"

Ike tried to nod, but his grizzled head was pressed so tight against the wall he could not move. Eyes rolled up in their sockets, his face became red as a turkey's wattles. Finally, breathing hard, Rainbolt relaxed his grip and threw the old man from him.

"Don't mention her again!" he warned. "Don't say her name. Do you hear me?"

Rubbing his throat, Coogan slumped against the scaling wall. When he spoke, the sound was like the rustling of old cornstalks in the wind. "I hear you." He spat. "No need to get violent!"

"I'm sorry I was rough with you, but—"

"Hee, hee!" Ike quavered. He gathered up his cards. "No offense meant, and none took, either."

After that, he watched Rainbolt carefully, and forebore to cheat.

The rain drizzled on, splashing into the cell, making black earth-smelling stains on the wall, running down into formless puddles that sank into the pounded earthen floor. After the card game Coogan took a nap, whiskers ruffling in and out with deep and regular breathing. Rainbolt could hear the imprisoned Kiowas moving about in their cells down the hallway, between him and the little anteroom where Sergeant Huckabee, the jailer, sat at a rough deal table reading his Bible.

The Kiowas were fond of the tin cans Army peas came in. They traded furs and hides for the shiny metal so they could fashion elaborate scrolls and twists and plaques to decorate the trailing fringes of their knee-high moccasins. When a Kiowa moved, Rainbolt thought fancifully, he moved to music—a sparkle of melody as the bits of metal clinked and tinkled. That was the way the lonely Rainbolt knew they were moving about, padding back and forth, restless and impatient, almost as if waiting for something.

From time to time, Coogan had called out to them, exchanging comments. The comanchero was fluent in their language, and knew their names: Wolf Sleeves, Milky Way, Won't Listen, Stone Teeth. "These fellers," he told Rainbolt, "are all *onde*—high muckety-mucks." They had been Satank's escort when the fierce old Kiowa warrior had come in to Fort Sill to parley. Now the general had seized Satank, and they were going to take him to Jacksboro, the Thirteenth Judicial District Court, for trial.

In the gathering dust Rainbolt heard "Retreat." Sergeant Huckabee shoved through the bars their evening meal: sour beef and Swiss canned peas in a glutinous stew, hard bread, suet "butter," tin cups of coffee.

Coogan turned up his nose. "Don't give me none of that slop!" he warned. Tomorrow, the old man boasted, he would dine on terrapin stew washed down with French wine in Jacksboro. So Rainbolt ate both portions, and was grateful. Since he had been a little boy at Nine-Mile Plantation, so long ago, he had had a big appetite, though his frame had always been spare and lank.

In the evening a lantern flickered in the hallway, casting staggering images across the walls of their cell. She was there. Huckabee, nervous, held the lantern high for her. She had charmed the jailer, too, as she had charmed so many others.

"You shouldn't be here," Rainbolt complained.

Anxious to please, she held out a copy of the Jacksboro *Pioneer and Gazette*. "I knew you would want something to read."

Huckabee, keeping an eye out for the Officer of the Day, was pacing the hallway with the smoking lantern. In the gloom Rainbolt could not see her face, but did not have to. Ellen Cameron was a beautiful woman—tall and regal, with a sweeping pompadour the dark mahogany of a fox's brush.

13

Delicate fine-boned features were modeled like a cameo. Altogether, Philip Rainbolt thought, too fine a figure of a woman for a muddy frontier outpost. Perhaps that had been the trouble.

"Thanks." He took the newspaper and turned away. But she held out her hand through the bars and touched him. The brush of her fingers made him tremble.

"Philip?"

"Yes."

"The enlisted men's garden is coming along fine. I—I thought you'd want to know." Pleased, she showed him a blister on her finger. "I hoed awhile out there today, to help. There's lettuce, already, and radishes, and the carrots are showing green."

"That's nice," he murmured.

"And Private Neilsen—he's the Swede with the missing front teeth, you remember—he read a whole page from the primer today without a mistake. You'd have been proud of him!"

Huckabee touched her sleeve then, saying hoarsely, "I can't let you stay any longer, ma'am! There'll be trouble."

Crossly, she demanded, "Philip, why won't you look at me?"

He didn't answer, only kept his head turned toward the shadows in the cell. Finally she sighed, and Huckabee led her away. Rainbolt heard the light tap of her slippers beside the leathern shuffle of the jailer's boots; then she was gone. All that remained was a light springlike fragrance—a fragile scent rising above the guardhouse stink of unwashed bodies, stale tobacco, wormy beef—hovering above it as foam rides the stronger current below.

Silent and impassive, Ike Coogan had been watching the two of them. Now, from some inner recess in his clothing, he took a stub of candle and lit it. Prisoners in the guardhouse were routinely searched, deprived of anything that might make their stay bearable. But Ike Coogan was a special case. They had let him keep money, tobacco, cards, all sorts of things. And tomorrow the comanchero's money would buy him other privileges. Coogan would be free; Philip Rainbolt on his way to the military prison at Fort Leavenworth with six months at hard labor for striking Sergeant Kruger. It was a queer world.

"Little coon-can?" Ike suggested.

He did not mention Rainbolt's visitor.

All that night the Kiowas prowled, making Rainbolt think of animals in a cage. The music of their bells decorated the night; it was always there, so he was not sure whether he was asleep or awake. Occasionally they spoke to each other in low tones. Their speech was quiet and guttural, like falling water heard from a distance. Ike knew the Kiowas well, and spent the tedious night explaining Kiowa territory and customs.

"Ain't no tougher fighters, I'd say. Man for man, Kiowas has killed more white men than any other tribe." He showed Rainbolt the ritual sign for *Kiowa:* gnarled right hand, back down, fingers curled, near his withered cheek, then making a rotary motion. "Allus cuts off their hair on the right side."

"Why?" Rainbolt asked drowsily.

" 'Cause that's the side they aims a rifle from, or a bow, and that's what they're adoin', mostly—shooting at somebody or something." The old man took a plug of contraband tobacco from his dirty buckskins and offered Rainbolt a bite. When he refused, Ike bit off a chunk and went on.

"I ain't never seen anything a Kiowa was afraid of, 'cept maybe a Tonk."

"A what?"

"Tonkawa." Ike put the Wedding Cake away. "A Kiowa hates a Tonk worse 'n anything. Tonks paints their faces blue, and eats people."

"What?" Rainbolt was startled.

Ike nodded vigorously. "They're cannibals. Like human flesh better 'n horse or beef or pig meat. I guess that's why Kiowas hates Tonks so. Think it ain't civilized to eat people." Ike guffawed, slapping a skinny thigh. "Hee, hee! As if a Kiowa was civilized hisself!"

The old man maundered on and on with his

tales while Rainbolt drifted into an uneasy sleep. The last thing he remembered was the sound of Kiowa bells, tiny bells.

In the morning he woke stiff and sore, covered with fleabites. Ike Coogan had finally run down. The old man slept, leaning against the wall, mouth open, snoring. In spite of himself, Rainbolt felt a grudging affection for Coogan. *Blue-faced cannibals!* He grinned painfully, and stretched.

The morning was gray and dreary. The air smelled of mud, of horse droppings, of moldy canvas, and frying meat from the mess hall nearby. Before regimental headquarters stood a canvas-topped Army wagon and a team of four mules whose hoofs were enormous balls of Indian Territory mud. There was a mounted escort, too; this was the morning they were taking old Satank to trial in Jacksboro.

Coogan snuffled, wheezed, and rose painfully to join Rainbolt at the window. Around the blue wagon hovered a feeling of approaching incident so strong that it silenced even the garrulous old comanchero. Down the hallway the Kiowas ceased their pacing. From their cells the Indians could not see the blue wagon, the headquarters porch, the flag drooping from the peeled jack pine staff. But they knew; they knew *something.*

"Do you feel it?" Rainbolt whispered.

He remembered a very old oak-framed picture on the parlor wall at Nine-Mile Plantation, an

17

ancient scene at a Greek temple. The painting or engraving or whatever it was had faded over the years to a murky brown, but there was about it the same feeling: figures, waiting figures, suspended in a mysterious haze, looking toward a columned temple with watchful eyes. The picture belonged to his Grandfather Penrose, who had helped Habersham seize the British powder magazine at Savannah in 1775.

"Feel it?" Ike wheezed. "Some feels it, yes, but I *smell* it. Trouble, I smell. Comin' fast, like a turpentined cat!"

A horse neighed impatiently, lifting a muddy hoof and then plunging it down into a puddle, splattering a nearby heavily armed guard, who cursed.

The sun hovered closely behind the clouds, giving off a dank and moldy warmth. The light bathing the scene was harsh and luminous. Suddenly there was a commotion on the porch of Regimental Headquarters. The general commanding the Department of the Missouri stepped out, boots ringing hard on the porch and spurs jingling. After him came the Kiowa chief, Satank, wrapped in a robe of gray wolfskin and looking fiercely about, an old eagle caught in a trap.

His robe was lined with red flannel, belted about with an elkskin sash, and heavily ornamented with scalps. "No squaws or whites!" he had told the general with some heat. "Only Mexicans and

Tonks!" But it had done him no good. Suspected of having led a recent raid on the Red River settlers, they were taking him to Jacksboro anyway.

A corporal motioned toward the blue wagon, and another man offered the old warrior a leg up. Satank only scowled at them, refusing to move. In an ancient crooning voice he began to sing.

Ike Coogan made a surprised croaking sound. "Look *out!*" he muttered. "He's singin' his death song!"

"What?"

"Look out, now!" Ike warned.

With a sudden gesture Satank whipped off the elkskin sash and threw it to the ground before him in a gesture of defiance. He tossed the robe aside to stand naked in the hard light, a whiplike supple man in spite of his years.

Alarmed, the corporal raised his carbine. But Satank, howling like a demon, grabbed the weapon. For a moment the two struggled. Then the frightened soldier broke away and ran.

Satank tried to lever a shell into the chamber of the Spencer, but the action jammed, as the Spencer action often did. Working madly at the lever, a solitary mud-spattered figure, Satank crouched, pointing the useless gun menacingly. The wavering barrel came to rest on the neatly tailored blue breast of the general. But at that moment a dozen shots rang out.

From all quarters—from the porch, from the mounted column, even from the roof of the stables where marksmen had been stationed against trouble—muzzles flashed, lead whined, clouds of powder smoke rolled damply into the air.

"They've finally done it," Ike murmured.

Old Satank slipped slowly, almost disdainfully, into the red mud. Alarmed, a magpie squawked and flapped away. Riddled with bullets, the old man swayed for a moment on his knees. He tried to clench his fist in a last gesture of defiance. Then he toppled headlong into the mire, looking incredibly small and childlike.

A great sigh rose from the imprisoned Kiowas—Milky Way, Stone Teeth, the rest. In some animal way they knew what had happened, and they keened with a high-pitched grief that sent shivers down Rainbolt's spine. Ike Coogan, staring unbelievingly through the bars, swallowed hard. "They wasn't goin' to take *him* to no white man's trial," he muttered. "Oh, no—not old Satank!" Biting off a fresh chew of Wedding Cake, the comanchero shook his head in awe. "By God, savages or not, sometimes you got to admire 'em!"

The tension was gone, draining swiftly from the scene as grain spills from a rent sack. The mounted column was dismissed, the blue wagon lumbered back to the stables. A detail plucked the slight body from the mud and rolled it in a blanket, dragging it toward the post hospital. Insisting he had been promised the scalp by Satank himself, a Caddo scout tagged after the body, knife fluttering. But no one listened. The two soldiers kept dragging the body, dead heels making parallel grooves in the wet earth.

"This," Ike muttered, "is a day to remember, Philip Rainbolt or whatever your name is. The eighth day of June, eighteen hunnerd and seventy-one. From now on the Red River's gonna run actual red with blood!"

Late in the afternoon, after a long ride from Jacksboro, Coogan's lawyer arrived. He was a florid-faced man in a flowered waistcoat, wise in the ways of the *habeas corpus.*

" 'Bout time you got here!" Coogan complained.

Before the comanchero left, he drew Rainbolt aside, pressing something into his hand while the Officer of the Day wearily examined the writ. "Here!" Ike muttered. "Take this!"

Rainbolt looked down in surprise at the old Green River knife. The blade had been honed so many times it was by now only a thin sliver of steel.

"Put it away, quick!" Ike hissed. "Don't go causin' me no trouble, now! Lawyers is expensive!"

"But—"

Ike clasped his arm. "Maybe," he muttered, "I

21

seen somethin' in you. And a man never knows when he can use a good knife."

Afterward, Rainbolt was never sure why he had accepted the knife. He slumped on his pallet, feeling it hard and cold under the waistband of his breeches. Escape, somehow? But he was already in enough trouble—six months in Leavenworth for striking Kruger. That was bad enough, but they *hanged* people for using knives!

Absently, he reached inside his shirt, touching the warmth of the bone handle. He thought about yelling for Sergeant Huckabee, turning the weapon over to him with the story that Ike had accidentally left it behind. But he didn't, and then Ellen Cameron was there, smiling at him through the bars.

He got unwillingly up and stood near her, not too near, with face averted.

"I told you," he said. "I don't want to see you again, Mrs. Cameron."

"Ellen," she pouted. "You always called me Ellen, before."

Huckabee hovered near her with his lantern. "Ma'am—" he whispered.

"I'll talk to Hugh," Ellen pleaded. When Rainbolt did not answer, she tried to reach his hand through the bars. "Maybe something can still be done, Philip," she said. "I have some influence with the general. Before he leaves I can—"

"No," he said.

She was miserable, in one of her quick changes of mood. "After all, it was my fault as much as yours. I see that now, and I'm sorry."

"Go away!" he said through tight lips. "Please, Ellen, there's nothing more to be said, or done!"

She was not used to being rebuffed by a man. Perhaps that had been part of the trouble, too. Angry, she stamped her foot. "All right, then, damn you! If that's all you've got to say to me, after—after—"

"Please, ma'am!" Huckabee begged. "I'll get into trouble!"

"It's all right!" Ellen Cameron snapped. For a visit to the mill she had thrown a cloak hastily over her shirtwaist and balmoral skirt; Rainbolt suspected that Major Cameron was busy where a coal-oil lamp burned late in regimental head-quarters. Now Ellen pulled the cloak tightly about her and looked at Rainbolt with mingled anger and frustration. "It's all right, Sergeant," she repeated. "I was just going. There's—there's nothing here to—to detain me any longer!"

After Huckabee had escorted her out, he returned, mopping his brow.

"I'm not in favor of things like this," he said. "Officers' wives visiting prisoners is a little out of my line. But she *is* a handsome woman."

"She is, indeed," Rainbolt admitted. He added, "And always interested in the welfare of the enlisted men."

Huckabee gave a sharp glance. Then he said, "Well, it don't need to bother either of us much longer. In the morning you're to be took to the military prison." He made a tiny adjustment to the wick of the lantern. Then he said, carefully, "No need to speak of this to anybody. About *her* being here, I mean."

Huckabee had been kind to Rainbolt, offering to read him comforting passages from Isaiah.

"No," Rainbolt agreed. "No need. Certainly, no need."

The watches of the night were long. Rainbolt even thought he missed old Coogan, by now probably cutting up in a Jacksboro whorehouse or buying drinks for the crowd at some saloon. For a while he stood moodily at the barred window, watching the lights in the mess hall, the NCO club, Evans and Fisher's Trading Store. Finally the rain stopped. Through Medicine Bluff Gap a miasmic fog rolled up from the swollen waters of the creek. Winking out one by one, the pinpoints of yellow light vanished. Creeping vapors muffled all sound; tattoo sounded whisperlike against the clinging silence. He could not even hear the Kiowas moving about next door. There was only himself and the night, and far down the hallway the faint glow and coal-oil smell of Huckabee's lamp.

One mistake, Rainbolt thought, *and I have paid all this.*

Or were there many mistakes? Somehow, it seemed, he had never had the time to make a wise, unhurried decision. Events had always forced him into foolish choices. Was it that way with most men?

For a while he slept, huddled damply on the pallet. He dreamed he was back at Nine-Mile Plantation again, proud of the new gray uniform Wirtz Brothers of Macon had tailored for him. His cousins gathered close around, all laughing and joking. He remembered Lily Cantrell, from up the river, saying to him, "I'll just bet those Yankees break and run when they see how magnificent you look!"

Not knowing whether he was awake or asleep, he squirmed restlessly under the dirty blanket. Somehow, he could look down and see the smoke, confusion, mingled uniforms, and horses and fieldpieces jumbled together in brown and blue and gray and red—bright red, the color of blood.

I have paid, he thought. *But I will pay more.* There was a price to bad decisions.

From his strange vantage point, high above the river, he could see the damned fool running. Desperately he called out, trying to turn the fleeing figure. "Those men! Back, go back! Tell them—hurry!"

But the gray figure did not turn back. Like an elegant jointed doll it ran stiffly, mechanically, fearfully. The limbered battery was swallowed up in a tide of blue coats, and the gangling mechanical figure ran on and on.

Though it was much too late, someone kept calling, screaming. "Turn back! Oh, go back!" Then he awoke, damp, miserable, panting for breath, to realize it had been his own voice. Even now it seemed he could hear the echoes dying away in the hallway of the guardhouse. Uncertain, he sat quickly up, wondering if anyone had heard him. A face hovered near his own, a shadowy form. Still in the spell of the old and terrible dream, he heard a ring of keys clinking.

"Who's there?" he called.

Suddenly he realized he had been hearing the tiny bell sounds for a long time; the tinkle of metal from the long-fringed moccasins of the captive Kiowas. But now they were no longer captives. Tumblers clicked, the heavy iron door swung open.

"Free," a voice told him "Free. You."

The voice was heavy and musical, falling water heard from a long way off. The Kiowas had escaped; in their flight they had paused to free Philip Rainbolt.

He scrambled to his feet. Sudden circumstance again, forcing him so unfairly into decision! He stood for a while, uncertain, hearing the musical pattering as his liberators fled the corridor. Quickly the sound died and there was only the night, the silence, the faint glow from Huckabee's lantern.

Why had they released him—a white man? Cautious, he crept from the cell. Around the corner, the jailer's lamp burned low and smoky. A Bible lay on the table, a pipe, a torn-open packet of tobacco. But Huckabee was dead. The jailer lay in a black pool of blood, throat cut so deep the grizzled head lay at an odd angle. Through the open door Rainbolt heard a rustling of leaves, a rain-washed drumming on the earth, a fragment of voices. Picking up the lantern, he went outside.

The Kiowas were gone. In the oil-smelling light he could see patterns of unshod pony hoofs. Their own people must have come to rescue them. Silent as the fog, the Kiowas had come, murdered, reclaimed their own, and vanished into the June night, leaving no clue but a few muddy hoof-prints, already fading into the rain-soaked earth.

Listening, he stood for a long time. Still no sound, no alarm from the sentries. But Huckabee was dead, the guardhouse doors stood open. He was not dreaming. He went back in and set the lantern carefully on the table next to the Bible. A murmur of rain, small hissing from the lantern. Absently he closed the Bible on a worn leather marker and looked down at poor Huckabee, whiskers stiffly erect, pointing into the air, eyes questioning. Perhaps, Rainbolt thought, Coogan had spoken of him to the Kiowas, and that was why they had paused to release him. *Maybe,* Coogan had said, *I seen somethin' in you.* What?

Squatting beside the body, he willed himself not to make any rash decisions. In his dream he had implored the crazy fool to turn back. Now, again, here was a chance to turn back.

Along Soapsuds Row a dog barked, then was silent. The chill of river mist seeped through the open door of the guardhouse. The lantern flickered, brightened, then guttered out. For a moment there was a rim of fire around the unnourished wick; then that too pinched out in darkness.

Rainbolt made his decision. Taking the blanket from his cell and the packet of Lone Jack smoking tobacco from the table where Huckabee had sat, he fled into the night.

At the stone corral Brutus came to him at his whispered call, the star on the gelding's forehead glowing whitely. The mist seemed to roll and flow as Brutus stepped daintily toward him. The rest of the mounts crowded around, snuffling curiously, but he pushed them back and patted Brutus' sleek neck as he led him from the corral.

The farrier sergeant slept in the stables; it was too much of a risk to try for saddle and bridle. Instead, he swung himself carefully up on Brutus, feeling the long backbone poke unfamiliarly into his crotch. When the gelding seemed about to whinny at the strange bare-backed presence, Rainbolt leaned far forward and pinched the gelding's nostrils tight; Brutus subsided with a sigh.

Guiding the gelding with the pressure of his knees, he draped the dirty blanket about his head and started off toward Medicine Bluff Gap. When dawn came, gray and chill and veiled in mist, Philip Rainbolt was far south of the post, clipping off the miles at an easy canter. He was headed south, toward the Red River. That would be the direction the escaping Kiowas had gone.

CHAPTER TWO

Surrounding the new post was Whisky City, one of dozens which sprang up in the Territory like toadstools to satisfy a soldier's needs where the Army did not provide. The place had a population of several hundred, and there was at least one murder daily. Most of the inhabitants were drifters, gamblers, whores, and thieves. There were a round dozen saloons, including the Emerald, the Island Home, and Flora Kibbey's Dance House, and even more bordellos. By now there was even a French Millinery Shop, a dry-goods store, and a grocery where sardines, soda crackers, and canned peaches could be bought to vary the sowbelly, beans, and hardtack of the mess hall. There was even a doctor, to treat the typhus, gunshot wounds, and venereal disease that were endemic.

Hugh had forbidden her the town, but Ellen Cameron went anyway, borrowing the adjutant's buckboard and talking Private Neilsen into driving. The dreary post stifled her: the telegraph operator had gone insane, three children on Soapsuds Row were dead of the milk fever, and the surgeon's Mexican woman was eating dirt. A bonnet from the milliner's, or perhaps three yards of flowered gingham to make herself a pretty basque waist—Hugh would like that!

Private Neilsen, uneasy, did not talk much, though she plied him with questions.

"It was a great shame about Sergeant Huckabee, was it not?"

"Yes'm."

"Have they heard anything about Philip Rainbolt?"

"No'm."

"The Kiowas that escaped—no word about them either?"

"No'm."

"I hear," she said, "that the general is very angry they got away."

"Yes'm."

She sighed. "It's a shame. Philip—I mean Private Rainbolt—was such a good man. In six months he would have been free."

Neilsen spat delicately through the gap in his front teeth, and wiped his chin. "No'm. I mean—yes'm."

They were rolling into Whisky City when she spoke again.

"We shall miss him at the school, and at the enlisted men's garden, too. He had a green thumb, I think." Trying to catch Neilsen's eye, she leaned toward him. "Did you know much about him? I mean—did he ever say where he came from, or what his background was?"

Neilsen's Adam's apple bobbed once, uncertainly,

but he kept his blue eyes on the ears of the mules. "No'm. Never said much."

She pursed her lips. "Maybe he used to be a teacher. He was very good at teaching you and the other men to read."

"He were that," Neilsen admitted. That was as far as he would venture.

The rain had stopped, the sun shone brightly, but the streets of Whisky City were a morass. Teamsters flailed oxen, wagons were hub-deep in mud, men rolled beer barrels up a ramp of planks. Most of them did not know who she was, but there was about her a stateliness and composure that proved she was a lady, and somehow important. One man even tipped his cap; she acknowledged it with a gracious tilt of her head.

"Now you just wait here," she instructed Neilsen. "I'll only be a minute."

The dry-goods store had as yet a scanty stock, and that chosen for the gaudy tastes of the whores. But seeing Ellen was quality, the proprietor took down a bolt of China silk, with humming birds and grassy marshes woven in. It took her eye immediately.

"Will you please put it on Major Cameron's account?" she asked.

The proprietor looked dubious. "Ma'am," he said, "I—I—" He adjusted the pince-nez on his nose. "A cash policy has always been my practice, and—"

"My goodness!" Ellen interrupted. "Why, in San Francisco I always charged things at Gillette's and Fouquet's!"

Comparison to such establishments weakened the dry-goods man. "Well," he faltered, "I suppose I—I—"

"And I'll take—oh, say a half dozen—of those embroidered handkerchiefs," Ellen went on. "Now wrap them nicely, if you please. The first of the month send your account or whatever it is called to Major Cameron at the post."

As she was leaving the store with her purchases, a skinny old man in buckskins bumped into her. He muttered an oath. Then, flustered, he stammered an apology. As he backed away, bowing and scraping, she recognized him.

"Aren't you—I mean—weren't you—"

"Yes'm." He bobbed his head, holding the ancient felt hat in both hands. "That was me, all right. Ike Coogan, ma'am. But I'm out of jail strictly legal. Y'see, I hired this lawyer—"

She shook her head impatiently. "I don't mean that! I was wondering about Mr. Rainbolt. You were in the cell with him. I thought perhaps you knew—I mean *someone* knew—where he was, where he was going."

She had said it all very badly, but the old man did not appear to notice her discomfiture.

"Not likely!" he cackled. "No ma'am! He's probably near the Red River by now!"

"But what would he do there, in that wild country?"

Coogan grinned. "Guess he c'n take care of himself!"

She frowned. "They say he murdered Sergeant Huckabee, and turned the Kiowas loose."

The old man shook his head. "Ain't likely. Rainbolt didn't seem to me the killin' kind."

She chose her words carefully.

"What kind of man *did* he seem to you?"

Coogan scratched his stubbly chin. He looked at her, rather sharply and impudently, she thought.

"Well?"

"Why, ma'am," he said, "Rainbolt was a man with a lot of problems."

For a moment she considered that, shifting the parcels in her hand. "The military prison, you mean?"

"No'm. Something bigger 'n that, I reckon."

The way he was looking at her, she became uneasy. "I—I was just curious." She laughed. "He was a model soldier—did so much for his bunkmates, I guess they call them."

"Yes'm," Coogan said.

She thanked him, and turned away. But he called after her.

"Don't you worry, though, ma'am! He'll come out finer 'n frog hair!"

She laughed at that, shook her head, and went into the grocery store to buy Private Neilsen a packet of long-nine cigars for his trouble. Why should that ridiculous old man think she was concerned about a deserting soldier?

When they got back it was late afternoon. The sun lay great swatches of gold across the peaks of the Wichita Mountains to the north and west. She gave the protesting Neilsen the cigars, told him how nice he was to accommodate her. Hugh, thank God, was not home yet. She hurried into the raw-wood-smelling structure they now called home. Hugh need not know anything about the trip to Whisky City, at least not till she draped herself in the China silk and showed him how well it became her—red hair, milk-white flesh he was so fond of, the slender waist and high swell of bust. Hugh—she knew how to handle Hugh Cameron. But that evening he proved difficult. Stamping into the small parlor, he threw a wadded-up telegraph message against the wall and slumped into the velvet-upholstered *fauteuil* she had bought at Gillette's when they were stationed at the Presidio.

"Why, whatever's wrong, Hugh?" she asked, setting the table. The Tables of Organization provided an enlisted cook and an orderly for the post commander, but at this frontier post the Tables of Organization were a joke. Ellen had sent away the sullen cook, and they never had an orderly. Capable in most things, she cooked for Hugh on the wood-burning range of the lean-to kitchen, once even making a pie out of moistened soda crackers and commissary prunes.

Angry, he slumped in the armchair, brows knit in the sign she knew meant trouble. Hugh Cameron was Scottish, but a black Scot; a stocky compact man with a forked beard and restless, impatient eyes, given to brooding and sullen silences.

"*That's* what's wrong," he muttered, gesturing at the wadded message. "The general keeps sending me orders to find Stone Teeth and Milky Way and Won't Listen and the rest before they cause trouble! God, I've got B Company and C Company both scouring the countryside! All that's left is F Company, and the sick, lame, and lazy! If I reduce my force any more I'll endanger the post itself!" Gnawing a knuckle, he stared up at her from under the bushy brows. But she knew how to handle Hugh Cameron. Let him talk, let him get it out of his system; don't have opinions.

In the plain, unpainted room, the wind sighing through the cracks between the boards and a coyote crying dismally in the dusk, it seemed absurd to set the rough-carpentered table with lace cloth and embroidered serviettes, the massy silver her parents had given her, the good china. But she did, and went into the kitchen to bring fried side meat and gravy, biscuits and molasses, a dish of lettuce and onions and radishes from her own kitchen garden.

"What do you think, Ellen?" he asked, eyes

following her about the room. "I mean—what more can I do?"

She laughed. "Nothing more, I suppose! You're a good cavalry officer, they all know that. If anyone can do the job, you can."

They sat down, and Hugh said a short Presbyterian grace. He ate silently, at times looking covertly at her in a way that made her uneasy. *It's coming,* she thought. *Oh God, not another quarrel!* But he said nothing further, only folding his napkin and lighting the Argand lamp on the pilaster table to read a month-old San Francisco *Call.* Hugh, she thought, missed San Francisco too, but was too good a soldier to complain.

After a while he said good night and went to bed, weary of responsibilities. Hurriedly she got out the hidden parcels from her shopping in town, admiring the sheen of the heavy silk in the rays of the lamp. With sudden resolve she drew the curtains and slipped out of her waist, her skirt, ruffled petticoats, chemise and suspender garters, pulling off her stockings and standing unclothed before the pier glass. The pier glass threw back at her an image of woman by lamplight, rich sheen of auburn hair, ripe flesh somehow glowing from within. She snatched up the bolt of silk and wrapped it about her, draping it carefully. Pleased with the way it encircled her bosom and coiled firm about her waist, emphasizing its tininess, yet letting a proud, firm thigh wantonly emerge, she held the fabric in place with one hand and picked up the lamp with the other.

Hugh, as she had thought, was awake. He lay blinking in the rays of the lamp, hands locked behind his head, dark curls stark against the whiteness of the pillow.

"Well?" She pirouetted, holding a hand over her breast to keep the material in place. "How do you like it?" She giggled. "I mean—how do you like *me?*"

For a long moment he looked at her, eyes dark and hard and distant. Then he moved suddenly, snatching her down beside him. He did not speak, only pressed himself tight against her, bruising her lips with his kisses, his hand fumbling under the clinging silk.

"Hugh, stop it!" she cried in mock ferocity, trying to fend off his hand. "My hair—you're ruining my hair!"

But he would not be denied; it was as if he had suddenly found a remedy for his problems. Bound together by the folds of the silk, they rolled across the string bed, the posts creaking and surging.

When he had satisfied himself they lay together, her head in the crook of his arm, cheek nestled against the hairy mat of his chest. Tattoo must have sounded long ago; the post was quiet. A remnant of breeze sifted through the cracks in the boards, and she was grateful for its coolness on her brow. For lack of fuel the Argand lamp had guttered out on the floor where she set it. The room was filled with June night and a distant scent of flowers where a laundress had planted sweet peas along Soapsuds Row. The coyote howled again, an eerie, long-drawn-out complaint, but it did not sound frightening to her now, lying in his arms.

There was still something on his mind. She felt it in the way he lay, slightly tensed, breathing shallowly and almost inaudibly.

"Hugh?"

He hesitated. "Yes?"

"Is something troubling you?"

He didn't look at her, only continued to stare at the ceiling. "No. No *trouble,* that is. I was just— thinking."

"About what?" She roused herself, naked, on an elbow. In the dimness of starlight she could see only the two black pools of his eyes, the stark demarcation between his cheek and the sable of the beard. "Is it anything you ought to tell me?"

He raised a hand as if to stroke her hair, then let it fall flat on his chest, fingers working. "It's about that fellow Rainbolt."

She felt a sudden chill. "Oh?"

"Bill Wagner came in today with the wagon train from Fort Arbuckle. You remember Bill— he was on the JAGD staff at the Presidio."

She remembered Captain Wagner—a curly haired pleasant man who had once been a lawyer.

"He's secretary of some War Department board now, making a survey of Indian Territory, the disposition of the various posts."

"But what about—about Rainbolt?" she asked.

"Seems Bill Wagner knew him once. He and Bill were classmates at a private school down south—Georgia, I think. After the war Bill was in Military Government for a while, and out of curiosity he looked through the rebel records. Your friend Rainbolt, it seems, had a checkered career."

She felt suddenly uncomfortable.

"At Petersburg," Hugh went on, "Rainbolt had command of an artillery battery with Heth's division. During the night, Lee withdrew to tighten up his lines. According to the court-martial records—"

"Court-martial?" she faltered.

"According to the records, Rainbolt was at division headquarters at the time. He ran back to limber the guns and get his men out of there, but the enemy fire was too much for him. He turned tail and fled—there were several witnesses—and the battery and all his men were destroyed." With sudden viciousness, he added, "That's your murdering Rainbolt for you—a yellow coward!"

At first she tried to pretend it did not mean anything.

"*My* Rainbolt? Why, Hugh, whatever do you mean? Why is he my Rainbolt?"

He laughed a short hard laugh. "You know what

I mean! You've been flirting with him ever since we came out here!"

Stung, she cried, "That's a cruel thing to say!"

He crossed black-haired arms over his face, refusing to look at her. "Cruel or not, it's true! You're a beautiful woman, Ellen—God knows you're beautiful—but you have a way of flaunting it that causes trouble. You got poor cowardly Rainbolt so flustered he punched Kruger in the mouth, and that's why he's going to the rockpile at Leavenworth."

"That's not true!" she cried, on the verge of tears. "And I think you put that brutal Sergeant Kruger up to hectoring the poor man out of jealousy of me, that's all!" Weeping, she went on, "You always told me an officer's wife should take an interest in the men! I organized the garden to give them fresh vegetables, and I got the chaplain to start the school for men who couldn't read! Mr. Rainbolt was very helpful—"

"*Private* Rainbolt," Hugh corrected. "And assaulting a superior was Rainbolt's idea, not mine."

"Anyway, he was always very helpful! We— we became good friends, that's all!"

He grabbed her arm and shook her, scowling. "Don't shout so! You'll wake up the whole post!"

His anger fueled hers. Perhaps it was because his criticism hit so near the mark. What was it she said to Philip Rainbolt just before he escaped?

After all, it was probably my fault as much as yours. I see that now, and I'm sorry.

"I'll shout if I want!" she screamed, wresting away her arm and knowing his grasp had left nail marks. "When you make accusations like that—"

Now he was shouting too.

"I won't have you making eyes at attractive men, Ellen, especially enlisted men! There's nothing so ruins an officer's chances as gossip!"

She stared at him, eyes brimming with tears of fury. "Enlisted men! Oh, my God! Is that the trouble? Rainbolt was an enlisted man?"

"You know I don't mean that!" he howled. "You're just twisting my words!"

"I know," she said between tight lips, "that Philip Rainbolt was a gentleman! In this godforsaken dismal post he was the only one I could talk to—the only one that took me on my own terms, as a woman and a lady! He knew Shakespeare and Locke and Dryden; he loved poetry; he made me see oh, so many things I'd been blind to! He wasn't ever jealous or spiteful the way—the way"—her breast heaved with the pressure of words—"the way—"

"The way I am?" Hugh demanded. He snatched at the silk still draped over her shoulders and pulled it away, wadding it in his fists and throwing it across the room. "And where the hell did you get this? Whisky City? I've told you before you're not to go there, ever! You disobeyed me!"

She struck at him with clenched fists. "I'm not one of your goddamned enlisted men! How dare you order me where to go and not to go?"

He trapped her flailing arms in his, trying to press her to him.

"Ah, Ellen, let's not fight! I didn't mean that! It was your own safety I was thinking about. If anything ever happened to you, I don't know what I'd do."

But she twisted free of him, furious, and sat on her naked legs, panting for breath, hair disheveled and falling over her shoulders. "I hate you!" she sobbed. "I hate you and this ugly place and the goddamned Army and everything!"

He tried to placate her. "Ellen, an officer's life can't be all dress balls and champagne and oyster suppers! I don't care for this place any more than you do, but a soldier's got to go where he's ordered! But if I put down the Kiowas along the Red River, it'll look good on my record. I've got friends in the War Department. Who knows—next duty might be military attaché in Paris!"

Still sobbing, she let herself be taken into his arms. From a long way off in the mountains the coyote called again. The coyote was free, she thought. And Philip Rainbolt was free. It must be nice to be free like that.

It was a wild land, down toward the Red River. Some of Colonel Grierson's Negro troopers from the Ninth had told Rainbolt about it. The wind blew almost always. Storms appeared from nowhere—the heavens discharged rain, thunder, lightning, sleet, snow. Tornadoes brewed; fires, started by settlers or strokes of lightning, burned grasses, trees, animals, carrying everything before them. Dust and sandstorms were frequent, carving scrolls and patterns into the most solid of rocks, then sweeping the work fine as if to show it to the world, or perversely hiding it with inches of dust so divided it was like talc, filtering into everything—food, drink, clothing, a man's most private parts. Clouds of dust made the midday sun a weak and wan moon, but the sunsets were beautiful.

The air was so clear that distances were deceiving. Mountains seemed to march toward one, but were never reached. The Staked Plains, the *Llano Estacado*, were without a reference, and resembled a landlocked sea, overwhelming any but the most determined traveler. In summer the midday heat was scorching and unbearable; trembling mirages danced before the eyes. The grass became parched brown, cracking underfoot like brittle twigs. But at the end of summer the northers came, blowing cool winds, and temperatures dropped fifty degrees within an hour. In winter blizzards howled down without notice, freezing man and animal alike, blanketing the land with impassable snow.

This was the land where Philip Rainbolt was riding. He knew good horseflesh. When he had drawn a jug-headed gray with plow-horse fetlocks from the remount pool, he immediately traded her off for Brutus. A Brooklyn recruit who didn't know horses but needed the ten dollars Rainbolt offered swapped the gelding and was content.

Now the sun sparkled on the distant peaks of the Wichitas, well behind him to the north. Ahead was a June morning, air fresh and clean after the rains, brown grass spangled with dew. If it were not for the Kiowas he would be manacled in a wagon crawling its way toward Fort Leavenworth. For a moment he had a twinge of regret. Six months, even at hard labor, was not so long. He should have refused the chance to escape. Maybe it was even worth the sentence to smash his fist into Kruger's piggish face. But now the wind was fresh in his nostrils and he enjoyed the smell of freedom. Away in the distance, a thin line of riders topping a ridge, he saw the Kiowas. When he clapped his heels into Brutus' ribs the gelding sprang forward with a joyful gathering of hind-quarters. Cavalry horses enjoyed freedom, too, and the smooth rocking-chair gallop comforted Rainbolt's seat, sore from the lack of a saddle.

At noontide he caught up with his rescuers. He did not quite know how to approach them. Not speaking a word of Kiowa, he must depend on signs to show them he was a friend, that he sought refuge from their common enemy the Army, that he wanted to travel with them. They had tethered their ponies along a little brook, a thread of green in the shade of a grove of chinaberry trees. Stolidly they watched him approach. They made no move, only sat in the shade, chewing food from a rawhide *parfleche* before them.

"How!" he called, and dismounted.

They only kept chewing, looking at him with a wary interest but no great concern.

What was that word Ike Coogan said meant *friend?* Rainbolt could not bring it to mind. Holding up his empty hands, he started to walk toward them, smiling, recognizing the one called Stone Teeth. There was another word. *Top* something. While old Coogan was maundering on and on, Rainbolt had been half asleep. But *top* something meant *leader* as of a war party. *Topadoki*, that was it! He called out the word, hoping they would understand he wanted to talk to their leader.

They were still silent, chewing and staring. Finally one brave picked up a fist-sized rock and hurled it, at the same time shouting something threatening.

Startled, Rainbolt broke into English. "I'm a friend, see? I only want to travel with you! The Army is chasing me, too!"

Stone Teeth picked up a rock, and hurled it too. In a moment, as if it were a game, the rest of the band sprang to their feet, hooting and laughing; the air was filled with stones and clods of dirt. The Kiowas didn't want him near—that was plain. Rainbolt was hard put to protect himself against the rain of missiles, and dodged and danced this way and that, holding up his arms to shield his face and head.

It was a ludicrous situation, though any one of the rocks might have caved in his skull. When he saw them, still laughing, mount their ponies and start to ride off, his desperate hope vanished. He didn't know this strange inhospitable country. The Kiowas had been his one resource. Now he saw it snatched away from him, and was angry and frustrated.

Quickly he threw a leg over Brutus and started to gallop after them. One of the warriors, cantering easily, swung in the high-backed saddle and fitted an arrow to his bow. There was a *tccchk* sound as the arrow ripped Rainbolt's sleeve and whined into the grass beyond.

He felt suddenly cold and shaken. It was a joke no longer. With a dry throat he slowed Brutus to a trot, then finally rode back to the chinaberry trees. While the gelding grazed on sweet grass and quenched his thirst in the stream, Rainbolt at in the shade, arms locked around his knees. After the excitement of the jailbreak, the shock of seeing poor Huckabee slaughtered, his wild ride through the night, and now his rejection by

47

the people he had thought of as his saviors, he felt drained of all emotion, all feeling.

Around him the grassy plain seemed to extend forever, the only sign of life a few grazing buffalo. Though this was nominally treaty territory, awarded to the Indians a few years before, commercial hunters had slain most of the buffalo. The few that remained were not prime. Far to the north the Wichitas took on shades of purple and gold as the sun slipped down the heavens. In the willows along the brook something moved, and Rainbolt remembered the knife at his waist. He pulled it out, suddenly fearful. Nothing moved; the only sound was the brook rippling over moss-covered stones, the sighing of the evening wind in the chinaberry trees.

Since the night before he had eaten nothing. Hoping to still the pangs of hunger, he lay flat on his stomach and drank till he was bloated. Propping himself on outstretched arms, cold water dripping from his stubble-rough chin and drooping mustaches, he pondered. They would have vedettes out looking for the escaped Kiowas, that was certain. They would be pleased to recapture Philip Rainbolt, too, and send him in irons to his punishment at Fort Leavenworth, probably adding six months for his escape. It was clear he had blundered his way into another deadly predicament.

In the twilight he stalked a half-grown rabbit

along the brook, but the suspicious creature bounded into a thicket of briers just as he threw the knife. It took a half hour of painful scratchy searching to recover the weapon. He did, however, find some half-ripe berries, and ate a handful or so. They gave him cramps; in half an hour he was bent double, vomiting miserably.

Through the night he slept in starts, waking to stare up at the stars. The belt of Orion marked the passage of the hours, and he watched it mount higher and higher in the blue-black vault of heaven. Night birds called, there was a wrenching sound as Brutus pulled up the grass and chewed it. When dawn came, he would ride south again. To hell with the clannish Kiowas! He would find a settler's cabin along the Red River, and they would give him food and shelter. Down there no one would know him. It was a rough country, where they did not ask questions of strangers.

Much later something waked him. Sunlight bore painfully on his sleep-blurred eyes. He sat up, blinking; then his heart seemed to stop in his chest.

Before him, poking at him with a ribboned lance heavy with scalps, stood an Indian. For an Indian, the man was tall, and wore a long buckskin shirt ornamented with tufts of human hair. Around his neck dangled a breastplate of carved soapstone studded with silver buttons and polished blue gems.

Speaking in guttural tones, the Indian prodded Rainbolt to rise. Behind him the man's pony, a deer-legged big-barreled paint, grazed companionably with Brutus.

Slowly Rainbolt raised his hands into the air in sign of surrender. In growing panic he stared at the man's face; it was heavy and menacing, cut into irregular planes as if carved in wood. But it was the paint that frightened him. Across the heavy brows, in the folds between the nose and cheeks, down the heavy jaw and extending to the taut muscles of the throat, were broad slashes of indigo-blue paint. Rainbolt's captor was a Tonk—a cannibal.

CHAPTER THREE

When he got shakily to his feet, Rainbolt towered several inches over the Tonkawa brave. Alarmed as the lank frame continued to rise, the blue-faced man fumbled at his belt and brought out an ancient Dragoon Colt, squinting along the heavy barrel at his captive's face.

When Rainbolt ceased to lengthen, the Tonk seemed satisfied. With gestures, he finally made Rainbolt understand he was to take off his shirt and pants, evidently so he might be assured Rainbolt carried no hidden weapon. But a kind of paralysis enveloped Philip Rainbolt. Perhaps the loss of his clothes was preliminary to his slaughter for a cannibal meal. Ike Coogan's wild tales could not be wholly disregarded. So he only stood transfixed, limbs turned into ice, heart pounding and brain churning with a thousand stratagems.

When he did not obey the blue-faced man's commands, the Tonk became angry. Aiming the old Colt steadfastly at Rainbolt's nose, he snatched up his lance and poked his prisoner in the belly.

The hurt was minimal; in Rainbolt's panic he scarcely felt it. But the contact, slight as it was, released him from his paralysis. Opening his mouth as wide as he could, he roared in protest, at the same time grasping the blade of the lance and hauling himself along it toward the Tonk as a sailor climbs a rope.

The Tonk had never heard the Rebel Yell. It unnerved him. Before the savage knew what had happened, Rainbolt was on him. The Tonk pulled the trigger of the Colt, but the barrel slid harmlessly along Rainbolt's cheek. There was a deafening report, and the sting of powder burns against his cheek. But by then he had wrapped his long arms around the Tonk and they were rolling on the ground, locked together.

The blue-faced man was a head shorter but powerful and sinewy. He got his scalp lock under Rainbolt's head and pushed up hard, forcing him to abandon his hold. But Rainbolt wrapped his long legs around the man's waist, and at the same time hit the Tonk hard in the face with his fist. The Tonk howled in pain, clapping a hand to his mouth and spitting out bloody teeth. Seizing the opportunity, Rainbolt scrambled on top. By pinning the man's shoulders with his knees, schoolboy-fashion, he freed both hands to choke the Tonk, at the same time driving the man's head up and down against the hard-burned earth as a maul drives a tent peg.

The Tonk's face and throat were slippery with the blue paint and it was hard to hold on, but Rainbolt kept squeezing and pounding, squeezing and pounding. Somewhere a voice was screaming, a high-pitched keening noise he suddenly decided was his own. He was still yelling the Rebel Yell, but now in victory. The Tonk's face seemed to lose all form and shape, and finally the tense barrel-chested body relaxed, turned soft and yielding, and finally collapsed.

Winded, exhausted, Rainbolt rolled off the inert body and slumped for a moment on his knees. His side hurt, and he touched his ribs gingerly, wondering if he had broken one. The Tonk stirred a little. Tasting the trickle of blood stitching from a corner of his bruised mouth, the man's tongue emerged. Finally the Tonk groaned, a sudden sound that sent Rainbolt scrambling across the sun-parched grass to snatch up the Dragoon Colt.

Groaning again, the Tonk managed to sit up. Seeming afraid his battered head would fall off, he put a hand to each ear, propping his skull upright. He opened one eye and looked at Rainbolt, then closed it again as if not believing what he saw. He groaned again. Finally he opened one eye, cautiously, and stared beadily at his captor.

"Stand up!" Rainbolt ordered.

The blue-faced man probably did not understand the words, but he comprehended the menacing flourish of the Colt. Still holding his head, he staggered to his feet.

"Turn around!"

In response to Rainbolt's gesture the Tonk did so. Rainbolt, gun jabbed against the Tonk's neck, searched him for weapons. The man wore a bead-ornamented cartridge belt with a hatchet in a fringed scabbard, but had no other weapons.

The paint pony still grazed companionably with Brutus. By gestures, Rainbolt commanded the Tonk to move well away, toward the chinaberry trees. At the same time, Rainbolt backed closer to the paint and Brutus, carefully holding a bead on his foe.

All might have gone well, but the Tonk suddenly understood what was happening; he was being set afoot without weapons or a horse. There was no greater shame for a Tonkawa brave. Rainbolt, mounted on Brutus and holding the paint's rope bridle in one hand, shouted a warning, but the Tonk rushed headlong at him, screaming what must have been Indian curses.

Even then, Rainbolt did not want to shoot. He did not want to hurt anyone—never had. But when the blue-faced man grabbed his leg, trying to pull him off Brutus, Rainbolt had no choice. He squeezed the trigger of the ancient Colt, and the contorted blue face turned suddenly red.

In a general way he realized, he had been following Cache Creek to its ultimate junction with the Red River, some fifty miles from Fort Sill. Now that he was approaching the Red he began to doubt the wisdom of too close an approach to the cabins of the settlers and ranchers along its reaches. He knew they distrusted the Army, in spite of their clamor for protection, and would probably keep his passing among them a secret. But someone might still give him away, perhaps seeking the standard fifty dollars in gold for a deserter. Then, too, he no longer needed food or shelter. In the rawhide sacks the Tonk carried slung across the pony's withers he found parched corn, dried plums, a store of small cakes made from a kind of meal mixed with wild cherries, stones and all, and a rich oil that was probably buffalo fat. Brutus was holding up well on a diet of willow shoots and the grass that was still green near the banks of the creek. The Indian pony appeared to eat almost anything, and was flat and sleek. Besides, Rainbolt now had the Dragoon Colt and a supply of ammunition.

Though he had no conceivable use for the pennoned lance, he carried that along, too, tied to the pony's rump. It was so beautifully worked, rich with carvings and chasings, ornamented with the same polished blue gems and silver buttons the Tonk had on his breastplate, that Rainbolt took a liking to it. So he rode on, gradually becoming trailwise, and finally swam Brutus and the Indian pony across the Red River at a place far upstream from the nearest settlement. It was a place he remembered called Henrietta, a scattering of sod shanties, tents, and brush lean-tos he had once ridden through with F Company; although lone-some for human talk, he avoided it.

The weather continued fair and hot, the sky a bowl of eye-aching blue. The sun was so hot he rode with a makeshift hat woven of willow greenery. At night there was sometimes a brief and violent electrical storm: little rain but a great deal of wind and lightning. Next morning the distant vistas would be marked by plumes of smoke where lightning bolts had set the parched prairie afire.

At the river, knowing that the occasional watercourses ahead would be dried by the summer sun, he had filled the bladderlike Tonk water containers, probably fashioned from buffalo paunches, and watered the animals well. But the country ahead did not look promising. Ahead, the Rio Bravo and Mexico were almost four hundred thirsty miles away, across a hostile desert swarming with bloodthirsty Comanches and Lipans. Yet Mexico now appeared to be his only haven. Mexico, he had heard, was filled with ex-Confederate officers who had entered into farming or business with success. Some were even high officials of the government, or colonels in the Mexican Army.

Swiveling in the carved and hide-covered Tonk saddle he had now strapped on Brutus, he looked back. The Wichitas were only a bluish shadow on the far horizon. He had come a long way, but where was he going to end up? In sudden decision he clapped his heels into the gelding's ribs, and they trotted southward again.

Once, that day, he saw a wagon train in the distance. Reining up in a patch of precious shade, he watched it toil along a rutted track. Even from that distance he could make out the tiny black dots that were oxen, see a few out-riders, probably from his own regiment. The Army had a difficult and thankless task: herd wild Indians, drive out trespassers on Indian treaty lands, chase whisky peddlers and horse thieves, furnish escorts so much as was possible for stages, supply trains, and mail. Rainbolt had drawn his share of these duties, and hated them. But suddenly he was so hungry for human contact that he might, if he had been closer, have ridden up to the slow-crawling train and risked discovery, just for the chance to talk to someone and hear the news.

That afternoon he surprised an antelope in a thicket, dropping it with a lucky shot from the old Colt. He camped in a narrow boulder-littered canyon, risking a fire of buffalo chips to roast bloody slices hacked from the haunch. Never had he tasted anything so good. After the meager Indian diet, he stuffed himself with half-cooked meat, juices dripping from his untrimmed mustache and grizzled chin. Slicing some of the remaining meat thin, he spread it on a woven frame of twigs near the coals to smoke and dry while he slept.

That night he dreamed of Ellen Cameron. He thought he had erased her from his mind, but she returned unbidden and unwanted, filling him with old feelings. He saw her again working in the enlisted men's garden, the old hat covering her red hair, the smooth creamy flesh of her cheeks and neck in the shade of the straw sombrero with the tassels knotted under the chin. He saw again her direct look, the laughter in her violet eyes when she protested. *Philip Rainbolt, is that the way I taught you to thin lettuce? My goodness, you're pulling it all out!*

Half awake, half dreaming, he twisted uneasily. From somewhere there came a faint fragrance, spicy and provocative. Maybe it was some bush near where he slept, or perhaps it was only the remembered fragrance of her as she stood near him, gently mocking, a vagrant strand of hair blowing across her cheek. *All right, damn you— if that's all you have to say to me after—after—*

After what? Certainly, she was a flirt. She had flirted with him, as she had with anything wearing a pair of pants. Certainly she knew what it did to him, so long without a woman, to have her stand so close, so feminine and so desirable. There was a story around the post that she worked with the men in the garden, helped teach them the three

R's, only to spite Major Cameron, who was known to be extremely jealous. The whole idea of the garden, as well as the library and the classes, had been hers, really; the post chaplain was a sickly ineffective man who did little but preach on Sundays and complain the rest of the week about the heat or the cold, the rain or the drought, the flies when the windows were open or the stuffiness when they were closed. The men loved Ellen Cameron.

He remembered the day he had been squatting in the garden, sowing lettuce seeds. "Oh, be careful!" she cried. "You're using too many!" Quickly she knelt beside him, and quickly, too, she toppled against him. The soft pressure of her breast against his shoulder sent a galvanic shock through him. He became a stammering red-faced fool, saying silly things about lettuce planting, insisting he knew what he was doing when in fact he had never before planted anything. At Nine-Mile the Negroes had always tended to the planting, while he rode his little pony.

But Ellen Cameron did not appear to notice the way her breast had for a moment encountered the hard jut of his shoulder. As if nothing had happened, she looked at him with her level violet-eyed gaze and said, "Philip Rainbolt, you are a handsome man, and a good soldier, I hear! But when it comes to planting lettuce seeds, you are an ignoramus! They are so fine, you see, that you will get too many of them in one place unless you first mix them with sand, and then dribble out the mixture—so—" She showed him. Red-faced and silent, he knelt beside her, wishing she would go away and wishing also that she would never leave his side.

He woke with a start, sitting for a long time in the first flush of dawn, arms locked around his knees and staring at a clump of Spanish dagger, its plumes moving restlessly in the dawn wind. Ellen Cameron was a flirt; she had probably planned the whole thing. He had fallen into a trap by blundering after her like a lovesick schoolboy. The rest of the soldiers laboring in the garden had noticed his infatuation, joked about it. But it had been no joke when the matter came to the attention of Major Cameron. Rainbolt knew the commanding officer had put Sergeant Major Kruger on him as a mastiff is put on a fleeing rabbit. The Prussian had bullied and chevied him until at last, goaded beyond endurance, Rainbolt turned and struck.

Again, the feathery plumes of the Spanish dagger moved. For a moment, deep in his thoughts, he watched them move, sway, dance. Then, with a feeling as of ice water suddenly poured into his boots, he knew he had lulled himself into a deadly apathy. It was not a Spanish dagger waving in the wind; it was a plumed Indian, stalking him in the open, taking short steps, then freezing lest he be noticed.

In panic he sprang to his feet, snatching the Dragoon Colt from its holster. He squeezed off a half-dozen fast shots, but the savage only stood there, watching him. Incredulously he stared, mouth cottony and heart pounding. Then realization washed over him, leaving him sweaty and trembling. It had been a harmless desert plant, after all. His imagination was working overtime.

He could still hear the echoes of his fusillade dying away across the dew-wet plain. Angry and sheepish, he ejected the empty shells and reloaded. Edgy—he was getting edgy, in this great expanse of loneliness. And he had wasted half a dozen rounds of scarce ammunition. Saddling up Brutus, he felt shaken. This endless expanse of burned grass and dry arroyos made him nervous. Or perhaps it was just the need to see a human face again, to talk to someone, to feel not quite so alone. But the desolate panorama stretched endlessly before him, barren as the mountains of the moon.

After several days' riding, he crossed one of the many forks of the Brazos. The tributaries were drying out, and his animals lapped the stagnant pools, unsatisfied. Once again he filled the buffalo-paunch water bags. He put on his shirt again, wet and slimy from use as a strainer, and squatted for a long moment, looking southwest. Mesquite, a little scrub oak, patchy grass—in the far distance a hazy bulk that might be mountains. But he knew now he would never make it across those mountains, even approach them closely. As fast as he rode, the mountains retreated faster. He would never reach the Rio Bravo, and the haven of Mexico. He would have to fight hard even to stay alive, here in this desert. How, he wondered, does a man die of thirst? Already his tongue felt thick and woolly, or was it his imagination? Someone—it had probably been one of Colonel Grierson's Negro troopers—had told him once about a patrol on the Llano Estacado when they had run out of water. The Negroes did what they had to do. They drank the blood of their tiring mounts. When they had killed all the dying horses they drank their own urine, sweetened with a little sugar that remained. Anyway, it kept them alive.

Late in the afternoon he decided to turn back before he was completely committed to this hostile desert. Maybe he would wander across a patrol that would take him into custody and end this miserable foolish flight. But a grove of cottonwoods to the southeast caught his eye in the slanting rays of the late sun. As he rode closer, he began to tremble with excitement. The horses, too, sensed something exciting. Water! Perhaps there was a settler there, a small *rancho*, a sod shanty—water!

Ears stiff, Brutus broke into a shambling trot.

The Indian pony whickered, and no longer lagged behind, dragged by the lead rope. Before his eyes the smudge of green grew, expanded. In the long shadows he could see the outline of manmade structures: a sway-backed shed, a ramshackle fence around a garden patch, an adobe shack. Washing flapped from a line, a dog barked, there was even a faint curl of smoke where someone was preparing supper.

Delighted, he clapped his heels into Brutus' ribs and they galloped into the patch of green that was the yard. Geraniums grew there, and a circular wall of laid-up rocks that must enclose a well or spring. He flung himself off Brutus and snatched the mossy rope going into the depths, hauling up bucket after bucket to appease the three of them. The dog came up, too, sniffing at him. Rainbolt poured water into the wooden trough for the dog, too, asking, "Thirsty, old boy?"

The dog only rolled eyes whitely up and slunk away, whining uneasily. Rainbolt shrugged and walked toward the adobe house, water bucket still in hand. "Hello, the house!" he shouted. "Need a little water?"

No answer. "Hello!" he shouted again. "Where is everybody?"

Still only silence. A breeze ruffled the scanty grass, the flowers stirred, the small nondescript dog looked at him with mournful eyes.

He had a sudden panicky feeling; something

was wrong. Drawing the Colt, he walked slowly toward the house, almost tiptoeing, though there could be no need for silence. The door hung askew on leather hinges. Behind him the dog whined, and would approach no farther.

Rainbolt stepped into the gloom. He wanted to cry out, to scream, to do anything to break the deadly silence, but his throat was thickened with fear. No one would have heard him, though. Snatching out a soiled rag of a handkerchief, he muffled his nose against the sweetish rotten smell of death.

It was hard to tell how long they had been dead, the bearded middle-aged man, the pleasant-faced wife in her bright gingham, the half-grown tow-headed boy. They lay together in a communion of death, sprawled across a comfortered brass bed that must have come from Ohio or Tennessee or Kentucky. A bright-feathered arrow was buried half its length in the woman's broad bosom; the man had been hacked to death with a hatchet, the boy shot many times in the head. Only the small face remained whole and unbroken.

Stumbling out into the red-streaked twilight, Rainbolt sat for a long time on the edge of the well, breathing deep of the cool air, trying to rid his nostrils and his memory of the smell. What was it Ike Coogan had said? *The Red River's gonna run actual red—with blood.* Three days ago, maybe four. Kiowas? Comanches? It wasn't important.

As he looked around in the twilight he could see things that first had escaped his notice. There had been stock—horses and cows—but they were gone, driven off by the raiders. An attempt had been made to set fire to the barn—that was the smoke he had noticed—but the fire had gone out, leaving some smoldering hay. There had been dried corn and beans, too; apparently, most of it had been stolen. Suddenly suspicious of the water in the well, Rainbolt probed its shallow depths with a stick. A few feet down, he felt something soft and yielding. Human—or animal? Sometimes they sought to poison wells by throwing bodies into them. Queasy and trembling, he threw the stick away and led the animals to the barn and its scorched hay.

Next morning he buried the three bodies in a common shallow grave, marking it with a rude cross fashioned from scraps of lumber he found in the barn, lumber precious in a treeless land. Kentucky, he thought, or Tennessee; the land would have been different, there. The family had known trees, in Kentucky.

Taking off his willow-shoot hat, he murmured a few vaguely religious-sounding words over the mound of earth. Afterward, he went against his will into the death-smelling adobe, searching for food.

The raiders had taken most of it, smashing and grinding into the dirt floor what they did not want. But Rainbolt found an overlooked tin of Rio coffee and a worn grinder, some parched corn, and a leather sack with a few California gold pieces in it, the total wealth of years of privation, hard work, and—death. There was a green glass bottle of calomel, too, which he took. If he ever got a bellyache from his rude diet, the pink pills might help.

The day too brassy-hot to ride, he passed the afternoon in the shade of the cottonwoods, eyes searching the blue-hazed distances. The dog came to him trustingly now, licking his hand and staring at him as if Rainbolt held the answer to some question. He found a few withered sprigs of onion in the sun-baked garden, and with them and the last of the dried antelope meat made a stew for his supper, grinding also a few of the precious hard brown coffee beans to make a cup of coffee.

At dusk he left the rancho with almost a feeling of regret. At least he had felt safe there; raiding Indians would not soon return to a place they had so thoroughly despoiled. There was water there, too, precious water, and the place had a feeling of people about it, of being lived in, that was comfortable, though the people were now dead under his crude cross and some wilted geraniums he had stuck in a tin can on the grave.

When he rode away, the small dog howled and ran after him. It hesitated for a moment, looking up with one forepaw raised. Then it ran back to the adobe house, barked a few times, and finally came shambling to sit near Brutus' hoofs, looking up at him in that puzzled way.

"I guess," Rainbolt said, "four of us to feed and water isn't much worse than three."

Dismounting, he scooped up the dog and deposited it in the now empty Tonkawa pannier, only the head and forepaws sticking out.

"Brownie," he decided. "That's your name."

He put out a finger and the dog licked it.

"Not much of a name," he said, "but then— you're not much of a dog."

Ambling through the twilight, he suddenly realized he didn't know where he was going. But it didn't seem to make any difference. Stolidly, Brutus paced through the gathering night; the Indian pony followed, the dog slept, small head bobbing with each step of the paint. Squinting at the stars, Rainbolt saw the Big Dipper and Polaris, and judged he was heading more or less southerly. *No difference,* he thought again. *No difference.* He was a ship without a rudder, wallowing in an endless landscape. Listless, drained of all emotion, he dozed, awoke, dozed again. Some Hindu mystic, he thought, might say he had reached a nirvana-like stage where life and body no longer mattered; only spirit remained. But Rainbolt knew better. There was not even spirit left—only an unimportant husk of a man stumbling toward nothingness. *The nothingness of sleep. The nothingness of death. No difference.*

Toward morning, Brutus' shamble led them into a rocky canyon still warm from the day's heat. The gorge seemed to slope a little toward the southwest. Content to let the gelding go where he chose, Rainbolt dozed again. Their path led deeper and deeper into the canyon, but soon it would be too hot to travel again, and he might welcome the shade of an overhanging ledge. Too, there might be water, a spring. And the canyon could harbor small game, give him a cover for a cooking fire.

If he thought he no longer cared for life, that it made no difference any more what happened to him, he suddenly changed his mind. In the starlit night rough hands seized him and dragged him from the saddle. Someone grabbed Brutus' bridle. Dark figures swarmed around him, and he could smell the odor of their bodies: a grass-like smoke-scented aroma.

Nirvana forgotten, he fought like a catamount for his life, the life so recently despised. Trying to get the Colt free of its holster, he felt an agonizing thwack across his wrist; his whole arm was quickly numb. With his good hand he tried to get to Coogan's Green River knife, but the scabbard was empty. Almost, he twisted free of the hands pinioning him, but someone tripped him then. He fell down hard, the wind rushing out of him in a great gasp.

Quickly, expertly, they trussed him and dumped him across his own mount. When the dog snarled at his captors, someone must have twisted its neck, because the small brave bark was suddenly snuffed out. A moment later someone was leading Brutus down the shale-littered slope. They were all around him—Indians, joking and laughing, paying no more attention to him than if he had been a slaughtered antelope they were bringing to camp.

A thought came to him to turn his wretched stomach anew. The Indians had been painted, but in the first streaks of dawn he had not been able to make out the colors. Had it been—were they—blue?

Ellen had never known a man so insanely jealous as Hugh Cameron. At first, when he was courting her, riding his horse all the way from the Presidio to her parents' house in the Western Addition, it was fun. Hugh glowered at all the other eligible young men on the veranda, and insisted on filling every line of her dance card with his own name. Two years later, Ellen Cameron knew her marriage had fallen apart. She was only another Army wife. On the post she was the sole woman, except for laundresses and Indian squaws; no one to talk to, to exchange feminine confidences, secrets, with. That was hard enough, being cut off from others of her own sex. But Hugh's unfailing vigilance was worse. He never wanted to let her out of his sight. It was almost like a disease; that, and now his passion to catch Philip Rainbolt.

After weeks of fruitless searching, Major Cameron had given up the hunt for the escaped Kiowas, and so notified the general. The Kiowas, Major Cameron reported, could be hiding in any one of a thousand gorges or brakes or canyons all the way to the Rio Bravo. But Rainbolt, Hugh told Ellen, was something different.

"Because," he said, "Rainbolt doesn't know that country. He's a soldier, and that's about all he's ever been. He's used to maps, field glasses, supply wagons with water and rations, traveling as part of a military organization, fighting the Army way. Alone, he'll never make it. Just you see, I'll catch up with the murdering bastard."

Remembering her conversation with old Ike Coogan, Ellen said, "I don't think he ever killed anyone. Why are you so certain? The Kiowas could have killed poor old Sergeant Huckabee, couldn't they?"

But Hugh Cameron only looked at her queerly and continued to pore over his maps of Indian Territory, spread all over the parlor floor. Lonely, she went to bed and lay for a long time in her shift, feeling beads of perspiration on her thighs and between her breasts. It was hardly July, but the summer heat had set in early. In spite of scattered spring rains the post wells were running low. Soon they would have to bring water from Medicine Bluff Creek in barrels. There would be little to spare for the enlisted men's garden she had been so proud of. Already her own little kitchen garden was beginning to dry up, and Hugh complained about the few buckets of water she carried from the dwindling well, saying plain Army fare was good enough for him. He didn't need fancy frills, he said, like fresh lettuce and carrots.

"Hugh?" she called, finally. "Aren't you coming to bed?"

He didn't answer. Sighing, she turned over, feeling the shift wet on her back and thighs. In her father's house, now, they would be sitting on the veranda. Pitchers of lemonade, sweat-beaded and tinkling with ice, would be passed around. A breeze from the bay would flutter the lace curtains at the open window. She could see the red coal of her father's Havana cigar glow in the dark as he puffed; her mother's knitting needles clicked gently in time with the rhythm of her favorite cane-bottomed rocker. Suddenly Ellen was homesick, violently homesick. She was a prisoner in a savage and forbidding country, and the black-bearded stranger in the next room her jailer.

Home, she thought. *I want to go home. I want to play kissing games again with the young men, and dance and flirt, and have beautiful dreams. I want—*

Turning restlessly on her stomach, she buried her damp face in the pillow, lest Hugh hear her sobs. She could not go home, of course. She could never, really, go home again—that was all behind her, in the sweet past. Now she had made her decision, married, accepted Hugh Cameron's lot as her own.

Just before she drifted into a troubled sleep, a bizarre thought came to her, one that at once repelled and attracted. She had money of her own put away. It was possible for her to leave Hugh, to leave this dreary post, the heat-burned hostile country. Of course, she could not go *home.* She could never face the surprise and hurt of her parents, the wagging tongues of friends, the knowing smirks of relatives. No, she would have to go someplace else. But could she not go someplace else? Could not a spirited young woman make a new life for herself, the way a man could?

CHAPTER FOUR

Hands and feet bound, dumped over Brutus' back like a sack of oats, Rainbolt tried vainly to see where they were going. In his head-down position he could tell little except they seemed still to descend a gradual slope, going deeper and deeper into the canyon. The men bantered among themselves, Brutus' shoes clattered and rang on the rocks, overhead the sky became gray, then blue. Morning came, although into this deep cleft the rays did not yet reach.

Suddenly, in the half-light, there was a halt to their progress. A hurried conference was held, with a great deal of palaver. One man came back and squatted beside Rainbolt, looking puzzled into his face. Others joined him, staring at Rainbolt with what seemed like incredulity, almost awe. It was as if they had discovered something about him, something that had at first escaped their notice.

In that ridiculous upside-down position there was nothing to do but suffer their scrutiny. But there was one comfort. He could hear the music of their moccasins as they shifted about, uneasy, standing first on one foot and then the other. They must be Kiowas, not Tonks. He was glad.

Finally, in response to a command from a

thin blade-nosed man wearing a white man's checkered vest, they cut his bonds, pulled him off Brutus, and set him on his feet.

"Thanks," he muttered.

He could smell smoke from cooking fires, and in the growing light saw a few scattered *tipis* along the descending path that lead to the bottom of the canyon. Some of the Kiowa party were examining the pony Rainbolt had taken from the Tonk, pointing out details in the painted and carved wood of the saddle. Others held the Tonk lance upright; one man traced with a finger the pattern of silver buttons and polished blue stones. Another held the Dragoon Colt in both hands, almost like a sacred relic.

Finally the party mounted again. This time they did not bind him. Instead they let him ride among them, keeping a wary eye on him. The man in the checkered vest, apparently a person of some authority, took Brutus and the high-backed saddle for himself, while Rainbolt rode a wild-eyed Indian pony, which snuffled and sidled a little when he threw a leg over her, but was otherwise reasonable. Another Kiowa carried the decorated Tonk lance like a scepter as he rode, and a third bore the Dragoon Colt, holding it as if he were afraid the ancient weapon might bite him. The party must have looked like a religious procession as they rode into camp.

With hundreds of lodges, the Kiowa village was

a huge one. The floor of the gorge-enclosed village was wide, covered with rich grass. Painted and smoke-blackened tipis were everywhere, conical forms thrusting upward like an endless crop of mushrooms. Far down the valley Rainbolt could see a brush corral with what looked like hundreds of horses and cows. The day was still; a layer of blue-gray smoke from cooking fires hung over the camp. The air smelled of roasting meat and horse droppings, of tobacco, of scraped hides drying in the sun.

The bustling activity of the camp ceased as the procession passed, the man in the checkered vest now bearing the feathered Tonk lance like a bishop's crozier, and carrying the Dragoon Colt also, stuck in his belt. A moment before there had been noise, confusion, women gossiping as they washed their hair in the clear stream running through the camp. Now the hubbub ceased. People stopped talking to stare. Children watched with wide eyes. A woman who had been slicing antelope meat thin to dry in the sun put her hand to her mouth in the age-old gesture of astonishment—or was it fear?

Rainbolt was uneasy. There was somethin eerie in the suspended silence. This was more than the return of a war party with a white prisoner. Not even the dogs barked. People hurried silently to line the path the procession followed. The children wore little or no clothing. The men, in this summer season, wore not much more—usually breechcloths and moccasins. But their coppery, glistening bodies were richly hung with breastplates of pipestone, dangling earrings, necklaces of bear or elk teeth, sometimes silver disks pinned to hair braids. Shy, the women hovered behind the men and wore poncho-like shirts decorated with dyed quills or beads or bits of broken mirror, along with wrap-around skirts and knee-hig moccasins. The women, too, wore jewelry—earrings, pendants, or necklaces of shells and beads. Their faces and hair partings were painted in a vermilion so bright it made Rainbolt's eyes tingle.

Their close scrutiny got on his nerves. What were they going to do with him? He wanted to flee, to find a place where he could burrow deep in the earth, and so escape. But there was no place to run to.

The party stopped at a huge lodge, a structure which towered at least thirty feet in height. Rich with decoration, it was obviously an important dwelling of some sort, or a temple. The skins covering it were painted with suns and moons and sticklike figures of horses and men done in red and yellow and brown and orange, colors of the earth in autumn. One of the party lifted the decorated door flap and called respectfully within. A moment later the man in the checkered vest gestured to Rainbolt to enter the great lodge.

"In," he said, pointing. "Y—y—you go—in!" He stammered slightly when he spoke, and it was the first intimation Rainbolt had that any of them spoke English.

Though the skins of the great tipi had been scraped paper-thin and translucent, he blinked for a moment in the dimness, trying to accustom his eyes. In spite of the growing heat of the day, a small fire blazed in a central fire pit lined with stones. Around the fire pit were strewn very good Axminster rugs of flowered design, and between the fire and a large leathern couch was a table made of painted fireboards a foot wide and several feet long, ornamented with bright brass tacks. On the odd table stood a tin coffeepot and the remnants of a meal.

In a way, it was almost like a white man's parlor. Heaped in the corners of the tipi were quantities of painted rawhide chests, blankets, a small rosewood harmonium of the type favored by traveling missionaries. There were other musical instru-ments also: a battered French horn and a violin with all the strings missing save one.

Lying on the couch was a sparely made old man whose skin shone like a burnished penny, even in the dim light. A kind of radiance seemed to emanate from him. He appeared more Spanish than Indian, with sharp features, restless eyes, and a sprouting of chin whiskers. Simply dressed, he wore only a breechcloth and a red kerchief bound around his head, without other ornamentation. The red kerchief made Rainbolt think of illustrations of pirates on the Main.

The men brought in the plunder Rainbolt had taken from the Tonk, arranging it carefully on the flowered rug before the chief: the carved and chased saddle, the cartridge belt and hatchet, the Dragoon Colt. The pennoned lance one of them held carefully upright.

"Who are you?"

The old chief's question came to him through the stammering interpreter. Rainbolt hesitated, trying to frame a proper answer. His nondescript clothing, faded and weatherworn, would give the Kiowas no clue that he was a soldier. But these people, even if they hated the Army, especially for its killing of Satank, might still be practical enough to turn him in for the standard fifty dollar reward.

"A—a traveler," he finally admitted, and gingerly laid Sergeant Huckabee's packet of Lone Jack on the table as a gift.

While someone poured the chief a cup of coffee from the tin pot, the old man combed his chin whiskers with his fingers and looked at Rainbolt. Rainbolt, staring tensely ahead, waiting for what he knew not, noted the tufted high back of the couch. That couch, he decided, was just like one in the parlor of his Aunt Malvina's house in Waycross, Georgia. The couch was no more, the house was no more, having burned when Sherman came that way. Aunt Malvina had died, too; suddenly Rainbolt realized with a queer feeling of loss that he didn't have anyone. His disappearance in this hostile camp would matter to no one. Almost as the act of a condemned man making a lost life take on significance, he pointed to the pile of Tonk equipment and said fiercely, "He wanted to kill me! So I killed him, and took all those things."

"You killed the Tonkawa chief?"

"Yes."

The gloom of the great lodge lifted as someone held aside the door flap and other men entered. Rainbolt recognized them as old Satank's Kiowas, the onde who had escaped the guardhouse and freed him too, that night that now seemed so long ago. Particularly he recognized Stone Teeth, the one who had driven him away when, desperate, he wanted to join their party.

"What did the Tonkawa chief look like?"

As best he could Rainbolt described the Tonk—the blue-painted face with its pattern of whorls and dots, the heavy menacing contours, the beetle brows. As he spoke he had the odd idea that he had stumbled onto something important; impor-tant to the Kiowas, judging by their intense faces, certainly important to him—Philip Rainbolt—because he was buying time, precious time, to intervene between him and death.

"When the Tonk stuck me in the ribs with this lance," he said, demonstrating with gestures, "that made me mad. I yelled hard at him, and grabbed the lance and knocked him down and took away his weapons and his horse."

That impressed them. There was a lot of whispering behind cupped hands. Rainbolt waited for the man in the checkered vest to translate, a speckling of sweat on his brow, wetness in his palms.

"When I started to ride away, the blue-faced man ran after me and tried to pull me off the horse. I warned him, but he kept on pulling and yelling. So I shot him. I killed him with his own weapon. Then I rode away. That is all."

A hubbub broke out. The Kiowas argued with each other, a jumble of insistent voices and flashing hand language. Stone Teeth looked contemptuously at Rainbolt, but another Kiowa came up to Rainbolt and wonderingly touched the ropy golden mustaches and the sun-bleached beard on his chin. Another put a hand on Rainbolt's chest, bending over with a frown in a caricature of a doctor listening to a patient's heart. Others crowded around Rainbolt, poking gingerly at him, feeling the shreds of his clothing, staring unnervingly into his eyes. Apparently there was an unsettled question.

Only the sharp-featured chief was still composed. He lay quietly on the plundered couch, looking somberly at Philip Rainbolt, while a lean hand continued to play with the wispy chin whiskers.

The Kiowas were still all about Rainbolt, like a crowd at the Wiggs County Fair struggling to see the two-headed calf. He stood rigidly, fists at his side, sweating and uncomfortable. A bead of sweat crawled down his nose and persistently hung there, yet refusing to fall. He smelled the Kiowas all about him, the curious mingling of sweet grass and paint and smoke; he heard their meaningless chatter, felt them press against him with a jangle of bracelets and breastplates and earrings, saw the black eyes staring into his own with such a concentration that he became finally unnerved.

"Get away from me!" he howled.

Flailing with his arms, he drove them from him; they shrank back, startled. The hubbub ceased, the Kiowas pressed back against the circumference of the lodge. Stone Teeth still only looked at Rainbolt contemptuously, and spat into the fire, saying something under his breath to the man in the checkered vest.

If his fate was now to be death, Rainbolt thought, he hoped it would come quickly. No more knotty decisions—he was done with decisions. Let them kill him, and have done with it. What was it old man Coogan had said? *Man for man, I guess the Kiowas has killed more white men than any of the tribes.* Well, let them kill another one, then!

But the Kiowas did not kill him. Instead, the chief gestured to the stammering interpreter, giving him certain instructions. They took Rainbolt away, putting him in a small lodge of his own with an incongruous brass bedstead in the middle, complete with grass-filled mattress and a blue and white quilt he remembered as the Double Wedding Ring design. Of course, there was a guard at the door, a silent and watchful young man with a late model 56-50 Spencer carbine. It was the same as the one Private Philip Rainbolt had been issued when he first joined the Eighth Cavalry, with a seven-shot magazine inserted into the stock through a hole in the butt plate.

That first night he got little sleep. Nervous and apprehensive, he lay for a long time on a blanket near the door flap. The brass bedstead and the patiently worked quilt reminded him too much of the settlers at the small rancho—the man and the woman and the tow-headed boy he had buried beneath a makeshift cross.

After a while, sleepless, he got up and stepped tentatively outside. The guard looked up, but apparently did not object as long as his charge stayed near. Breathing deep of the cool night air, Rainbolt looked about him. The Kiowa village slept in the moonlight, conical lodges glowing strangely pale and luminous in the crescent moon, almost as if ghostly lanterns burned within. Somewhere a dying fire crackled in one last surge, and on the rim of the jagged walls of the canyon a scattering of bushes was outlined blackly by the moonlight. For a moment any one of the crouching black forms might have been an invader—the Eighth Cavalry, Tonks, whatever—but as he watched, one of the dark forms moved. He heard a lookout call to another. This impenetrable Kiowa camp, well shielded in the rocky gorge, was guarded.

After the heat of the day, the brassy dusty heat of Indian Territory, the night shimmered with spicelike scent from plants and bushes that grew in the canyon. From a series of rocky shelves a thread of water dropped into larger and larger pools; night birds flitted around the spring. From far down the sleeping canyon a horse whinnied, then another. Once Rainbolt thought he heard a cow, too—a long and dismal lament quickly swallowed up in the splashing of water. But when he took a step toward the spring, thinking with pleasure of a cool drink, his Kiowa guard menaced him with a twitch of the carbine barrel, ordering him back into the tipi.

Perplexed, Rainbolt went back to his blanket and closed his eyes. Prison at Fort Leavenworth, or this—he was a prisoner either way. But he *was* alive. He did not open his eyes again until it was broad daylight, the early sun laying dancing black shadows on the lodge wall.

For several days he remained a guarded prisoner in the Kiowa camp, enduring his ambiguous captivity. There was something strange about it. They were bloodthirsty savages—he knew that—so why did they not kill him? But how explain the strange respect some of them seemed to have for him; this comfortable tipi, the brass bedstead, certainly a mark of importance that attached to him? And if they were keeping him for eventual barter, why not just tie him up and throw him aside to await the day?

Perhaps they were still deciding what to do with him. They did give him clothes—Kiowa clothes—even a young woman to cook for him, and share the brass bedstead, if he chose. Though the guard still kept a watchful eye on him, by now he had apparently been given the freedom of the camp. An active man, he was glad for the opportunity to stretch his long legs. But it was unsettling to have a crowd of curious women and children following him wherever he went, staring wide-eyed when he had to make water. And while most of them regarded him only with uncertainty, some were downright hostile, scowling and making ritual gestures when he passed. It was all very unsettling.

Apparently under orders, the stammering interpreter in the checkered vest visited him often, asking if there was anything he wanted, any particular food he craved, did he smoke? Respectfully, the man laid before him a rawhide sack of the scraped willow bark the Kiowas smoked when they could not get white man's tobacco, along with a carved soapstone pipe and a block of phosphorus matches.

Having watched the Kiowas, Rainbolt stuffed the pipe with the fragrant bark and lit it. After a few puffs he passed the pipe to his visitor, who seemed surprised, but accepted.

After they had both puffed for a while, observing the Kiowa amenities, Rainbolt spoke. "Thank you for the smoke. I am grateful."

The interpreter shrugged. "It was not my gift. B—b—but I am glad you liked it."

Seizing the moment, Rainbolt blurted, "What's going to happen to me? Why are they keeping me here, under guard?"

But the interpreter only shrugged again, and said, "This is not for me to say. Some time, you will find out."

After that, though, a kind of rapport grew between them. Rainbolt learned a great deal about the Kiowas: their camp, their life, their customs, their language, both spoken and signed. So long as he did not press for information on his status, Two Time Talk was an agreeable informant. The man's proper name was some unpronounceable string of gutturals, but because of his stammer he was known as Two Time Talk.

The chief, the old man in the red turban Rainbolt had last seen on the couch in the big ceremonial lodge, was Water Turtle, successor to the murdered Satank as chief of this, the largest Kiowa band roving Indian Territory and Texas. The shy doe-eyed girl who cooked for Rainbolt was Star Sister, a niece of Water Turtle and his favorite. Rainbolt wondered again, what a chief's blood relative was doing in a prisoner's lodge, cooking for him, washing and mending his clothes, lighting his pipe each day with a coal plucked from the fire with a split green twig?

But the summer mornings were pleasant. In the heat of the day Rainbolt napped in the lodge, side flaps rolled to catch the breeze. Star Sister brought him choice tidbits of roasted meat, picked wild berries for him, sat long hours at his feet, patiently awaiting his whim. Perhaps, Rainbolt concluded, a man did better not to question fate.

Deprived of books, Rainbolt began to take a studious interest in the Kiowas—their tribal organization, their theology, their history. The hand talk fascinated him, the quick gestures that enabled a Kiowa to communicate with a Caddo, a Comanche, an Apache, even the Sioux and the Cheyennes when the Kiowas wandered that far west. They did indeed travel so far at times, since the buffalo that once grazed in countless thousands along the Red River were now scarce and poor in flesh, decimated by the hide hunters with their big Sharps rifles.

Tutored in the guttural Kiowa tongue by Two Time Talk, instructed in the sign language by Star Sister, Rainbolt even began to appreciate Kiowa humor. It was based generally on a ridicule of pompousness and vanity. They loved to make fun of the white men. A Moravian missionary once lived briefly with them; it was considered howlingly funny to make a pair of imitation spectacles from woven willow twigs and stalk through the camp pretending to read a book.

According to their legends, a supernatural being gave the Kiowas the sun, fashioned for them the day and the night, instructed them in the hunting and the arts of war, then went up into the stars to watch over them. A great hero in their early days was Sun Boy, child of the sun and an earthly mother, who gave them the sacred Tai Me fetishes, powerful medicine dolls which were kept in the care of the chief of the tribe. Sun Boy, it was said, now lived among the stars also, and would come down to rescue the Kiowas from a great disaster.

What fascinated Rainbolt most was the Sett'an Calendar. As the official record of their people, the calendar was almost as holy as the Tai Me dolls. It was an ancient buffalo hide, Two Time Talk explained, scraped so thin it was almost transparent. Drawn on it was an outgoing spiral which represented a timeline. As nearly as Two Time Talk could explain, it went back almost fifty years.

Two Time Talk made a rough sketch to illustrate. Each winter along the spiral was marked by a vertical black bar, each summer by a triangular symbol to indicate the annual Medicine Lodge and its accompanying Sun Dance. Along the spiral, each at its appropriate time, were drawn the events important to the Kiowas. One year showed a spotted man; that was the year of a smallpox epidemic that almost wiped out the Kiowas. Another year displayed dismembered bodies. That was the year the Osages treacherously attacked and cut off a lot of Kiowa heads, putting them in the Kiowas' own copper cooking kettles. A third year, perhaps as far back as 1820 or so, Rainbolt figured, showed crude drawings of what appeared to be gold coins. He was right. Two Time Talk said that |was the time the Kiowas ambushed a train of Santa Fe traders and captured a small keg filled with money.

Actually, the Kiowa language was relatively simple, having only three tenses: past, present, and future. Soon Rainbolt was able to stroll about the camp with his guard, a youth named Painted Bow, and call out an appropriate greeting. When the people seemed friendly, he stopped to talk with them, listening carefully to the various pitches, intonations, and clicking sounds that changed the meanings of words. But there were many lodges where he was apparently not welcome. When they saw him approach, the women would hurry within, taking the children with them. The husbands, sitting cross-legged combing their hair or painting their faces, went stonily on with their toilettes, refusing to recognize his presence. In a way, it was a replication of his status: on the one hand, a carefully guarded prisoner—on the other, an honored guest.

He always enjoyed seeing the Kiowas break horses. At the great corral down the valley were hundreds of stolen horses and prime cattle. A carnival atmosphere prevailed in the camp, and Rainbolt learned that it would soon be time for the arrival of the comancheros, bringing kegs of rum, bolts of calico and gingham, tobacco and trade goods in exchange for the stolen stock.

The young Kiowa men had a strange way of breaking unruly horses. Mounting with a blanket wrapped tightly around their body and legs, they simply grabbed the mane and threw themselves lengthwise on the horse. Rising up, their blanket-bound limbs functioned like pincers, gripping the horse's ribs so securely they could hardly be dislodged, even by the wildest bucking and sunfishing. After a while the fractious horse, wheezing and blowing, simply gave up.

In holiday mood, spectators lined the walls of

the corral, laughing, joking, applauding a good ride with cries of *"Hau! Hau!"* or jeering a thrown rider. Rainbolt saw Milky Way, Stone Teeth, and many of the Kiowa onde looking on. For an especially good ride these aristocrats would throw into the corral a favored knife, or perhaps a bracelet or string of shell beads.

After a deer-legged, wild-eyed and crazily splotched paint had thrown three men in a row, a young man suddenly seized the braided nose rope and led the animal, whuffling and trembling, to where Rainbolt and his guard sat on a pile of rocks. By gestures, he made it known that the prisoner was to try his luck.

Afterward, Rainbolt suspected that the malevolent Stone Teeth had planned the whole thing. But it was an embarrassing situation, and he did not know what to do. But the problem was solved when Painted Bow, his guard, gave him a good-humored shove into the ring.

Indians, Rainbolt knew, always mounted from the right side. But he was a cavalryman, and would ride like one. Taking two or three turns of the nose rope around his hand, he grabbed a handful of mane and vaulted onto the sweating hairy back.

Rolling its eyes, the pony sprang stiff-legged into the air, coming down with a hammerlike jolt he was sure shattered every vertebra in his spine. Both to protest the pain and to relieve his fears, he yelled. The paint responded by veering violently, forequarters going in one direction and spotted rump in the other.

His teeth slapped together and he bit his tongue painfully. At the same time the pony reared high, pawing the air. Desperately Rainbolt clung to the mane, having lost the nose rope entirely. But the bucking pony suddenly flung its heels in the air and put its head between its forelegs in an incredible reversal. Rainbolt flew off like a rocket, having left only the sense to tuck his head between his shoulders in an effort to prevent his neck from being broken. Then he was lying flat in ammonia-smelling horse droppings, staring up at a red sun only dimly seen through the settling dust.

Staggering, he got to his feet. But where the unsuccessful rides of the young men had been greeted with good-humored jeers and whistles, there was now silence. In a way, it was almost like a scene from a Roman arena. A defeated gladiator, Rainbolt stood alone in the middle of the corral, dusty and disheveled. The crowd was silent, face-less, waiting for a sign. Stone Teeth lounged among his friends, and the faces turned toward him in mute inquiry.

Stone Teeth, successful in disgracing the white man, let the silent tension build. Chewing the hard-parched corn that gave him his name, he smiled, the patronizing smile of the man who has won. Taking the cue, the spectators tittered, and fingers pointed at Rainbolt. Then a wave of laughter started, and soon they were all laughing, catcalling, pointing ridiculing fingers. Someone picked up a fresh ball of horse dropping and threw the sticky mass at Rainbolt. It hit him on the cheek and slid wetly down; the crowd roared approval. This was not the good-humored poking of fun that had gone on before. This was frightening. Somehow, it was almost as if some larger issue than Rainbolt's horsemanship was being decided.

Flushed and angry, he looked down at the ball of manure. He remembered a gesture he had seen on his walks through the village. It was a filthy sign—one that Star Sister had blushed at and did not even want to explain to him. Staring hard at Stone Teeth so there should be no mistake, he pointed to the smoking ball of dung and then made the remembered gesture: thumb protruding between first and second fingers. *Eat excrement,* it meant. *Horse manure is the food for a man like you!*

Stone Teeth's smile faded. Someone tried to restrain him but he pushed them aside, vaulting over the low corral poles and drawing his tasseled knife from its sheath.

Rainbolt, watching him come, jabbed his thumb out again. *Eat excrement! Eat excrement!*

Stone Teeth was furious at the insult, given before the large audience. But in his time in the cavalry Philip Rainbolt had learned barracks brawling. With his quiet and studious ways, it had become a necessity in the brawling world of Eighth Cavalry paydays and drunken poker games. As Stone Teeth met him, knife held low before him as if ready to gut a trapped antelope, he threw himself suddenly backward and to one side, avoiding the murderous glide of the tasseled knife. At the same time he caught Stone Teeth's ankle between his own legs and rolled over, twisting hard, so that Stone Teeth tottered and fell, the outflung knife burying its point in the corral dirt.

One man against a knife was not good odds, but the fight ended as abruptly as it began. Dimly Rainbolt was aware of someone pulling him to his feet, squalling in his ear, at the same time planting a moccasined foot on Stone Teeth's bare chest to fend him off. Behind his savior was old Water Turtle, the turbaned chief, calling for peace.

In response to a command from Water Turtle, Stone Teeth put his knife sullenly away and stalked off, followed by a band of friends. He would, Rainbolt knew, hear more from Stone Teeth; panting for breath, he watched Stone Teeth go. But someone was still jabbering in his ear, making a great commotion, pulling at his sleeve to draw his attention.

"Hee, hee!" Ike Coogan chortled, pumping his hand. "Looks like I got here just in time!" He backed off, looking at Philip Rainbolt with a critical eye. "So this is where you holed up, bucko!" He shook his grizzled head admiringly. "And you surer 'n hell learned a few tricks since I last seen you!"

CHAPTER FIVE

It was certainly true—he was a long way from Private Philip Rainbolt, F Company, Eighth Cavalry, late inmate of the Fort Sill guardhouse. At first Coogan did not even recognize him with his shaggy hair, uncut mustaches and beard, the Kiowa shirt and leggings.

Rainbolt himself realized with a start he was even further away from Philip Ramsey Rainbolt of Nine-Mile plantation in Wiggs County, Georgia, near Macon; even further from Captain Rainbolt of Heth's Division at Petersburg. In this strange new life with its wealth of stimulus and event he had even forgotten about the lost battery. Now, seeing a white man, even the whisky-smelling old comanchero, he felt the lost battery again take form and shape in the back of his mind. The consciousness was not dramatic, nor compelling—the battery was simply *there,* part of him in the same way as his fingers and toes and ears, a continuing witness.

For a while, sitting cross-legged on the buffalo robe across from Coogan, he hardly heard the old man's words.

". . . and I allus *knew,* even in that stinkin' jail, that you was my man, so to speak!" Coogan dug

Rainbolt in the ribs. "Hee, hee! Didn't I say I seen somethin' in you?"

Shaking his head as if to clear his vision, Rainbolt asked, "You knew *what?* What are you talking about?"

Coogan was delighted. He prowled the tipi, drinking from a tin cup of rum, seeming not to have heard. "By Jesus Christ and every damned apostle there is, it's the biggest chance ever a man had! Why, you and me—we can clean up in one big haul, live out the rest of our days eatin' patty foo graw and drinkin' champagne in Paris, France!"

Rainbolt was annoyed. "Sit down and tell me what you're gabbling about!"

Coogan stopped pacing. He sat down on the robe and emptied the tin cup, staring at Rainbolt over the rim of the cup. Then he put the cup down, wiping the thicket of whiskers with the back of his hand.

"You mean you don't know?"

"Know what?"

"About you and Sun Boy?"

Rainbolt began to be angry. "Stop talking in riddles!"

Rocking back and forth on his skinny bottom, hands clasped on his bony knees, Ike opened his mouth and roared, a single yellow tooth sticking up from his lower gums. "Oh, my good Christ, what a joke! Of course you don't! You didn't know *what* was goin' on, did you?"

"I knew," Rainbolt admitted sulkily, "that they put a guard on me day and night, watched me like I was some kind of a prize pig at the fair!"

Coogan leaned forward, grinning. "You don't see no guards now, do you?"

Rainbolt sprang up and went to the door flap. It was true. Painted Bow, the young man with the Spencer carbine, was nowhere to be seen. The camp seemed almost deserted. From the corral, however, he heard a lot of noise: yells, laughter, an occasional gunshot. The comancheros had come, and it was a day of celebration. Puzzled, he came back and sat down, rubbing his forehead.

"Why?" he asked. "Why no guard?"

" 'Cause they finally decided who you are! At least, most of 'em. There's dissenters—Stone Teeth and his brothers. But most of Water Turtle's Kiowas gives you a fair chance of being Sun Boy hisself!"

He knew of Sun Boy and the ancient legend. But—Philip Rainbolt?

Seeing his confusion, the old man want on.

"It don't make a half-bad case, and we dassn't tamper with it, long's that's what they want to believe. Sun Boy was born of the sun and an earth woman, right?"

"That's what they say."

"The story goes that in time of big trouble Sun Boy's gonna come down, kill one of their great enemies, then save the whole tribe from bein' wiped out and go up in the sky again. What could fit better? Satank was killed by the soldiers. Accordin' to their medicine men, that means their gods are mad and there's goin' to be a heap of trouble from now on. Then you killed Cat—"

"Who?"

"You mean you don't even know who you drew down on?"

Rainbolt shook his head.

"Why, that was Cat!" Coogan howled. "The biggest baddest Tonk there ever was! Some of these here savages believed Cat was a god hisself, he killed so many Kiowas and got away with it! And here you cashed in Cat's chips for him and come ridin' in with his medicine lance and joolery and everything!" Wiping his eyes, he settled down again. "I ain't clear in my mind how you done it, but someday when there's time you can tell me."

Rainbolt had a feeling of unreality, a disorientation that made him uncomfortable.

"Not only that," Coogan went on, "but Sun Boy's father is the sun itself. The story goes that Sun Boy, when he comes back, will have hair bright yellow, like the sun." He pointed to Rainbolt's flowing hair and beard. "Kinda bleached out now, but it's fair to call it sort of goldy yellow."

Not that he believed the tall tale, but assuming it was even halfway true, something intrigued Rainbolt.

"Why doesn't Stone Teeth believe?"

Coogan chuckled. "You upset his applecart! Stone Teeth's medicine said he was goin' to kill Cat and be a big hero among the Kiowas. But you beat him to it! Oh, Stone Teeth never had any ideas of bein' took for Sun Boy, bein' a little too dark-complected. But he did favor the idea of gettin' to be a big man, at least a topadoki, and now you ruined everything. I reckon that's why he set you up to ride that wall-eyed paint; figgered it'd prove to the people you wasn't no Sun Boy. But I set 'em all straight. When Water Turtle asked me what I thought, I said you probably *was* Sun Boy."

"You told them *that?*"

"Hee, hee! I sure did. My maw didn't raise no idiots! Why, you and me—we got a gold-plated deal here that's gonna make us rich!"

"I don't understand."

The comanchero poured himself a third or fourth drink—Rainbolt didn't know which— and clapped him on the shoulder. " 'Course you don't! Your brains is just a mite addled from associatin' so long with these savages, 'thout no white meat around!" Tossing down the rum, he went on. "So far I done had to share the horses and cattle the Kiowas rounds up with a bunch of other fellers—comancheros like me. But *now* I got Sun Boy right here in Water Turtle's camp! Sun Boy is my boy! He's gonna tell Water Turtle not to do business with nobody but Ike Coogan!"

"But—"

Coogan tottered to his feet, putting on his ancient greasy hat.

"Think of that! Rich men—you and me! Patty foo graw and silk sheets, the Roo de la Pay and French ladies to pleasure us any time of day!" When Rainbolt, astonished by the comanchero's proposition, tried to make him sit down, Coogan only pushed him away and took another drink, saying, "Don't stand in my way! I got to see to my goods!" He stared bleary-eyed at Rainbolt, wiping his mouth with a stained sleeve. "Sun Boy!" he chuckled. "Right? You and me!" He tottered away toward the corral and the noise and the scattered shots, swinging the jug from a crooked finger. "Sun Boy!" he chortled. "Ain't that rich?"

The celebration went on for three days and three nights. In their wagons the comancheros brought kegs of rum and brandy, bolts of bright cloth, wooden boxes of knives and hatchets, cooking pots, mirrors, beads, red and yellow and green paint. The biggest attraction, aside from the liquor, was the store of weapons. Crate after crate was opened with blows from an ax, and the eager Kiowas fought each other for the newest model firearms. The Kiowas were, Rainbolt thought, better armed than the Eighth Cavalry. Tipsy from rum and whisky and brandy, they ran, excited, through the camp, firing repeating carbines and fine revolvers. Rainbolt saw an entire crate of the new Remington's Double and Single Action Belt Revolver, the .38-caliber model with the six-inch barrel, so new it had only been announced in the *Army and Navy Journal* a few months back. And of course there were barrels of powder, even a supply of the new smokeless kind, preloaded metal cartridges of every caliber, load, and bullet weight, even pig lead, ladles, and molds for casting bullets and reloading metal cartridges. Rainbolt would not have been surprised to see the comancheros bring out one of the new Gatling guns for use against the Eighth Cavalry. Raiding the Red River settlers and stealing their stock must, he realized, be a tremendously profitable business.

The comancheros were a ruffianly lot. Some were Mexicans, others renegade Texans, still others Negroes and Indians. One of the most successful, Ike Coogan's chief rival, was a gigantic Caddo named George Washington. Quick and businesslike, the comancheros got down to cases after the initial round of gifts. A Maynard carbine for a white-faced steer; a red blanket for a bay horse; a gallon of best Indies rum for a milk cow and calf. The calf would probably die on the long trail drive across the Canadian and the Cimarron to the rail head, but that was part of the expense of doing business.

While the hired Mexican *vaqueros* were

forming the herd for the drive north, Rainbolt rode Brutus over to where Ike Coogan sat his fine sorrel. Now that he was an important man among the Kiowas, Rainbolt had demanded and got his old cavalry mount back. Brutus was shy among the Indian ponies, the milling herd of lowing cattle and unruly horses. He gentled the gelding with the nose rope that was now his accustomed rig, and spoke to Ike Coogan.

"You know what I think about this dirty business. I told you, back there in the guardhouse, you were a dirty old crook and should be hanged. I haven't seen anything here to change my mind."

"That so?" Ike asked mildly. He scratched his nose with the butt of his quirt. "What do you aim to do, then?"

The question caught Rainbolt unprepared. Finally he said, "I've been thinking things over. Maybe I'm tired of running away. I've got Brutus and the Kiowas will give me supplies. It might be a good idea to go back to the post and turn myself in. I broke jail, that's true, but I doubt if I'd get more than another six months. I'm only twenty-nine. In a year I'd be out."

Ike laughed so hard the sorrel became frightened and started to prance. He cut her across the ears with a savage blow of the quirt and sawed hard on the checkrein. Cowed, the animal came to a trembling halt.

"Why, you egreejus idiot!" the comanchero

cackled. "Who in hell you think you are, to make up your mind just like that?" He pointed the quirt at Rainbolt. "You'll butter up old Water Turtle just like I ordered you to! You'll tell him Ike Coogan is the best thing to come along since coal oil! You'll see that the next time he has a corral full of stock to let *me* know—just me— and run these other fellers off!"

"You can go to hell!" Rainbolt protested.

"You won't do it?"

"I won't!"

Suddenly Ike shrugged. He became matter of fact, almost casual.

"All right, then! If I can't make you see how much money's in it for the both of us, I'll have to come up behind a different bush. Understand this now, bucko! You ain't goin' no place, 'thout you plans on being hung!"

Rainbolt could only stare at him.

"Because," Ike Coogan went on, "you're wanted for murder!"

The air, the sun, the milling stock; all seemed unreal. All that was real was Ike Coogan and the moving lips framed in porcupine-needle whiskers. Finally, after a deep intake of breath, Rainbolt managed to blurt, "Murder? Me?"

Ike nodded, licking cracked lips with a small delicate tongue.

"Cut poor old Huckabee's throat, didn't you? With that knife I give you?"

Dazed, Rainbolt shook his head. "I—I—"

"Then turned loose Milky Way and Stone Teeth and Won't Listen and the rest, and run away with 'em to this here Kiowa camp?"

It was ridiculous, but Rainbolt could not find words to deny the accusation.

"Old hard-ass Cameron would love to catch up with you," Ike chortled. "You played fast and loose with his wife, killed Huckabee, busted out of the major's jail, and took a whole slew of Kiowa troublemakers along with you. Made Cameron look ridiklus, and that's a fact."

Rainbolt found his voice. "Why, that's a lie! You know not a damned word of it is true! The Kiowas let *me* out, and then rode away! Huckabee was dead when I got out of my cell!"

"Who's goin' to believe such a cock-and-bull story? You had a knife—I *told* Cameron that."

"But you gave it to me!"

"I guess," Ike said roguishly, "I seen some good in you no one else seen! I says to myself, now here's this young buck in jail here. I don't like jails—they're cold and they're drafty. It's a shame, I says, to keep a promising young fellow lawbreaker in such onsanitary conditions. Maybe, I says, he can use a knife to dig his way out of that 'dobe jail when I'm gone." He rolled his eyes heavenward. "I never figgered he'd cut somebody's *throat* with it!"

Rainbolt still could not believe.

"Sure, I had a knife," Ike admitted piously. "But it was stole out of my clothes in the guardhouse while I slept! I told Major Cameron that."

"The Kiowas!" Rainbolt blurted. "They came in the night, on horses! Somehow they slipped past the sentries and broke into the guardhouse. They killed poor Huckabee, they took his keys—" His voice rose in despair. "Didn't anyone find their tracks?"

"Wasn't no tracks that night," Ike said coldly. "It was raining, remember? If there *was* any Kiowas come to rescue friends, the rain done washed out their tracks." He turned in the saddle to call out an order to one of the vaqueros. "No," he resumed, "I'd say it was a pretty fair case against you. Anyway, there's federal warrants out for you from here to Californy and back, and I daresay the presses is turnin' out more. If I was you I'd know right away which side of my bread had jam on it. You better stay right here, Sun Boy, and get old Water Turtle crackin' to round me up some prime stock. I'll be stoppin' by soon to see how our little business deal is acomin'." He pointed the quirt again. "Just remember—I'm the onliest one knows who you are and where you are, Philip Rainbolt or whatever your name might be! So cross me, and you got a date with a noose at Leavenworth Prison early some morning!"

With a great deal of bellowing the herd began

105

to move out. Rainbolt sat Brutus for a long time watching them, the vaqueros dashing expertly this way and that, straightening the line, galloping to turn a wandering heifer. After a while there was only a haze of dust to mark their passing. Stunned, he rode back to the camp, which was now sleeping off a monumental drunk. For the first time he accepted Star Sister's advances, and lay with her in the big brass bed. He felt lonely; he needed any comfort he could get.

The night her husband struck her, Ellen Cameron started to lay her plans. It had been a foolish quarrel about nothing; she did not even know how she had crossed him. But Hugh Cameron, badgered by the general's insistent telegraph messages, frustrated by the escaped Kiowas, was in a black mood. It was rumored the Kiowas had joined Satank's old band somewhere across the Red River, and wanted revenge. The summer wore on, with repeated lightning raids by the Kiowas on ranchers and settlers all the way from the Red to the Mexican border. The Kiowas hated Texans. They pillaged and murdered, driving off stock and burning the homes. Major Cameron and the Eighth were ineffective, and the settlers were already making political representations to Washington in protest.

Afterward, of course, Hugh was sorry, and kissed the red weal on her cheek. Ellen tolerated him, knowing she was already as good as gone. A wild tide of adventure rose in her; she wondered if it was unseemly in a lady to feel so stimulated. But she went ahead, quickly and covertly, with her plans.

There were her Uncle Nestor and Aunt Alice Beecher in Memphis. They would be sorry to hear of trouble with her marriage, but her father's brother had never approved of her marrying into the Army, anyway. Looking at the map by the light of a candle while Hugh was at headquarters one night, she pondered her route. There was no way out of the post except by Army supply train, of course. But if she could find a teamster in Whisky City with wagons going more or less south—say to Bell Plain or Bonham—she could catch the Texas Pacific there and be in Memphis in a few days. After that, what? She didn't know. But it would be fun to be free again.

Private Neilsen was the only one she could trust. The Swede was an occasional "striker" for the major—an enlisted man doing household chores for extra pay. Besides, Neilsen was grateful for the school and her help with teaching him how to read and write and cipher. But he was appalled at her plan.

"Why, I couldn't do *that,* ma'am!" His Scandinavian eyes were blue and wide with astonishment. "He'd—he'd have me flogged!"

Ellen knew Army regulations. "Fiddlesticks!

It's not allowed any more. Flogging, I mean. And think—twenty dollars! Why, that's as much as you make in two months! Besides, you're in debt gambling, aren't you? I heard the sergeant major say so!"

Neilsen was watering the parched garden for her, with forbidden water at that, and he was frightened. She played on that fear. "You know my husband has forbidden gambling. You can pay off your debt to Corporal Biggers with the money, and have some left over to send your family. You have a family, haven't you? Two boys and a girl. Or is it two girls and a boy?"

In the end, wheedling, cajoling, she won him over. On a day when Hugh was out on scout with B Company and Lieutenant Conyers, Private Neilsen drove a wagon into Whisky City to pick up supplies from Tyler's Fancy Groceries. The Army furnished only coffee, bread, beans, and beef, with occasional molasses, cornbread, or sweet potatoes. Each company had a fund to which the men contributed. When there was enough money, someone went into town to buy treats like canned tomatoes, dried apples and peaches, sauerkraut, or potatoes and onions. In her best gray serge traveling dress, she hid under a blanket in the bed of the wagon till Neilsen reached Whisky City. Then, in response to his whispered command, she followed him, clutching her valise, through a maze of fetid lanes and alleyways. The next morning, fifty dollars in gold having been exchanged, she left with an ox train for Fort Worth; it would pass near Bell Plain, and she would take the train for Memphis with the rest of her money. In her reticule she still had almost a hundred dollars in greenbacks, and the small ivory-handled derringer Hugh insisted she keep with her when he was away.

At first she was excited by the great adventure. Only a few hours away from Whisky City the enormity of the land overwhelmed her. She imagined the toiling wagons the *Nina*, *Pinta*, and the *Santa Maria*, taking her on a new voyage of discovery across uncharted seas. The grassy plain seemed to extend forever. Burned by the sun, it took on a golden hue, broken only by sparse patches of mesquite and scrub oak. The man who owned the wagons was a morose broken-faced giant she knew only as Mr. Mason. He said little to her, and the two Mexican boys who drove the oxen spoke no English. So she sat beside the silent Mason and made up stories to while away the time.

"When we get there," she asked him after several hours of heat-heavy silence, "how will we cross the Red River?"

Mason stared at her, teeth clenched on a soaked stub of cheroot. His eyes were heavy and blood-shot, breath thick with a musty odor that repelled her.

"Ferry," he said, and spoke no more.

All that day she sat on the high seat, watching the slow weave and bob of rumps as the oxen toiled along the rutted trail, listening to the endless squeaking of the wheels. After a while the heat haze made her eyes ache. Feeling faint, she left the seat to lie on a pile of sweat-smelling blankets in the bed of the wagon. But the dirty canvas overhead seemed to attract and focus the heat. After a while she modestly pulled together the curtain between her and the driver and took off her clothing, down to her camisole.

A little before sunset each night they stopped, grained and watered the oxen, and made a small fire to fry bacon and boil coffee. This was the only time she could in delicacy relieve herself. She was aware of the Mexican boys watching her with dark intense eyes as she sauntered away, looking for a clump of mesquite or a stand of the dwarf oaks. But the stars were beautiful; overhead they lay like a handful of diamonds scattered on a rich blue-black velvet. In spite of the heat of the day there was always a breeze to rustle the burned grass.

Ellen liked to ride. Since Mason had a couple of pluglike horses tied to the rear of the tandem wagon, she occasionally persuaded one of the Mexican boys, a fat and pimpled youth named Luis, to saddle the mare and let her ride out on the plain as a relief from the tedium of the slowly toiling wagons. Fortunately, her gray serge had a very full skirt. She could mount astride without revealing more than a little ankle and a few inches of stockinged flesh. But one day when Luis made a cradle of his hands to assist her to mount, he suddenly whispered something under his breath and slid his hand up her leg, almost to the knee.

She gasped and slapped his face. But he only grinned at her, licking his lips.

Angry, she galloped away. When she returned she tied the horse to the wagon and took off the saddle and bridle herself. Climbing up on the high seat, she said, "That boy Luis—he touched me today!"

Mason turned a lackluster gaze on her. He had not been feeling well; the fetid smell of his breath sickened her. Was she mistaken, or were those patches under his eyes and on his neck some kind of a rash?

"I—he—" She faltered under Mason's heavy-lidded gaze. "He ran his hand up my—my limb when he was helping me get up on the mare." She blushed, and pulled the lacy collar of the serge more tightly around her neck.

"Damn greasers!" Mason snorted. "They ain't worth a hill of beans! But I get 'em cheap. I'd have to pay a white man twice as much!" Shaking his head, he promised to speak to Luis. But at suppertime Mason was obviously ill, shaking as with an ague. The Mexican boys only grinned at her and shrugged when she tried to get them to help, so she made Mr. Mason lie down in the lead wagon while she gathered mesquite twigs and made a fire.

That night there was no breeze. The air turned heavy and sticky, the full moon shone murkily through a veil of ragged clouds drifting slowly and ominously from the north. Mason slept fitfully; afraid of the Mexicans, who squatted at the edge of the firelight and looked at her with dark and passionate eyes, Ellen sat on a blanket and from time to time stirred the coals. Between her breasts the tiny derringer lay, loaded and ready to fire.

At dawn Mason climbed unsteadily out of the wagon and ordered the boys to harness the oxen. But by the time they had eaten hardtack and cold grease-frosted bacon and were ready to move out he was deathly sick. Trying to climb on the high seat, he staggered and fell. It was only her strong arm under him that kept him from sprawling at full length. The patches were bigger now, and more inflamed, the color of ripe mulberries. "My head hurts," Mason complained, "and my heart pounds in my chest."

Now she knew that musty odor; Mr. Mason had the typhus fever. One of the laundresses on Soapsuds Row had caught it, and she helped the post surgeon treat the woman with Blue Mass pills and calomel. The same rash, the same fetid breath, the same complaints of headaches and pounding pulse. The typhus.

All that day she sat beside him, giving him sips of water from a tin cup. What was it the surgeon said? *Keep the room and the patient thoroughly clean. Give abundant and easily digested food. Stimulants might be needed.* But there was nothing to help Mr. Mason. He began to wander in his head, talking about a farm he once owned in Missouri.

Fortunately, the cloud cover made the heat less oppressive. But in late afternoon, when her patient slept, she climbed down from the wagon to find the Mexican boys gone, and the horses. When she looked in the trail wagon she found a jumble where they had gone through the supplies and taken what they needed. There was a little bacon left, an unopened box of Army hardtack, a can or two of peaches. She was almost certain Mr. Mason kept a shotgun there, but if he had, the boys had stolen it too. Perhaps as well as she, they had recognized the typhus and fled.

Not knowing what to do with the oxen bothered her. Still yoked, they looked at her with sad eyes and browsed at the scanty grass. She made trip after trip to the water kegs and finally sank down on the plain, spent and wet with perspiration. She had not known animals could drink so much water, and the level in the barrels was running low.

The sun set low and red, in a sea of ragged dark clouds. There was still no breeze, only an ominous quiet. The oxen were restless and pawed the earth, looking about with rolling eyes. Painfully she got to her feet. The good gray serge was soiled and dusty, the lace collar had come loose and she had stuffed it into her bosom, there was a jagged rent near the hem where she had caught her foot and stumbled, her hair fell around her face in annoying tangles. But she made a fire and heated leftover coffee for Mr. Mason. He was too sick to eat anything, so she sat beside him in the growing darkness while he sipped the coffee. "Hurts my throat," he said in a husky voice, "but it lifts my sperrits a little." Handing her back the tin cup, he said, "You're a fine woman, Miz Beecher." That was the name she had given when she paid him the fifty dollars. It was not a lie, really; Beecher was her maiden name, back there so far away and so long ago in the city by the bay.

She had not yet told him about the flight of the Mexicans, fearing it would upset him. Now, frightened by the oncoming night and the knowledge she was alone on this limitless prairie with a sick man and no way to help him or herself, she started nervously when the patched canvas of the wagon cover slapped against the stays in a quick gust of wind.

Wondering, she left the sick man and stood

outside in the lee of the wagon. It was almost dark, yet in the remaining red-streaked gloom she could see furious black clouds boiling in the sky. The wind had freshened, blowing cold and steady against her cheek. The oxen rolled their eyes at her and seemed to want her to do something. Though it was foolish, she got a rope from the trail wagon and tied the lead span to the biggest mesquite bush she could find, in case the animals decided to bolt.

All that night the wind blew in a steadily rising crescendo. Huddled beside Mason, she trembled with fear as the canvas rippled and cracked. The wagon swayed from side to side in the gale and bolts of lightning lit the sky, casting everything into stark lime-white relief. She wondered if he was dead, the way his grizzled beard and chin stuck straight up, his eyes closed, and his cheeks sunken and hollow.

She expected rain, but in this strange land the lightning and wind and thunder brought no hint of moisture. But toward morning pellets of hail started to drum on the taut canvas. After a while the uproar was tremendous, like being inside a gigantic drum. She pressed her hands against her ears and cowered, trying to scream but not hearing herself in the uproar. Some of the hail bounded into the wagon from the seat; it was huge, the size of apricots. Slowly but surely the pellets assaulted the canvas. A rip started over her head, spilling a fresh downpour. The pellets hit her head, her cheeks, her bosom; when she put up her hands to protect herself they came away with blood on them where the icy bullets had struck. Moaning in fear, she tried to pull the blankets over Mason's unsheltered face. The wagon pitched and heaved; she was thrown heavily across the sick man, bruising her forehead against the oaken ribs of the bed. For a moment she lay dazed, wondering if this was all a bad dream. Finally she struggled to her knees. Inching her way forward to the high seat, she pulled aside the canvas.

In an eye-searing flash of white light from the heavens, she saw everything with the clarity and precision of a photographic plate: the rolling heavy backs of the oxen as they ran in panic, the mesquite bush on its rope dragged by the lead span, the limitless horizon toward which they ran with no barrier to stop them.

She saw something else too. It made her gasp, and she was quite sure her heart stopped. The lightning had set fire to the prairie. All around them blazed patches of flame, merging into larger and larger patches as the wind fanned the inferno.

CHAPTER SIX

Rainbolt learned never to walk between Water Turtle and the fire. It was part of the chief's personal medicine, given to him in a dream. If someone walked between him and the fire, Water Turtle would have bad luck. His horses would get sick, maybe he would be killed in battle before he had a chance to count coup. Everybody knew about the chief's medicine and was respectful of it, taking care never to come between him and the fire.

Summoned to the big tipi for an audience, Rainbolt allowed Star Sister and Two Time Talk to fuss over him, getting him ready for the event. It was, they assured him, a great honor; something, Rainbolt estimated, like an invitation to a White House smoker by President Grant.

Star Sister made him sit still while she arranged his long and tangled hair with a comb of horn. While he refused Two Time Talk's offer of the checkered vest, he did accept a magnificent breastplate of soapstone cunningly worked with inlaid bone, disks of polished blue that must have been turquoise obtained through trading with the Apaches and other tribes far to the west, and lozenges of polished glass—blue, green, and red. From the breastplate depended by rawhide

117

cords a curtain of wrinkled objects like dried apples. With a start Rainbolt realized they were human ears. The barracks tales were true, then; the Kiowas ritually cut ears from their victims. With gingerly curiosity he tried to determine if any of them were white, but they were so smoked and desiccated it was impossible to tell. Two ime Talk was very proud of the breastplate, saying it had belonged to his grandfather. While Rainbolt was trying to decide whether to take off the grisly thing, Two Time Talk in a mixture of Kiowa and English and signs, primed him for the event.

"First, stand for a while outside, and see if anything happens. If it does not, call 'Father, I am here.' That is *soyan beahya gadombit* in our tongue. Then he calls to you, invites you to come in. But remember what I have said! Never walk between our father and the fire!"

Star Sister nodded vigorously; the black braids, wrapped in otter fur, bounced. "Do not talk, either, until our father speaks to you. And remember— do not come between him and the fire!"

In a way he was impatient to go, yet uneasy. His status was still uncertain. What old Coogan had told him—that he might pass for Sun Boy— could be true. Yet he knew how mercurial, how changeable, Indians were. Swallowing hard, he could not get down the lump in his throat. Suddenly he felt a flush of the panic that had driven him from the field at Petersburg. That was six years ago, but it felt the same. Willing his legs to support him, he pushed his mentors aside and went out into the summer sun.

Watching him pass, the people were silent. *The People,* they called themselves in their own language, as if there were no others. When Rainbolt had first heard the term—*the People*—from Star Sister, he had been amused at her naïve solemnity. Now, walking through the camp, the weight of the prairie sun on his bare head and the gruesome breastplate swinging against his chest, he wondered if he had been wrong to laugh at Star Sister. His life now depended on the People.

Looking neither left nor right, he stalked toward Water Turtle's lodge, considerably taller than most of the watching Kiowas, yet dwarfed by their silent scrutiny. *They know,* he thought. *They know something is to be decided today.*

After a polite wait, he finally called out as he had been instructed. Water Turtle himself pulled aside the door flap and gestured for him to enter. Rainbolt bowed his head and stepped inside, carefully looking to the fire, while Water Turtle lay back down on his favorite couch.

It was hard to tell the age of an Indian. Rainbolt guessed the chief to be in his sixties, but the old man fixed his guest with a penetrating eye containing none of the rheum of age.

"Sit down."

Most of the Kiowas seemed to know a little English. While the soldiers were in hot pursuit of one band, another would be at the agency in Jacksboro, demanding the flour and bacon, the beans and black powder and guns they had been promised at the recent Medicine Lodge treaty talks in Kansas. But Rainbolt was surprised at Water Turtle's English. There was something queer, almost unsettling, in the way the chief chose his words, the deft turn of phrase, all in fluent English though hinged heavily with the guttural Kiowa accent.

"Some people say you are Sun Boy."

Rainbolt volunteered nothing.

"Others say you are not. You are just a white man, they say, and should be killed."

Rainbolt only squatted uncomfortably, limbs cramped and aching in the unaccustomed cross-legged position.

"Coogan says you are Sun Boy. But that old man lies a lot of times. Maybe it is just a trick—a trick for you and that dirty old comanchero to make some money."

This savage in the red kerchief—an untutored aborigine—was shrewd. He might have made a good politician in the halls of Congress. Then Rainbolt remembered that Water Turtle had been one of the skillful Indian negotiators at the Medicine Lodge treaty talks.

"On the other hand," the chief continued, loading a decorated pipe with poor Huckabee's prized Lone Jack, "you might be Sun Boy. Such things are possible." He plucked a coal from the fire between horny fingers and lit the pipe. The coal flared into flame as the old man drew deep, and was soon extinguished and lost in clouds of fragrant smoke.

"Such things are possible," the old man repeated.

He lay back on the couch, puffing, and a shaft of sun entered through the open smoke flaps at the top of the tipi. The ray lit his bronze face, made the kerchief glow like flame. Rainbolt felt some-thing almost like reverence. But that was foolish; he was a Baptist.

"After all," Water Turtle said, "Jesus was a—" For the first time he searched for a word.

"A carpenter," Rainbolt murmured.

"Yes. A Jew carpenter. So—what is funny that Sun Boy comes to us a soldier from the post? It is possible."

This morning most of the lodges had the side walls rolled up to catch the breeze, but not this one. Rainbolt sweated, swallowed hard, inwardly cursed the cramps in his long legs, but did not move. It was protocol. Besides, the black eyes were weighing him. Soon they would arrive at a decision, and nothing he said would make any difference. Everything had been put into the scales—now they were waiting for the swinging beam to come to rest.

"So," Water Turtle murmured.

He puffed for a long time on the pipe, while the lodge filled with tobacco smoke, sun-lit dust, the expectance of decision. A fly darted around Rainbolt's head and lit on his cheek, stitching its way over the bridge of his nose and down under his shirt.

"So," Water Turtle repeated, "we will see. We will watch. If you are Sun Boy, there will be a sign. If you are only one more bad white man, we will know that too. You stay in my camp. You live as one of us so the People can see and decide too. Then, someday, we know. The People will know. I will know." He laid the pipe down. "You will know too, when that time comes."

I will know, Rainbolt thought, his throat dry and thick. He tried to swallow, but could not. *I will certainly know.*

The weather continued clear and hot, ideal for Kiowa raids on the hated settlers. This country was so huge, so vast, that it would take several divisions of troops even to begin to police it. As it was, the Kiowas controlled the land. They rode almost unhindered where they wished, fearing the Army not at all. Water Turtle's Kiowas led the attack, avenging the death of old Satank.

Rainbolt had a lot of time on his hands, and used it to good advantage in learning about the

Kiowas and their ways. For example, the Army always thought of Indians as distinct tribal entities, governed by a hereditary chief as the citizens of the several states were ruled by an elected governor. The many Indian treaties signed and broken were, he grew to understand, a consequence of that mistake. The Kiowas, for example, were a jumble of warrior societies, camp chiefs, honorary clubs, councils of elders, medicine men and shamans, and other powerful influences. Though Water Turtle was greatly respected, it was plain that his decisions could be rejected or overturned. An example were the raiding parties that almost daily left the camp, returning with many head of prime stock and a miscellaneous collection of booty; framed mirrors, ironstone pitchers, quilted comforters, crayon portraits and landscapes, even flowered chamber pots.

Anyone could organize and lead a raiding party. All a man had to do was to get a drum and ride among the tipis singing the *guadagya* song, the travel song that summoned the adventurous. There would be booty for all, the guadagya song said, with plenty of chances to count coup and take scalps. There was a hierarchy of scalps; Mexican scalps did not count much, settlers or ranchers were more valuable, especially scalps with red or blond hair. Highest in value were Caddo and Tonkawa scalps. Pony soldiers ran a close second. So almost daily the raiding parties went out.

When they returned after a few days or weeks, the women would line the trail into camp, chanting, playing flutes, singing, "*Imkagyá gya! Imkagyá gya!* [They are coming in triumph!]" Even if old Water Turtle wanted to stop the avenging raids, the raids that were sure soon to provoke a powerful Army retaliation, there was little possibility he could do so.

The only break in the raiding came with the advent of the annual Sun Dance. The great occasion lasted for four days and four nights. The sacred Tai Me dolls were taken from the great tipi and carried through the camp by a file of dancing and singing warriors, the *Koitsenko.* These latter were a much-respected society limited by tradi-tion to only ten men, the bravest of the brave, wearing their distinctive black elk-skin sashes. After every one had seen the sacred dolls, the Sun Dance began, with the Tai Me installed on a kind of dais at the center of activity.

The purpose of the dance was to cure illness, to ask for good fortune from the holy fetishes. It was also a symbol of the regeneration of life, as well as a powerful bond for displaying loyalty and patriotism. The dancers were mainly young men, though women could dance too, if they chose. The dancers, stimulated by a drink prepared from dried roots and herbs, started slowly. But soon the dance became wilder and wilder. Uncertain of his status, Rainbolt watched from the edge of the circle. Painted red and yellow, shouting, singing, beating ceremonial drums and blowing whistles, shaking rattles and brandishing medicine lances, the dancers shuffled and capered in endless motion. Although Rainbolt thought there was little grace or style to the dance, there was a hypnotic effect to the drumming, the shuffle of the dancers, the intensity with which they took part. The dance raised clouds of dust. At times it was hard for him to see anything but a glimpse of a red and yellow face, the pennoned tip of a lance, a fist grasping a feathered rattle.

Though the women were allowed to join in the Sun Dance, and took a small part in other rituals, they were in general only drudges and menials. They cooked, cared for the children, tanned hides and robes, fetched firewood and water. There was one striking exception. Favorite children, whether male or female, were often given special consider-ation and high status. They were called *ade*, and usually had the run of the camp, entering any lodge as honored guests to sleep, eat, or simply visit. No one seemed able to explain to Rainbolt how children became ade. Sometimes they were the offspring of topadoki; others might be from the *kaan* or lower-class people, who made up about half the population.

Star Sister and her brother Red Sleeves were ade, and Rainbolt's status in the camp seemed augmented by the fact that an ade shared his bed and obviously loved him, whether he was Sun Boy in fact or not.

Lying with her at night, he often thought about Ike Coogan, the comanchero, wondering when Ike would return. Each day, as raiding parties came back to camp with their complement of freshly captured horses and cattle, Rainbolt pondered what to do. If he sought an audience with Water Turtle, trying to advance Coogan's status as favored trader to the Kiowas, it might damage his own uncertain condition. If he did not, and Ike returned to find himself only one of the many comancheros vying for favor of the Kiowas, there was always Ike's threat—*I'm the onliest one knows who you are and where you are, Philip Rainbolt! Cross me, and you got a date with a noose!* In this vast land the Army might be ineffective, but he did not doubt that if Major Hugh Cameron ever got wind of where Philip Rainbolt was, the Eighth Cavalry would pursue him into this very camp.

Faced by dilemma, he procrastinated, did nothing. He was beginning to like the Kiowa life, the freedom from work and responsibility. Star Sister loved him, pampered, lay with him in the brass bed, asked nothing in return from him. Life was good, the weather fine. Someday there would be a reckoning, he supposed—not only for Philip Rainbolt but for the Kiowa nation. But until that day, he would strive to put troublesome things from him.

But one day his idyl came to an abrupt end. Stone Teeth decided to go on a raid himself. Pounding his drum, singing the guadagya song, and riding his favorite horse Red Pet, he paused before Rainbolt's lodge, followed by a long line of young warriors he had recruited.

"Will you go with us?" he asked Rainbolt.

Startled, Rainbolt did not reply. Stone Teeth tossed a handful of parched corn into his mouth from the beaded bag he always carried with him. Pointing the drumstick at Rainbolt, he asked again, "Will you go with us?"

He felt, rather than heard, Star Sister's soft presence behind him, her little intake of breath.

"I—I do not know," he finally stammered.

Stone Teeth grinned a big-toothed grin. "You will bring us good luck," he insisted. "If you are Sun Boy, who can doubt our good luck? Sun Boy is a powerful medicine. If Sun Boy really rides with us, we will come back with a lot of fine horses, many fat cattle. We will bring back with us paint, sewing needles, knives, jugs of liquor!"

"No!" Star Sister whispered in his ear. "Do not go! He is a bad man!"

But the rest of the braves took up the guadagya

song, gesturing to Rainbolt, inviting him to join the band. Thoughtfully, Rainbolt fondled his golden beard, now grown long and glossy. Sun Boy was a legendary hero—half-man, half-god. If a man taken for Sun Boy stayed in camp, knowing only the soft and delicious comforts of a woman, he would not last long among these savage people. Whether he wanted it or not, Rainbolt was committed. He knew it, Stone Teeth knew it. When he nodded briefly in agreement and turned toward Star Sister, it was plain to see she knew it too. Stone Teeth had neatly mousetrapped him.

On a blistering August morning they rode out from the Kiowa camp: Stone Teeth, Philip Rainbolt, and a dozen or so young braves, eager to count coup and establish their standing as seasoned warriors. Most of them rode the prized *t'a kon*, the black-eared horses they prized above all others. Rainbolt rode Brutus, and carried Cat's pennoned lance; the Dragoon Colt was at his waist in the beaded and decorated holster with the trailing fringes that the Tonk warrior had once carried. One young man wore a dented and rusty cuirass, probably found in some sun-drenched canyon with the moldering bones of an early Spanish explorer still within it. Stone Teeth himself, proud of his command, was in his finest clothing. He wore a plumed headdress and richly decorated leggings, with the black sash of the Koitsenko around his waist. Rainbolt at last understood old Satank's defiant throwing down of the elk sash the day he was killed at Fort Sill. The Koitsenko, in times of peril to the People, drove an arrow into the ground, pinning the trailing end of the sash as a statement that the enemy could not drive them from that spot.

"A fine day!" Stone Teeth exulted, throwing his arms wide to the heavens. "Look how Sun smiles! He knows a great man rides with us!"

Rainbolt's brain was a jumble of conflicting emotions. The thing had come about so quickly that he rode confused and apprehensive, hoping against hope they would not come on any likely prey. A renegade, an escaped murderer—that was what they called Philip Rainbolt now— might well join a savage band to torture and slay as the bearded man and pleasant-faced woman and tow-headed boy had been tortured and slain. After all, what was left to Philip Rainbolt in a white man's world? But if he did not join in the slaughter and rapine, tried on some pretext to keep himself clear of it, they would know him for the pretender he was, and slay him too. Stone Teeth had set the trap well. Reason now did Rainbolt no good, no more than when he tried to reason why he had fled the field at Petersburg, why he had joined the damned Army again, why he had been vulnerable to Ellen

Cameron, why he had struck Sergeant Kruger, and grasped at quick freedom that night the Kiowas broke jail. What fatal flaw was in him? Shakespeare had once used a word . . . *star-crossed,* that was it. Philip Rainbolt was star-crossed.

From the start, Stone Teeth's expedition turned out to be a disaster. The weather was bad, with frequent dry thunderstorms, hail, and great winds. Water was scarce. In the middle of this summer the streams had dried up and the pools among the rocks were brackish and gypsum-impregnated. To protect themselves, the Kiowa-wise settlers had withdrawn from their vulnerable and widely scattered adobe houses and sod shanties. Now they congregated in well-armed settlements, going out each day under armed guards to till the soil and herd their stock.

Angry at finding one abandoned shack after another, Stone Teeth ordered an assault on a small settlement along the Boggy River. But the settlers drove them off with volley after volley from a stone blockhouse. Two of the Kiowas were killed. A third, an eager young man named Whirlwind, was shot in the stomach. Stone Teeth himself braved a hail of fire to ride to the young man and drag him to safety. But it was obvious that Whirlwind could not survive the wound; already, bluish loops of intestine showed in the jagged rent in his stomach.

Quickly, without apparent emotion, Stone Teeth shot the suffering youth through the head and they rode away, the Kiowas angry and baffled at the increasing resistance to their raiding.

The killing of Whirlwind shook Rainbolt. He knew the Kiowas often put out the old and sick to die—"putting them on the prairie" was the expression they used. Whirlwind could not have lived long with that gaping wound, but to abandon him, alive, was to know that the angry settlers would find him and wreak their vengeance. Still, Stone Teeth had been almost casual about shooting the boy. This was a strange new world—a hard world.

The attack on the fortified settlement had come about so quickly, the Kiowas riding furiously in and then being driven off by accurate fire from the concealed blockhouse, that Rainbolt and many of the other warriors had really seen no action. Now, under clouded and thickening skies, they rode down a parched valley between two boulder-studded ridges to discover a small rancho with a brush corral containing a cow and several horses. A man was plowing a field with a span of mules—a man who ran heavily, stumbling and falling, toward the stone house when he saw the Kiowas top the ridge. A woman screamed. Small figures that must have been children ran to her, and they all went in the house and barred the door.

"Not much," Stone Teeth muttered, "but we take what the Great One Above gives."

Quickly the Kiowas rounded up the horses and mules. The cow they drove to the shelter of a rocky ledge and butchered, roasting steaks over a fire of buffalo chips and twigs. It had been a long time since they had tasted fresh meat, and they ate till their stomachs were bloated and their hands and faces smeared with blood and juices.

While they feasted, the stone house seemed deserted. Rainbolt knew the man and his frightened family were inside, watching, hoping the Kiowas would go away—take the stock, but spare their lives. He, too, hoped that was what was going to happen. But after they ate, one of the braves took a smoldering brand from the fire and tied it to an arrow. Circling the house, he shot the flaming arrow from a nearby hill. His aim was good. The fire arrow fell on the mud-plastered wattles forming the roof. Though it did not break through, it lay there for a long time, smoking and sputtering.

Rainbolt squatted silently, chewing on a half-crooked rib and watched the rest take up the game. All, even Stone Teeth, shot fire arrows at the house. Finally, one corner of the roof caught fire and started to burn. A small wind, harbinger of an approaching storm, helped the blaze along. In a few minutes the whole roof had caught, and one gabled end started to sag.

He got up, wiping greasy hands on his leggings, feeling frightened and helpless. What to do? What *could* he do? This was the moment of reckoning—the time he had dreaded. With growing horror he saw the sagging roof fall inward in a shower of sparks, a puff of smoke. A moment later the heavy plank door opened; the man and his family stumbled out, blinded by smoke, black with soot, their clothing stitched with sparks.

Stone Teeth, carbine propped easily on a rock, shot the man through the chest. The settler stood for a moment, old musket at wavering port. Then, slowly, he pitched on his face and was still. Screaming, the woman ran to him, trying to turn him over, while three small children pressed against her, pulling vainly at her skirt and crying.

There was no need to waste ammunition on women and children. They could be run down and gutted with a knife, like new-foaled antelope. Some of the Kiowas went casually into the stone house to plunder. The brave in the Spanish cuirass took out his knife and went toward the huddled family. Stone Teeth got back on Red Pet, looking disgusted at the scanty haul.

"Stop!" Rainbolt shouted.

Though he had called out in English, there was something in his voice that caused them to pause. The Kiowa with the drawn knife, one hand gripping the long black hair of the woman, turned. He looked puzzled.

"Stop it!" Rainbolt called, and flung himself off Brutus. He ran to the group, pushing the brave away and standing between him and the woman and her children. "Goddamn it!" he snarled, "let them alone!"

Stone Teeth's face was passive, immobile. Yet Rainbolt fancied he could see the glint of triumph in the dark eyes, a lifting of muscles around the mouth that might have been a smile.

"What is the matter?" Stone Teeth asked.

Standing his ground, Rainbolt spoke in his mixture of signs, halting Kiowa, and some English words when he could not think of Kiowa expressions or even the proper hand talk.

"Nobody is going to hurt this woman and her children! It is wrong, and a coward's thing, to kill women and children who cannot fight!"

Whether he understood or not, the young man in the Spanish armor drew back, looking at Stone Teeth for guidance. Stone Teeth slid off Red Pet and walked toward Rainbolt, his gait swaggering, confident.

"I sang the guadagya song," he said. "I beat the drum. I called people to come with me." With a stiffened thumb he poked himself in the chest. "I am the topadoki! I do not like other men"— he spat—"white men, telling me what to do!"

134

He gestured to the Kiowa with the knife. "Go ahead—kill them!"

As the man started forward again Rainbolt drew the Dragoon Colt from his belt and aimed it unwaveringly at Stone Teeth. Understanding that in some strange way Rainbolt appeared to be their savior, the woman cried out and grabbed his legs. The children wept, and one of them tried to seize his hand.

"If anyone touches these people," Rainbolt said, "then I will kill you."

Stone Teeth sucked in his breath, and stared at the muzzle of the Colt. Slowly, very slowly, he took out his scratching stick and poked it thoughtfully into his dark locks.

"We always kill white people in our lands," he said finally. "What difference does it make if they are women—children? Women have babies, children grow up to kill our buffalo, to put on soldier suits and chase us."

It was a reasonable speech, delivered in a reasonable tone. Intent on Stone Teeth's meaning, Rainbolt almost did not see the flicker of his eye, the covert gesture, almost did not notice the Kiowa slipping away, running low and quick to the hillock behind the burning house. From there, Rainbolt could be shot in the back. But he did see. Turning quickly, he managed to keep Stone Teeth between him and the marksman on the rise.

"Do you count coup on children, then?" Rainbolt demanded. "You are brave men, all of you, to fight women, little babies. It is no wonder the Great One Above looks down and laughs at you, sends you home empty-handed!"

They all understood the contempt in his tone. Stone Teeth's heavy brows drew together in a scowl.

"Besides," Rainbolt went on, reaching down and trying to break the woman's frantic grasp on his thighs, "this is what makes white men angry. To kill their soldiers is one thing. But to kill their women and children is another. That will bring the pony soldiers into our country faster than anything." He gestured toward the captured horses and mules. "Take them and go! It is enough!"

He had not meant it to sound so brusque, so much like an order. Vainly he tried to think of the signs for *talk it over, consider;* the Kiowa words for *let us smoke over this.* But his mind failed him. The woman had pinioned him tightly, the children were clawing at him like small animals. Their fear began to unstring him.

"I do not fear the pony soldiers!" Stone Teeth said haughtily. He took a threatening step forward, one hand on the carved bone handle of the knife at his belt. "I do not fear any white man! I—"

Rainbolt raised the muzzle slightly and sighted

along the splined barrel. Stone Teeth's angry face hovered darkly on the beaded front sight.

"Sun Boy," Rainbolt said, "does not kill women and children, I think."

He did not know exactly why he said it. The words came to him out of the sky, a desperate effort to recover the initiative. But they had their effect on Stone Teeth. The rest of them, too, heard and understood. The brave on the hillock looked uncertain, and lowered his rifle.

"What do you know of Sun Boy?" Stone Teeth's lip curled, but there was a shadow of doubt, of uncertainty, in his savage eye.

Perhaps it was only coincidence, but at that moment the low scudding clouds broke. A spot of sun painted the burning house, tinging the smoke with gold. For a moment Rainbolt and the woman and her children were washed in its coin-yellow rays. Aware of the sudden flush of warmth, Rainbolt blinked in the light that kindled fire in his long hair and sweeping mustaches.

"Because," he said, "I talk to Sun Boy. He talks to me. And I tell you all what he says. He says— leave these people. Take the horses and mules he has given you, and go. That is what Sun Boy says."

Stone Teeth blinked. The hand on the haft of the knife twitched a little. Seeming perplexed, the man on the hillock stuck his shoulder through the sling of his rifle and padded down toward them. But no one was looking to Stone Teeth for instructions. They only stared at Philip Rainbolt in an uneasy way. The man in the Spanish armor put a hand over his mouth in awe.

"Take the horses and go!" Rainbolt repeated.

He made the classic plains sign for *horse*— first two fingers of his left hand astride the barrel of the revolver to indicate a man riding. By rights, the fingers of the left hand should have been astride the index finger of the right hand, but that hand was busy holding the Colt. Then Rainbolt made the *go away* sign, adding in his broken Kiowa, "Sun Boy says this is what you should do. He has spoken."

Slowly, carefully, Stone Teeth put away his scratching stick. He did not say anything, only got up on Red Pet and rode slowly away. The rest of the Kiowas looked at Rainbolt for a while, gestured and talked among themselves. Finally the man in the Spanish cuirass got on his horse. The rest followed, leading the horses and mules.

When she saw they were leaving, the woman ran to the body of her husband. He lay almost as if sleeping, but the gray homespun shirt was soaked with blood. It lay plastered wetly to his chest; flies already buzzed around it.

"I'm sorry," Rainbolt told her.

When he knelt beside her, the children clung to him, knowing there was no more comfort from the dead father.

"Who are you?" the woman asked, raising her eyes to Rainbolt.

He didn't answer. Nothing seemed appropriate. *Philip Rainbolt—one time schoolteacher, cavalryman, renegade, murderer?* For a moment he had a desperate impulse to stay with this woman—to help her bury her dead husband, plant new crops, be a father to the fatherless children. He was weary, weary of running away. But almost as quickly the realization came to him that the only safe place for Philip Rainbolt was the Kiowa camp. Even that was now doubtful as a haven. Sooner or later, Stone Teeth would kill him. Stone Teeth had to kill him. He knew that.

"Nobody," he murmured. "I'm nobody. Nobody you'd want to know."

Far to the west rode the Kiowas, leading the captured horses. They crawled, an antlike procession, over a low ridge splashed with sunset gold. When he joined the column they made room for him. Some pulled respectfully aside, others only stared at him with dark, perplexed eyes. Stone Teeth himself appeared not to have noticed that Rainbolt had joined the party.

That night he slept a little apart from the others, rolling himself in his blanket at the edge of a granite outcropping where it would be difficult to surprise him. Listening to the howling unseasonable wind, he slept only fitfully. But nothing happened. The Kiowas broke their fast on more roasted cow meat and rode westward again, toward their camp. It had been an ill-starred journey and they were all anxious to get home.

That morning they ran on a string of abandoned freight wagons. A few emaciated oxen, still yoked, grazed nearby, looking at them with searching thirsty eyes. But Stone Teeth was sure it was a trap. Many times before, he said, he had run into similar ambushes, attacking wagons only to find them filled with waiting soldiers. The lead wagon, tipsy from a broken wheel, lay at the edge of a rocky escarpment. Behind that escarpment could, Stone Teeth insisted, lie pony soldiers in wait. He pointed to Rainbolt.

"Go in the wagon. See what is there." He signaled the rest of the party to take cover, and wait. "Go ahead!" he shouted at Rainbolt. "What is the matter? You are such good friends with Sun Boy! He will not let anything happen to you!"

Rainbolt slid down from Brutus and went toward the wagon, his Colt drawn and lance at the ready. It was a silly precaution—the wagon was obviously abandoned, burned in a prairie fire and then deserted. But he lifted the ragged flap and stared into the gloomy smoke-smelling interior. That was when he saw the woman.

Face smudged and blackened, dress torn and hanging in shreds, she pointed the toylike derringer at him and screamed, "Don't come nearer, or I'll shoot!"

CHAPTER SEVEN

One moccasined foot in the interior of the wagon, he stepped on something soft and fell headlong toward the menacing eye of the muzzle. As he toppled, the muzzle bloomed, a small red flower shot with streaks of yellow and orange. Sprawling, his outflung hand touched her ankle. In desperation, he grabbed and pulled.

In a flutter of skirts and embrace of flesh, the woman came down on him, still screaming. For a moment he threshed, caught in the enveloping folds of her skirt. A wild fist caught him in the eye and planets flashed through his vision. But now he had her located. Brushing aside the billowing skirt, he got her by both wrists and held her tight.

"You goddamned little fool!" he snarled. "What in hell did you have to shoot at me for?"

Still holding her wrists, he felt the sting on his cheek; his fingers came away speckled with blood. "Why—why—" He broke off in amazement. The woman was Ellen Cameron.

"My God!" he blurted. "You! You! What—what are you doing here?"

Dazed, she stared uncomprehending. "Who are you?" Briefly she struggled, trying to free her wrists.

"Ellen!" he finally marveled. "Ellen Cameron!"

Her face was smudged and dirty, the fine red hair in disarray, falling over her cheeks, almost hiding an eye. The proud swell of her bosom was barely contained by the torn fabric of the camisole and serge traveling dress. Another woman in such extremes would have wept. But Ellen only faced him, chin up and hostile.

"How do you know my name?"

Almost as she said the words, she knew.

"Mr. Rainbolt," she whispered. When he dropped her wrists, one hand stole to her cheek in wonder. "Philip Rainbolt!"

He was afraid she was going to faint, but she was made of sterner stuff. She closed her eyes, her cheeks paled into marble, a faint beading of perspiration bloomed on her forehead. Then she opened the violet eyes again. In her hardships, they had not suffered.

"But you—you—" She touched his cheek with a finger. It came away smeared with Kiowa paints—red and yellow and blue. Suddenly he realized how he must look to her—an apparition with a colored rag bound around his long hair, cheeks daubed with war paint, bare to the waist, wearing long Kiowa leggings and tinkling moccasins.

Suddenly he knew they were not alone. Hard eyes were staring at them through every rent in the wagon canvas. Stone Teeth himself climbed in through the driver's end and demanded, "What is the matter here?"

Now Rainbolt saw the body of a man lying across the bed of the wagon just behind the high seat. That was what he had stumbled on. Pointing, he asked her, "Who is that?"

She swallowed hard, brushing dirty fingers across her eyes. "The driver. A—a Mr. Mason. Last night he died. Of the typhus, I think. The wind came up, and the lightning set the grass on fire."

Rainbolt took her hand. "There is sickness here," he told Stone Teeth. "Fever sickness." He pointed to the spots on the cheeks, the neck, the chest of the dead man.

Stone Teeth and the Kiowas understood. They scurried away from the contaminated wagon.

"I ran away," Ellen murmured tonelessly. "I ran away from Hugh. He was so mean to me. You see, I only wanted to go to Memphis, where I have relatives. My aunt and uncle live there. They—"

"You can explain later," Rainbolt said curtly. "Let's get out of here."

But the wagon had been a kind of home for her. She hesitated, trying to arrange her tangled hair. "Mr. Mason got sick, and the Mexican boys ran away. Then there was the storm—the fires on the prairie. The oxen ran away. They ran and ran till the wheel broke. There was water in a barrel, and I managed to put out the fire in the wagon top, but then—"

Annoyed, he pulled at her. "Come. Now!"

"But your cheek!" she protested. "Here, let me—" With a wisp of soiled cambric she dabbed at it. "I'm so sorry! I thought you were an Indian!"

Grabbing her wrist, he pulled her from the death-smelling wagon. "I am!" he howled. "Now will you hurry?"

Stone Teeth and the rest of the party had rounded up the oxen and now sat their mounts, waiting impassively. The sun was high and brassy; beneath the horses were black pools of shade. Stone Teeth's face was somber, but Rainbolt paid him no attention. Instead, he made a cup of his hands and nodded to Ellen to get up on Brutus.

She was hesitant; he saw a flicker of panic in her eyes when she saw the painted savage faces. "But—but I—"

"Stop talking!" he snapped. "Do as I say!" When she still hesitated, looking back at the burned wagon as if there were salvation there, he blurted, "Goddamn it, get up there! Do you want me to leave you for the coyotes?"

She shrank back as if struck, but put her small foot in his hands and swung herself on the high-backed Tonk saddle. "You don't need to shout at me!" she cried.

He knotted a rope around the nose of one of the captured horses and then around the neck to make a halterlike bridle, the way he had seen the Kiowas do it. It was a clever device; the nose loop and single rein gave the horseman a strong contact with the animal's head, and a hard pull on the rein choked the animal, bringing it quickly to a halt. Vaulting onto the mare's back, he warned her for a moment with the tight grip of his knees and a jerk at the rope, then reached down to take Ellen's bridle. "*Hopo!*" he barked. "Let's go!"

Stone Teeth still looked at him in that somber calculating way. The rest looked at Rainbolt and his female captive, then at Stone Teeth, waiting.

Finally Stone Teeth said, "Hopo!" They filed off, horses shambling in the heat, Mason's oxen driven before them, a haze of dust rising from unshod hoofs. Overhead a solitary buzzard floated; the way west shimmered in a vast mirage that made it appear they were approaching an inland sea. But there was no sea, nothing but dust, the sweating animals, the sun that bore on them like a heavy weight.

Rainbolt and Ellen rode at the rear of the column, he judging that was best, but they were soon half choked with dust. From time to time she tried to talk to him, but he would not respond. *Ellen Cameron,* he was thinking *Ellen Cameron!* A careless god was playing tricks on him. *Iktomi,* the Kiowas called that god. Iktomi, the prankster, who dangled men from unseen strings and made them dance to a strange tune.

That night they camped in a rocky draw. Though the evening was cool, the walls of the canyon still radiated the heat of midday. Only one more day's ride from the Kiowa camp, they ate the last of the cow meat, washed down with brackish water from buffalo-paunch bags. One of them had a green glass bottle with a kind of liquor in it, brewed from fermented mesquite beans.

Ellen sat on a rock beside him, chewing the tough meat. "Where are we going?"

He looked at her morosely. "To their camp." He jerked his thumb toward the Kiowas, sprawled around the fire and enjoying the bottle.

Grimacing, she plucked shreds of meat from her lips and threw them into the bushes. "My goodness! It's like leather!"

"An old cow," he said. "Anyway, it's all there is."

She began again. "How did you—I mean—whatever are you doing here with these people, dressed like that and all painted up?"

Not looking at her, he scratched a design in the dust with a stick. "I ran away, too. The Kiowas captured me, took me to their camp. Somehow, I survived. They tolerate me—at least, so far." He broke the stick in two and tossed the pieces away. "But you certainly complicate things."

The Kiowas around the fire were having a good time. There must, Rainbolt thought, have been more in that bottle than he thought. Still, Indians were notoriously susceptible to liquor, and the fermented mesquite stuff was strong. In the leaping flames he saw a figure silhouetted, tipping the bottle high. It was Stone Teeth.

"I'm sorry," Ellen apologized. After a moment, she added, "I guess we're both fugitives."

Bitterly he said, "You are so from choice! I *had* to run away!"

"What choice?" The sudden bitterness in her voice matched his. "I would not be treated by any man the way I was used by Hugh Cameron!" Vindictively she added, "At least I didn't murder anyone!"

"Neither did I!" he shouted.

The leaping flames of the fire were reflected in her dark eyes, showing a question there. "What do you mean? Surely poor old Sergeant Huckabee—"

"I didn't kill Huckabee, no matter what they say! The Kiowas came, during the night, let Stone Teeth and Wolf Sleeves and the rest of the prisoners out. They killed Huckabee—cut his throat so there would be no noise—and opened my cell door. I don't know why they freed me, except that they and I both had something against the Army. So I ran away, on a horse I stole from the corral." Angry, he gripped her by the flesh of the upper arm and stared into her eyes. "But I never touched Huckabee!"

147

Her eyes softened, and his grip on her relaxed. "I knew it!" she cried.

"Knew what?"

"That you didn't kill poor old Huckabee! You couldn't! You're not that kind!"

"I don't know what kind I am," he muttered. "I just don't know any more. But I didn't kill Huckabee, anyway."

"I told Hugh!" she exulted. "I told him you didn't kill the poor old man! But he just laughed at me!"

"Anyway," he said, "they're looking for me for murder, aren't they?"

"Yes."

"So what difference does it make? Anyway, I'm with the Kiowas for better or worse. One murder more or less is nothing to them. So far, they put up with me. But bringing a white woman into camp is something I doubt they'll stand for."

One hand stole to her throat. "What—what will they do?"

"I don't know. We'll find out, I daresay."

She sighed, then said awkwardly, "I—I think I have to go over there—behind those bushes." Perhaps it was the glow of the firelight, but her cheeks looked very red.

"All right." He shrugged.

He walked over to the fire and sat down. The bottle now was nearly empty. Stone Teeth was standing up, though wavering, telling about some exploit or other he had performed once in a snow-storm. The young man in the dented Spanish armor handed Rainbolt the bottle with its sloshing dregs. His name was Crow Bonnet.

"Have a drink, friend."

Rainbolt tipped up the bottle. Even the few drops that were left stitched a fiery path down his gullet. Trying not to wheeze, he wiped his mouth with the back of his hand, eyes burning, and thanked Crow Bonnet.

"Good," he said. "Very good."

After a while he realized he did not see Stone Teeth.

"Tomorrow," Crow Bonnet said, "we go home. That is good. A man likes to ride out, but he likes to come home, too."

Rainbolt felt a queasy feeling. Where was Stone Teeth?

"We did not take many horses," Crow Bonnet said. "But that is the way it is sometimes. The gods—"

"Ellen?" Rainbolt called. He got to his feet, eyes searching the darkness beyond the firelight. "Ellen? Where are you?"

From somewhere in the darkness, she screamed. The piercing sound bounced from the rocky walls of the canyon, echoing farther and farther down the granite cleft till it whispered away.

"I'm coming!" he shouted. Snatching a brand from the fire, he pulled the old Green River knife from his belt and ran toward the scream.

"Where are you?"

As he ran, the smoking torch made shadows on the granite wall. "Where—" Suddenly he stopped. In the light of the torch Ellen Cameron cowered in fear. Stone Teeth was holding her tightly against him. He had cast aside his beaded belt with its knife and hatchet, and shed his fringed leggings. When he saw Philip Rainbolt he blinked for a moment in the flare of the torch, but did not relinquish his hold on his prize. Instead, he made a low growling noise reminding Rainbolt of the growling of a bear F Company had once brought to bay with their dogs.

"Let go of her!" Rainbolt ordered.

Stone Teeth only stared insolently.

"I said let go of her!" Rainbolt took a step forward, gesturing with his knife. The rest of the Kiowas pressed behind him, and he wondered if one of them might grab him from behind.

"She is mine," Stone Teeth insisted. "She is mine just the same as all those horses and mules and oxen we took are mine! When we get back to camp, I will share the horses and mules and oxen with the others, just as I will share this woman. But right now she is mine!"

He was not so drunk as Rainbolt had thought. When Rainbolt menaced him with the knife, coming so close as to prick him with the point, Stone Teeth threw Ellen angrily from him and stood defiant, arms folded. "You need killing," he said. "For a long time you have needed killing, white man."

"Then kill me," Rainbolt offered.

"I have no weapons. You can see."

Rainbolt threw the knife aside. It clattered on the rocks, and was silent. "Nor have I," he said.

Someone threw fresh fuel—grass or twigs, from the sudden way it flared—on the fire, and they circled each other, low and crouching, hands reaching out like the antennas of insects. A Kiowa started to move toward Rainbolt, raising a hatchet, but Crow Bonnet said something quick and hard. The man drew back into the ring of spectators.

The Kiowas loved to play cards, to race horses and gamble, but especially to wrestle. Many times Rainbolt had watched them, naked brown bodies straining against each other. Anything was fair; a wrestler could kick, bite, gouge—nothing was barred. But that had all been in fun, though violent and sometimes dangerous. This encounter, Rainbolt knew, was deadly. Stone Teeth would kill him, or he would kill Stone Teeth. There was nothing in between.

Quick as a cat, Stone Teeth suddenly flung himself at Rainbolt, moccasined feet first, trying to catch his adversary's legs between his and turning, so to throw him. But Rainbolt jumped, the groping legs missed their mark. He tried to fall on Stone Teeth, to pinion him, but the Kiowa wriggled free. They crouched again, circling this time in the other direction.

This time Rainbolt was the aggressor. He caught Stone Teeth's fingers in his and twisted hard, at the same time pulling the naked body to him and getting an arm about Stone Teeth's waist. But his opponent twisted free. Putting his foot in Rainbolt's chest, he kicked hard, breaking the grip on his fingers.

Again they circled, charging at each other in little rushes, then withdrawing. Stone Teeth reached out a foot and tried a hock trip, but Rainbolt eluded him. Rainbolt suddenly reversed the direction of his circling and rammed Stone Teeth in the stomach with a butt of his head. Once he had seen a corporal in F Company do that, and win fifty dollars in bets. But he caught Stone Teeth only a glancing blow, falling to his knees in the process and bruising his shins on a ledge of rock.

Panting, chests heaving, bathed in sweat, the slippery bodies matched each other, hold for hold, breaking loose, slipping and sliding in the shale, first with advantage to Stone Teeth, then to Rainbolt. The spectators were silent, with only a quick intake of breath, a muttered "Hau! Hau!" in approval of a clever move. The match was still a draw.

Finally, Stone Teeth, eager to break the dead-lock, managed to catch Rainbolt around the waist. Pinioned from behind, Rainbolt writhed desperately in an effort to break that iron grip that cinched him like a vise, driving the breath from his body. In desperation he threw up his arms and staggered backward, hoping to press Stone Teeth against the rocky wall behind them. Locked together, they crashed against a ledge. Stone Teeth let out a surprised gasp, and for a moment his grip slackened. Rainbolt turned, catching his foot in a tangle of splintered rock and fell. His head hit something hard; brightly colored lights flashed through his skull. He put a hand to his injured head, opening his eyes just in time to see Stone Teeth towering above, a cabbage-sized boulder held in both hands, ready to dash it down. In panic he threw himself side-ways, at the same time kicking out with both legs.

The down-rushing boulder hit where his head had just been, and bounced away. Stone Teeth, staggering from Rainbolt's wild kick, blundered against one of the intently watching Kiowas. His groping hand came away with the man's feather-plumed knife grasped in it. He rushed on Rainbolt to slash and destroy, but Rainbolt caught his wrist. For a moment they swayed together, sweaty chest against chest, as the knife slowly, implacably, started its downward path.

Rainbolt was winded and dazed. His lungs

labored, he could not suck in enough air to sustain him. Now the knife was between them, and he could feel Stone Teeth jerking at it against the restraint of his own grasp, trying to free it for the last deadly glide into Philip Rainbolt's belly.

Gasping, sobbing with the effort, he got his head under Stone Teeth's chin and pushed him off balance. Still locked together, they fell heavily. For a moment, for the tick of a clock, Stone Teeth lay stunned. Rainbolt acted. Still holding the Kiowa's sweaty wrist, he twisted hard and drove his fist against the naked chest. The knife, in Stone Teeth's own grasp, went in surprisingly smoothly. At first there was a hesitation as the point pricked the taut skin, probed, dimpled. Then the blade popped in full length, stopping only when the guard pressed against Stone Teeth's painted chest.

Gasping for breath like a grounded fish, mouth open, sweat pouring from him, Rainbolt swayed to his knees. Stone Teeth lay quietly, eyes open and looking upward in surprise. His hand moved slowly, wonderingly, to touch the haft of the knife that had killed him. Then he closed his eyes, and that was all.

Painfully Rainbolt got to his feet. The inside of his mouth tasted like old tarnished copper— bitter and astringent. No one spoke. He looked around, taking time to eye each of the Kiowas challengingly. Finally he pointed to where Ellen

Cameron lay, watching him, the back of her hand against her mouth. Her face was white and pale, but her look was steady.

"She is mine," Rainbolt said, pointing. "I will kill any man who touches her." Taking her by the hand, he led her away to where his blanket was spread.

"Lie down there," he said, almost flinging her from him. "No one will bother you!"

He was not as sure as he had sounded. Yet, by morning, nothing had happened. The Kiowas buried Stone Teeth among the boulders of the canyon, wrapping him in his blanket and piling his gun, his hatchet, and other weapons on top. From a stake driven in the ground fluttered his Koitsenko sash of elkskin and his war rattle. It was their custom to put away their dead on pole scaffolds, but in this parched dry land there were no trees large enough from which to cut poles. At the last, one of them brought Red Pet to the tomb and cut the horse's throat. Red Pat slipped quietly down at Stone Teeth's feet, eyes rolling for a long time as the blood gushed. The horse would be waiting, in the spirit land, to carry Stone Teeth again.

"How awful!" Ellen shuddered. "Why did they kill that beautiful horse?"

He paid no attention to her question. Instead, he helped her up on Brutus, saying, "You ride here, at the tail of the column. Stay well back. You'll eat a lot of dust today but it'll keep you out of trouble."

She looked at him anxiously. "But where are you going?"

He left her, cantering on the captured mare to the head of the column, now his by right of conquest. Crow Bonnet sat there; as the senior of the young warriors he might now expect to take over command of the war party. But Rainbolt coolly dug his heels into Brutus' ribs and trotted up in the lead, the Tonk lance held vertically like a staff of office.

For a moment he looked at them. They looked at him. No one said anything. Finally he called out, "Hopo!" Almost casually the Kiowas followed him, as if nothing had happened. He breathed a sigh of relief.

It was not until they were almost in Water Turtle's camp that he noticed an addition to the plumes and scalps, the rattles and strings of shells and beads decorating his Tonka medicine lance. The beaded pouch Stone Teeth always carried with his supply of parched corn now hung gaily there. It was Rainbolt's medicine lance now —his *zebat*, the Kiowas called it. The Kiowas decorated their lances with scalps, amulets, trophies of victory. Now Stone Teeth's beaded pouch hung on Rainbolt's zebat. It was their way of commemorating his victory over

Stone Teeth, and accepting him as a great warrior.

When they reached the camp the women were singing their welcoming song—"Imkagyá gya! Imkagyá gya!" But this time the warriors were not returning in triumph. Their haul was scanty, and sharp eyes counted two men missing. A woman saw the beaded corn pouch on Rainbolt's lance, and her hand went quickly over her mouth in awe and dismay. Soon it would be all over camp. The white man had killed Stone Teeth in a fight over a woman—the flame-haired white woman who rode dusty and disheveled at the end of the column. One man scowled at Rainbolt, and another called out something that must have been a curse. Others wailed, and women tore their garments; some slashed their arms with knives, the symbol of bereavement. They were, Rainbolt guessed, Stone Teeth's relatives, and he knew the matter was not yet over. But he looked neither right nor left, riding proudly between the lines of dark Kiowa faces. When he reached his own lodge he dis-mounted and helped Ellen Cameron from the patient Brutus.

She almost fell, from weakness, emotion, and long hours in the unaccustomed saddle. In response to his curt nod she stumbled through the doorway and sank down on a pile of robes, looking wonderingly at the big brass bed and its quilted comforter. Star Sister, who had been waiting patiently outside the tipi to welcome

Rainbolt, stared wide-eyed at the white woman. When they had gone inside, she followed, silently, and squatted beside the fire, tending the chunks of meat that were spitted on green sticks.

Ellen took a deep breath, and tried to arrange her tumbled hair. She looked at the brass bed again, and then at Star Sister. "So this is where you live," she said to Rainbolt.

"Yes."

Modestly she tried to arrange the shreds of her gray serge dress around her shoulders, her bosom. The hem had been torn away, and she blushed when she saw Rainbolt staring at the stockinged calf of her leg.

"I'm hungry," she said to cover her embarrassment.

He spoke to Star Sister in a guttural phrase. The Indian girl brought some of the meat. It was hot and burned her mouth, but Ellen found it satisfyingly crisp and brown and juicy. It dribbled annoyingly on her bosom, but she was too hungry to care. After a while she wiped greasy hands on her skirt—she was beyond manners and did not care—and asked Rainbolt, "Do you speak their language, then?"

"A fair amount," he admitted. He ate some of the meat himself, and when the Indian girl brought it to him, he let his hand rest affectionately on her sleek locks. "A lot of it is beyond me," he added, "but I learn each day."

Trying not to let her voice quaver, she asked, "What will become of me, now?"

He shrugged. "I've learned not to worry too much any more." Rising, he tossed a gnawed bone into the fire. "I wouldn't either if I were you. For now you're safe. Maybe I am too. Anyway, we'll find out soon."

"I shall pray," she decided.

He nodded. "You do that."

When night came, he might have offered her the brass bed. But he only motioned her to the pile of buffalo robes and lay on the bed himself. In the light of the guttering fire she pondered whether it was quite right for her to sleep there, in the same tent with him. But after a few moments he was asleep, breathing easily and deep, and she decided it was all right. The Indian girl, at least, did not sleep with him, Ellen Cameron thought with satisfaction.

In the morning Water Turtle sent for Rainbolt. Careful not to come between the chief and the fire, Rainbolt entered the great lodge. Water Turtle sat for a long time smoking, saying nothing. Then he looked up, his eyes impassive.

"So you killed Stone Teeth."

Nothing was to be gained by lying. "Yes," Rainbolt admitted. "But it was a fair fight."

Water Turtle's wrinkled face broke into new fragments as he grimaced. He shook his head doubtfully, puffing a propitiatory cloud of smoke upward toward the Great One. "And over a woman."

Rainbolt nodded. "She was my friend."

Water Turtle frowned. "Your friend? How was that?"

"I knew her. From back there." Rainbolt gestured northward. "At the post. She was lost, and—"

"I heard all about it," Water Turtle interrupted, a little peevishly. "Women! Pah!" He spat. "They always cause trouble. So now Stone Teeth is dead, and his brothers and uncles call for revenge."

Rainbolt shrugged, and said again, "It was a fair fight."

"Yes," Water Turtle agreed, blowing a perfectly formed circle of smoke and watching it bend, elongate, finally drift away upward into the smoke-blackened lodgepoles. "Yes. That is true. I was told that."

Autumn was coming early this year, the shamans predicted after examining certain birds and small animals and plants. In spite of the noonday heat, the brilliant bowl of sky, the leaves on the trees were already withered and brown. There had been a frost, too. When a cold wind rippled the skins of the lodge, Water Turtle pulled his red blanket around his shoulders as an old woman might a shawl. He was usually cold; it was part of his medicine, he said, to be always cold.

"Stone Teeth," Water Turtle said, "was a brave man. That is the truth. But he was ambitious. He wanted a lot of power among the People. Sometimes I thought he wanted to take my place." Water Turtle's face crinkled in what might have been a grin, with a hint of slyness to it. "You are lucky you did not kill someone else, someone the People liked better." Then his face became somber. "I heard also that you spared women and children —white women and children. Why did you do this?"

Water Turtle had, Rainbolt reflected, heard a great deal.

"Men fight," he explained. "Men fight each other. That is right. Men are made to fight each other. But to fight a woman, to harm children—"

"At the Washita," the old man shouted, "the white men killed *our* women and children! 'Lice make nits'—that is what Gold Leaf Cameron said at the post one time—I heard him say that!" Furiously the old man rocked back and forth in his bright red blanket. Only gradually he quieted. Finally he quit rocking, and loaded his pipe. Rainbolt politely forked a coal from the fire and lit the pipe.

"But that is not what I wanted to talk about," Water Turtle said. For a while he puffed hard, getting the pipe going. Then his face took on a gentler cast. "It is hard to be a chief," he said. "I do not complain. My father was a chief, and his father before him. But it is still hard, to always know what is the right thing to do."

He closed his eyes, still puffing, and suddenly he looked incredibly old and withered, like an ancient oriental idol.

"The medicine men, the associations, the topadoki, all these have their own ideas, and each speaks for a different course. It is hard, sometimes, to listen to them all and still keep a straight mind."

The wind mourned around the tipi; Rainbolt, shivering, took the liberty of putting a handful of twigs on the dying fire.

"A chief," Water Turtle said, "a born chief, like me, knows well how to do certain things." Eyes still closed as if looking a long way back, he recited a kind of litany. "My father told me all these things. When you go out on the warpath, look out for the enemy and do something brave. Study everything you see, try to understand it. Have goodwill to all your people. Don't tell lies. Keep an even temper, and never be stingy with food." Water Turtle opened his eyes. "In the old days that was plenty to make a man's name great in his tribe. But now things are different. Some-times, even though I am a chief, I do not know what is best for the People. I am ashamed to say it, but it is true." He picked up the dented brass horn and rubbed a horny finger over it. "There are many white men in our lands now, lands they say they gave to us but which they act like were their own. There are the pony soldiers, the walk-a-heaps, the traders and farmers and the rest. They pour in like water in a river. If you stop them in one place, they break out like water over a beaver dam and come from another direction. My father, and his father, never had to put up with this. I don't think my father ever saw a white man. But now I have to deal with all these things. It is very hard." He picked up the dented French horn and tried to blow a blast. But all that emerged was a strangled gasp. "I cannot play that thing!" he cried, flinging it angrily away. "They gave it to me at the Medicine Lodge meeting, but it is like all the white man's things—it is no good!"

Outside, it was gray and gloomy, and the wind howled. The great lodge was lit only by an occasional flaring of the fire as the heat reached a pocket of pitch in the wood. Finally, almost grudgingly, Water Turtle said, "What do you think?"

Rainbolt chose his words with care. He liked these people—Two Time Talk, Star Sister, Crow Bonnet, others who had been kind to him. And the Kiowas, even with their uncertain attitudes toward him, were still his refuge.

"I am not very smart," he said. "During my life I did many wrong and foolish things. I should not even speak before a great chief like Water Turtle, leader of the People. But certain things are true. The traders—the comancheros—are bad people. Ike Coogan, the Caddo George Washington, the rest—they are all bad people. They trade the People whisky and guns for stolen horses. When the People steal horses from the settlers along the Red River, that is when the white men get mad and ask the Great White Father in Washington"—he waved—"away back there—for more pony soldiers, more walk-a-heaps, more guns and cannon, to protect them."

Water Turtle snorted. "We do not fear soldiers!"

Rainbolt nodded. "My father speaks truth. But there are a whole lot of soldiers coming—more soldiers than the Kiowas and Comanches and Kwahadis put together. Some Indians have joined the soldiers, too. The Tonkawas, the Caddoes—they are scouts for the pony soldiers. And the white men have a new gun. They call it the Gatling gun. It shoots hundreds of times in the snapping of a finger." To illustrate, he snapped his fingers, and said, "Hundreds of bullets. Bullets all around. So—what good is it to be brave when the enemy is ten to one against you, and has a fast-shooting gun like that?"

"That is true," the old man muttered. "But I would put on my best clothing and go out to fight ten thousand of them!"

"That would not help the People," Rainbolt pointed out.

"True. True."

"So," Rainbolt went on, "first—I would send these evil men—these traders, comancheros— away. I would tell them that the People have enough guns and bullets and do not want any more of the white man's whisky. I would stop dealing in stolen horses. Then, maybe the white men, the soldiers, will leave us alone."

Us? He felt uneasy that he had said the word. But that was how it came to him. Was he now, in fact as well as in appearance, a Kiowa? An Indian? Philip Rainbolt?

Water Turtle smoked for a long time, his face stolid and unrevealing. Finally he said, "Well, I will think about it." When the pipe gasped, bubbled, and then went out for lack of tobacco, he laid it down and said, "But it is a big step—an important step—to take. Maybe it looks like we are running away from a fight. So first—I will need a sign. I don't know when it will come, but I will look for it. I will look for the sign."

He did not refill the pipe, only sat there a long time rubbing his ancient hooked nose with the bowl, as if savoring the warmth. After a while, he gestured toward the old harmonium. "You are a—a—" He wrinkled his brow, holding the bridge of his nose between thumb and forefinger. "I cannot think of the English word." Finally, he said, "Clever. That is it. The word is *clever.* You are a clever man, I think. You can do a lot of things. I see you doing card tricks for the

165

children sometimes. Can you play that thing?"

Rainbolt's Aunt Malvina in Waycross had had a fine rosewood organ in the parlor. He remembered picking out tunes, experimenting with chords, while his cousin knelt below working the pedals for the wind. Rainbolt had been too small to reach them; his gangling legs came much later.

"I don't know," he said. "But I will try."

Fingers stiff on the unaccustomed keys, he pumped up the air and got out a handful of wheezy notes. But some of his ear came back to him, some facility with fingers. Remembering the tune, he experimented with "Nearer My God to Thee." It had been Aunt Malvina's favorite. He ended on a shattering discord, but Water Turtle was pleased.

"*Hau*! *Hau*!" The old man's furrowed face broke into a grin. "That is very good! Play more!"

His aunt had been religious. Most of what Rainbolt remembered were sacred songs— "A Mighty Fortress," "Jesus Loves Me," "Shall We Gather at the River."

After a while, Rainbolt's memory and his legs and fingers alike were exhausted; old Water Turtle had gone to sleep. Quietly Rainbolt left the great tipi. No more comancheros, he had advised Water Turtle. No more Ike Coogans, no more stealing horses and cattle. Now the fat was probably in the fire. But the old man had not objected to Ellen Cameron's presence in the Kiowa camp. That much, at least, was good.

CHAPTER EIGHT

A Quaker missionary named Mr. Battey once had supper with Ellen and Major Cameron at the post, talking a long time about the Kiowas and his experiences as a missionary among them. The Kiowas, Mr. Battey said, were very warlike, and hated white men as Mr. Battey hated Lucifer. Yet, he went on, the Kiowas had often gone out of their way to escort him through hostile Comanche territory on his work for the Lord. When he had once been granted the hospitality of a Kiowa camp, Mr. Battey said, he was thenceforth treated with deference by everyone, invited to sup with them and sleep unmolested in their tipis.

That reassured Ellen Cameron. At first she had greatly feared the Kiowas, but Mr. Battey's words reassured her. Too, she was not the kind of woman to remain long daunted by anything. So she quickly settled into the life of the camp, but knew soon a different and perplexing concern. Philip Rainbolt was at the core of it. He was her savior, and she remained grateful to him; she decided also that he would soon find a way to permit her to resume her journey to Memphis and the welcoming arms of Uncle Nestor and Aunt Alice. Yet Rainbolt remained cool to her— uncommu-nicative, hardly even polite. After all, he *had* been only a private, while she was the major's wife. Surely, on those grounds alone she deserved more consideration.

That first night, the Indian girl had left the two of them—she and Philip Rainbolt—alone in his lodge. It embarrassed Ellen, but what could she do? There were probably snakes outside, so she slept in the tipi on the pile of robes Rainbolt had indicated.

But the second night—that time the Indian girl slipped easily into bed with Rainbolt, as if it were her right. Ellen's face turned red; she rushed from the lodge in embarrassment and confusion. Behind her someone laughed a smothered laugh, and she was not sure whether it had been Star Sister or Rainbolt himself.

That night, in spite of her mortal fear of snakes, she slept in an abandoned wagon bed. The Kiowas, it appeared, had plundered a lot of household goods and furnishings from the settlers, later discarding much of it in a huge pile of old bureaus, cracked ironstone pitchers, broken chairs, wagon wheels, pots and pans with handles missing or bottoms rusted through. She spent an uncomfortable night in the jumble. In the morning she marched proudly into the tipi as if nothing had happened. Rainbolt, wolfing a stew the Indian girl had prepared, looked up at her.

"Sleep comfortably?"

"Very comfortably."

"That old wagon bed," he said, "is oak. Very hard oak."

Not looking at him, she accepted the bowl of stew he handed her. "So you followed me."

"Not far." He laughed. "Star Sister thought it was very funny."

Angry, Ellen said, "I do not care what that girl thinks."

"She is very sensitive," Rainbolt explained, spooning up the last of the stew and wiping his mouth with the back of his hand. The small scar on his cheek from Ellen's derringer was healing well. "The night we came back with the war party," he said, "she ran off because she thought I had brought home a new woman to sleep in the brass bed. I had a devil of a time coaxing her back."

"I see you were successful," Ellen snapped.

He nodded soberly, no hint of mischief in his eyes. "I told her she was still my number one wife. You, I said, were number two or three—I forget which—but she was not to worry."

Ellen slapped his face. Star Sister, angry, came running with a skillet to defend Rainbolt, but he caught the girl around the waist, laughing.

"I am not concerned," Ellen said icily, "with your immoral arrangements for sleeping, Mr. Rainbolt. The only thing I would like to know, if you can spare me the time from your paramour, is when I may continue with my plans to visit Aunt Alice and Uncle Nestor in Memphis, Tennessee."

"I don't know." He shrugged. "I truly don't."

She shook her head, exasperated. A tangle of hair came miserably down to engulf her face; she brushed it aside. "How—how can you expect a woman—a white woman—to live under such conditions?"

Rainbolt sat cross-legged, like a Buddha, while Star Sister, casting unfriendly glances at Ellen Cameron, combed his long yellow hair with a horn comb. After a while he asked, "Would you rather be back in that wagon with a dead teamster? I think he was beginning to smell already."

She shuddered, and felt faint. "No," she said in a weak voice. "And I am of course grateful to you for saving me, Mr. Rainbolt. But it is only natural for me to—to—"

"You used to call me Philip," he said coolly. "When there is news to tell you, I will tell you." That was all he would say.

She learned, however, he was not jesting about her status. A lot of work was required to keep the savage household going. Star Sister cooked for Rainbolt, but he made it clear Ellen Cameron was to do the chores. There was always wood to split, water to carry, an endless succession of menial tasks. Star Sister found Ellen skillful with a needle, and made her mend clothes. Ellen was strong and Star Sister handed her a sharp-edged rock to scrape deerskins and hides, removing the clinging bits of dried flesh. Ellen worked for hours curing pelts by rubbing into them some mucilaginous stuff that Star Sister brought her in a bucket. When she found, later, the stuff was deer brains, she rushed to the nearest bushes and vomited. But she was strong; she would endure just to spite Philip Rainbolt. *You used to call me Philip,* he had said. Now, in her fury, she had other names for him.

Enduring, however, bred frustration. As often as she could escape from Star Sister, she took long walks through the camp, arms wrapped about her as if to prevent some inner pressure from bursting. The Kiowas, for the most part, were afraid of the tall red-haired woman in rags and tatters and bits of torn lace, pieced out now with an old buckskin shirt and scuffed moccasins.

Though the nights were growing cold and there had been several hard snaps of frost, Ellen still refused to sleep in Rainbolt's lodge. That would have looked like capitulation. Instead, each night she dragged the buffalo robe outside and rolled herself in it. The grass was at least softer than the oak planks of the wagon bed, though in the grass she was still fair prey for late-season snakes. She shuddered and closed her eyes against the stars, wishing she could somehow punish Philip Rainbolt.

There were, among the Kiowas, many clubs and societies—the Biters, the Elks, the Big Shields, the Black Boys. All took part in tribal decisions and politics. There were even soldier societies for the young boys—the Rabbits, the Young Sheep, the Horse Headdresses. Now there was formed the Sun People, disciples of Philip Rainbolt. He found himself suddenly the head of a secret society.

It started with Crow Bonnet. Convinced by Rainbolt's victories over the blue-faced Tonkawa warrior Cat and over their own Stone Teeth that Rainbolt was indeed touched by some divine medicine, Crow Bonnet started the Sun People society.

He invited the young warriors who constituted Stone Teeth's ill-fated raiding party to join him in the new club, with Rainbolt as leader. Two Time Talk asked for membership, and was admitted. There were Bird Bow, Tsoli, Bull Tail, and several others. They were henceforth Rainbolt's to com-mand. Their creed was *Adalbeahya*—the worship of Sun Boy. They called Rainbolt—not to his face, but among themselves—*Pai Talyi*. It meant Sun Boy.

Like the other societies, the Sun People had to have their own medicine shields—circular leather bucklers from the tough neck hide of buffalo, dried and hardened in the fire and painted with totemic designs. In the center the shields carried a many-rayed representation of the sun, the disk decorated with raven feathers, beads, and an attached whistle carved from the principal bone of an eagle's wing. The Sun People used the whistle to communicate with each other.

Rainbolt's elevation was to him a mixed blessing. One of the Sun People was always on guard at the door of his tipi, tootling to the others on his bone whistle. It was unsettling, and kept him awake at night. Still, as head of the newly formed lodge, Water Turtle and the others were bound by custom to permit him to sit at the edge of their councils.

Now that his Kiowa was more fluent, he could understand the many problems confronted by the chief and the elders and societies; whether to move camp to a better buffalo country, how to decide a dispute between two hot-blooded young men who claimed the same horse, what to do about the increasingly frequent horse soldier patrols deep into their territory. As the head of a very new and junior society, Rainbolt could not speak, but he listened intently.

There were frequent emissaries from the Comanches, from the Kwahadi of the Staked Plain, even from the fierce Kiowa-Apaches far west of Water Turtle's land. They all faced a common problem: the incursion of the hated settlers, the decimation of buffalo by the greedy hide hunters, the growing number of Army outposts like Fort Griffin, Fort Concho, and Fort Duncan which were beginning to hem them in.

Some wise men counseled caution, gradual withdrawal westward, the avoidance of confrontation. But many firebrands were in favor of fighting to preserve ancestral lands. Allied, Rainbolt concluded, the Indians might manage to make the price of conquest high enough so the government would withdraw its troops from the Red River country; the settlers, deprived of Army protection, would flee. But these were Indians. The concept of allies, real allies, the concept of a united effort, a single leader to weld them into effective effort, was foreign. In the waning months of the summer and into autumn they wrangled, argued, and came and went as separate entities. Each was unwilling to concede leadership to any other, and each was individually concerned only with coups counted, horses captured, scalps taken.

In spite of Rainbolt's resentment of Ellen Cameron as the genesis of his problem—the fact that he was now a fugitive in an Indian camp—he was responsible for her, and he knew it. Soon he hoped to find a wandering missionary or trader to take her to one of the Red River settlements. Rainbolt would be glad to see her go. He had too many problems already. Still, remembering Fort Sill, the enlisted men's garden, the school she had started, the shameless way she had exploited him, flirted with him, gotten him into trouble, he could not forego his revenge.

He enjoyed the sight of her bedraggled, weary hair falling dankly about her face, hands worn and soiled from a never-ending round of chores. She looked, now, like any other careworn squaw.

But he overestimated her patience.

"Come and smoke" meetings were common among the Kiowas. When a man was bored, with little to do but preen himself at the door of his lodge or watch his woman split wood, draw water, and cook, he would go out among the tipis to call "Come and smoke with me!" It was the equivalent of a call in Eighth Cavalry barracks for stud poker or a payday crap game. Men would gather before the host's lodge, smoke his tobacco, discuss the topics of the day in the immemorial manner of menfolk all over the world.

One morning Rainbolt went off to such a meeting. With his card tricks, his mirth-provoking Kiowa, and his growing stature in the tribe and its councils, he was usually a welcome guest. He had enemies, of course, but who knew? Rainbolt might actually be Pai Talyi, after all. It was well to know a man who might be divine.

As always, Rainbolt was followed by one of the Sun People. Tsoli's name was actually Tin Knife, but at the post a farrier sergeant was in the habit of calling him "Charlie." "Tsoli" was the nearest a Kiowa could come to saying "Charlie."

The smokers sat for a long time, arguing, discussing, bragging, exchanging gossip. They smoked their host's store of tobacco until it was completely gone. Then they loaded their pipes with the crumbled dry sumac and other leaves that constituted their own tobacco. The rank stuff made Rainbolt almost sick, but he kept stolidly puffing, listening to the talk.

The Sun Dance this year was very good.

I will trade you my spotted mare for that one-eyed horse of yours and a red blanket.

Heap of Bears is afraid of his mother-in-law. She beats him sometimes, and chases him.

This last caused hilarity. The Kiowa man from long custom was expected to avoid his mother-in-law, not even permitted by custom to look on her. The concept of Heap of Bears trying to avoid contact with his mother-in-law while being chased by her made the Kiowas scream with laughter, pound their thighs, giggle like schoolgirls.

I know a man among the Kwahadis who can take live coals from the fire and walk on them without hurting his feet.

Rainbolt half-dozed, listening pleasurably to the chatter, by now even enjoying the strong Indian tobacco.

Stone Teeth's brothers are plotting against the white man.

In the midst of the chatter, the flashing fingers, he was not even sure who had spoken. Leaning forward, he gestured *repeat,* holding his left forearm stiffly out, hand extended, tapping his left wrist several times with the back of his right forefinger. *Repeat. Who said that? What is this about Stone Teeth's brothers?*

Old No Moccasins leaned forward, his gnarled fingers working furiously.

I have heard this. Stone Teeth's brothers want to kill you. Be careful.

Now they were all silent, looking at Rainbolt with eyes gone blank and uncommunicative. In the way of Indians he smoked for a while, then he laid down his pipe.

"I know," he said. "I know this. Thank you, father."

There was a breaking of tension. The quick sign talk, the delighted chatter, began again. Fingers flashed in a sunlit haze of tobacco smoke; there was laughter, boasting, more gossip. But as Rainbolt was preparing to take his leave, other sounds intruded in the clamor of the come-and-smoke meeting. The shrill cries of women were heard, and the men broke off their talk. Some rose to gaze under palms raised against the sun toward the scene of the disturbance. Already children, dogs, women were hurrying toward the noise, the shrieks and wails.

With seemly deliberateness, the come-and-smoke meeting dissolved and the men strolled toward the commotion. Rainbolt was horrified to see Ellen Cameron and Star Sister confronting each other before his lodge. Bust heaving, Ellen held a handful of long black hair that had come from Star Sister's dark locks. Star Sister, weeping yet belligerent, brandished a tin frying pan, chattering Kiowa.

"Did you see her, that she-devil? She pulled my hair!" Sobbing, Star Sister flailed with the skillet. Rainbolt, embarrassed, stepped between the two women, getting for his pains the edge of the skillet across the bridge of his nose. Staggered for a moment, he finally caught Star Sister's hand, snatching away the deadly skillet.

"What's going on here?" he demanded.

Ellen was furious. "I'm tired," she shouted, "of being a damned squaw! And I'm even more tired of having that baggage order me around! Ever since you brought me here I've been put upon and exploited and ordered to do this and to do that!" She threw out her hands, almost in Rainbolt's face. "Look! Red and coarse, nails broken, callouses all over!" Despairingly she raked at her hair. "Look at this tangle! I'll never get it to look decent again!" She tugged at her buckskin shirt, and the ancient leather tore apart under her fingers to reveal the décolletage. "What kind of clothes are these for a—for a lady?"

Rainbolt, aware of delighted giggles among the spectators, patted awkwardly at her with his hand. "Now just quiet down a little, can't you? We'll talk this over, and—"

Ellen pushed him away, eyes filling with tears. "Don't touch me! I'm not your woman! And I'm damned well not your number two or number three wife or whatever it is!" Weeping, she flung herself away, running toward the pile of old furniture and implements which had been her first refuge.

Seeing her go, Star Sister felt vindicated. She slipped into Rainbolt's arms and put her head against his shoulder. "That woman is evil. She will bring bad luck. You ought to get rid of her." Reaching up a hand in a gingerly gesture to feel her scalp, she asked, "Did she pull out much hair? Will I be bald and ugly?"

Rainbolt sighed. "No. You are beautiful."

"But you ought to get rid of her!"

"I can't do that!" he protested. "She is a—a friend."

Star Sister started to pout, but he rubbed his nose against her cheek and kissed her. Kissing was unfamiliar to the Kiowas, and Star Sister delighted in the strange custom. Later he heard her singing in the tipi as she cleaned a rabbit for his supper. Perplexed, a man with two women, he started toward the junk pile to comfort Ellen. Tsoli, grinning, followed him, but Rainbolt shook his head and gestured the young man back. He did not want anyone to witness his further embarrassment.

He found Ellen quite composed, sitting in the

old wagon bed, reading an ancient copy of *Appleton's Weekly* she had found in an abandoned bureau. Her eyes were red, but otherwise she appeared poised and unconcerned.

He sat heavily beside her, chewing a stalk of grass he pulled up.

"Look here, now," he said uncomfortably. "You —you've got to stop fighting with Star Sister." As best he could, he explained the delicate situation. "So you see, I've got to stay on her good side." There was more to it than that, of course, but he didn't want to get trapped in detail.

She was silent, turning the pages of the magazine, not looking at him.

"Believe me," he said after an awkward pause, "I'm doing the best I can to get you out of here. Soon, maybe, you'll be on your way to Nashville—"

"Memphis," she said between tight lips.

"Memphis, then," he said wearily. "But in the meantime—"

"In the meantime," she cried, throwing down the magazine, "in the meantime do you have to keep on sleeping with that—that Indian woman?"

He blinked in surprise.

"It's an affront to me!" she charged. "Why— why, it makes you no better than a savage yourself! And it's against the Commandments! In Isaiah, too, it says—"

"I don't give a goddamn what it says in Isaiah!"

he blurted. "Don't preach to me! What gives you the right to be so high and mighty?"

She started to cry again, putting her worn hands in front of her face, but he pulled them away and made her look at him.

"This is a good time to have it out! Let's start with the beginning, shall we?" For a long time his resentment had been simmering; now it boiled over. "In the first place, I wouldn't be here if it wasn't for you! And maybe you wouldn't, either!"

She tried to wrest her hands free, but he held on.

"If you'd loved your husband, and cleaved to him, as it says in the Bible somewhere that you ought, then maybe you wouldn't have come around flirting with enlisted men, brushing your damned bust up against the poor homeless bastards and making them lovesick and calf-eyed! They're all poor homeless fools, you see, anxious for someone to care for them. All they've got is a two-bit whore, maybe, in some Whisky City crib, when they can get two bits ahead. And you—*you*—come flouncing in with your red hair and French perfume and good works for the enlisted men and drive the beggars crazy!"

"It's not true!" she cried, but Rainbolt went relentlessly on.

"You should have loved your husband, and let us poor devils alone! But no—your goddamned husband got jealous of me—of *me,* Phil Rainbolt, a lousy fleabitten private—because I fell in love with you! He put Sergeant Kruger on me, like a hunter puts his hounds on a coon! So I'm here, for running away from six months in Leavenworth!" Locking his hands around his knees, he rocked back and forth on the wagon tongue, shaking his head in unspoken grief. "Now it seems I'm charged as a murderer, too! And all for being a soft-headed bloody fool, though there was no malice in me!" He looked down at his fingers, rubbed a thumb across his knuckles. "I even felt sorry for poor Kruger when I hit him. You see, he really didn't know any better. He was only a stupid man, taking orders from your husband!"

The afternoon was waning. The curious had drifted away; women were cooking supper, children played stickball on a grassy plot, horses neighed and cattle lowed from the big corral. Slanting rays of sunlight threw a warped shadow of the wagon on the rocky ledge behind them.

Rubbing her wrists where he had grasped her, Ellen looked at him strangely.

"I—I loved my husband," she faltered. "But he—he didn't love me. I guess he loved the Army more. It was his whole life. Why do you think I was so unhappy? Why—why do you think I spent so much time with the enlisted men, buying them garden seeds, teaching them arithmetic, complaining to the quartermaster about the spoiled pork and the weevilly flour?" She took a deep sobbing breath; her bust heaved under the rags of serge. "But it was no good. I—I wanted friends, maybe even—even affection. I was foolish, I suppose, but more than anything else I wanted *you* to like me! I wanted—"

"You wanted!" he jeered. "*You* wanted!" He shook his head. "It strikes me you're the kind that *always* wanted things, and got them, too! But did it ever strike your foolish little mind that life is bound to be different from what you want? That no matter what they want, people are bound to come up with hurts and shames and crosses to bear? And maybe *their* needs are important, too! You ought to think of other people once in a while, and what *they* want and need! I daresay even Major Hugh Cameron, U. S. Army, wanted and needed something he didn't get, at least not from *you!*"

Shaken by his vehemence, she recoiled. "I gave him everything!" she cried, angry at the injustice of his words.

At first he seemed not to hear, going doggedly on.

"I never asked," he said, "for trouble to be thrust on me. I never wanted to make important decisions, to take on responsibilities."

While he rambled on, seeming to talk almost to himself, she took a little courage.

"What is it you want, then?"

His face was sad, and his long intertwined fingers worked at each other. "I thought I would live out my life peaceably; teaching, maybe, or perhaps even going to seminary and becoming a minister. There was a little seminary in Macon, all trees and vines and stained-glass windows. It was peaceful. Was that too much to ask?"

"But what is it," she asked, "that you want *now?*"

He gave her a long agonized look. "I want—I want—"

He had been sitting on the wagon tongue, head bowed, staring at his hands. Slowly he raised his eyes and looked at her. For a long moment he stared, blue eyes fixed on her melancholy violet ones. And at that moment the arrow struck between them, feathers trembling as it quivered in the oak boards. A split second later and it would have buried itself in his throat.

Ellen Cameron stared at it, fascinated, eyes wide and cheeks pale. She put a hand to her mouth as if to scream, but did not.

Quickly, Rainbolt ran around the wagon and plunged into the bushes, searching for the assassin. He called for Tsoli, and the guard came running. Together they crisscrossed the bushes, finding only a trampled place where the bowman might have knelt. Tsoli cut the iron point of the arrow loose with his knife and examined the shaft, the feathers. It was a nondescript hunting arrow, with none of the special feathers, paint, or decoration to identify it as belonging to a particular man.

"You should have let me come with you!" Tsoli rebuked him. "There are some bad men in this camp!"

Rainbolt took Ellen's hand and led her back to his tipi. Star Sister was still angry, but Rainbolt made the two women sit down and touch cheeks. "For," he said, "I am in trouble, I think. I need both of you to help me."

When Star Sister later complained of not feeling well, having a sudden chill, Ellen Cameron put her briskly to bed in the brass leviathan and took over the cooking of the rabbit herself.

"For," she said, "the girl's not well, that's easy to see."

She offered the spoon to Rainbolt.

"Taste this, will you—Philip? I—I think it needs a little salt."

It was the first time in a long time she had called him by that name.

Sergeant Kruger stuck his close-cropped head in the door of the orderly room and reported, "Sir, the general is here."

Hugh Cameron nodded. "Thank you, Sergeant Major."

He buckled on his saber, put on his kossuth hat with the plume, and went out into the autumn sunlight. It was not every day the general commanding the Department of the Missouri came to Fort Sill. However, to Major Cameron it seemed like every day. Since the escape of old Satank's bodyguard and the murderer Rainbolt, the general had plagued him unceasingly with telegraph messages urging him to greater effort. As if he had not spent almost every day in the saddle himself, practically denuding the post of effectives to scour the Red River country with his patrols!

The general traveled in a blue Army wagon drawn by mules. It was fitted up with a rocking chair, a cot with an incongruous flowered quilt, and a mahogany table with an Argand lamp bolted to it. The general had always shown great style in everything, including the late War of the Rebellion. Now, assisted by his aide, he clambered stiffly down a small stepladder, slapping his tunic to rid it of dust.

"There you are, Hugh," he said in a fatherly tone.

"Yes, sir." When the general took on that fatherly way, Major Cameron knew the old man was unhappy.

They went into the commanding officer's quarters, where the general sat gingerly in the lyre-back chair Ellen had brought from her father's house in San Francisco. Seeing the old man settle into the padded seat, the major felt a pang in his heart. Ellen—poor Ellen! She had been a difficult woman, and probably not the best choice for a career soldier's wife. But he would not have wished her fate on any female.

"Now, Hugh," the general began, tasting the glass of cognac the younger man offered and setting it on the piecrust table, "you must—you must—" He broke off, narrowing his eyes and leaning forward to peer at the major. "Good lord, you've gotten thin and haggard-looking since last I saw you!"

"Yes, sir," Hugh admitted. "I've been in the saddle a great deal."

The general took another sip of the liquor. "And quite a cross to bear, too, eh?"

"Cross, sir?"

The general twirled the stem of the glass between stubby fingers. "It's all over the department, Hugh. No need to be embarrassed. Happens to a lot of people. Ran off, did she?"

Hugh Cameron flushed. "Yes, sir."

"Seems to me I heard they found Mason's wagon."

"Yes, sir. Sergeant Major Kruger did. I—I located the enlisted man who helped her get away—drove her to Whisky City and made some arrangements for her with the teamster. That was Mason. He was going back empty to Fort Worth, and she paid him fifty dollars."

The general nodded, straightening the leg he

favored from an injury in the Peninsula campaign. "You located the enlisted man, eh?"

Major Cameron stiffened. After a moment, he said, "Yes, sir."

"You damned *well* located him! Had him flogged, didn't you, till he spoke up?"

The old man had his own spies. Hugh swallowed, and said, "Yes, sir. But he wouldn't talk. That was the only way."

The general drained the last of the cognac, shaking his head when the major offered him more. "You know goddamn well," he snapped, "that flogging was outlawed in '65!"

Hugh Cameron's patience was strained. For weeks he had held himself in, trying to maintain a normal appearance before men who knew his pretty wife had run away from him, perhaps even for a rendezvous with Philip Rainbolt. The fugitive Rainbolt could even have sent Ellen messages via Neilsen, though the Swede denied it.

"Yes, sir," Cameron said. "I knew it. And I take full responsibility for whatever I did, sir."

The general grunted. "Well, I'm sorry. Ellen was a beautiful woman. I hope she died quickly, without pain."

The bones, Sergeant Kruger said, were widely scattered by coyotes. It was hard to tell how many people had died there in the burned wagons. But the sergeant major had brought back

Ellen's scorched valise, clothing still neatly packed inside. Probably she had wandered away from the wagon, if she still lived, and died in some nameless canyon.

". . . goddamned troublemakers—"

Starting from his musings, the major realized he had not been paying attention.

"Sir, I beg your pardon?"

The general looked at him strangely. "You act damned preoccupied," he observed.

"I'm sorry. I—I haven't slept for a couple of days."

"The comancheros," the general repeated. "Goddamned troublemakers! Keep the tribes stirred up with guns and whisky! Yet when I put a comanchero in jail, fancy lawyers get 'em out faster 'n an alligator can chew a puppy! And all the while the coffee coolers in Washington are yammering at me to protect the settlers! God*damn* the settlers!" The general chewed wetly on a cigar. "Why in hell can't they stay home in Indiana or Kentucky or wherever and stop populating this godforsaken desert?"

"Yes, sir," the major said. "I'm doing my best."

The general shook his head. "It isn't good enough, Hugh. Now listen. I'm reinforcing your command with three companies of Ninth Cavalry —Grierson's Negroes—and a battery of the new Gatling guns. I want you to find the main body of the Kiowas. Confront 'em, take their weapons, maybe keep their chiefs as hostage. I don't want another Washita or Sand Creek—there are too many soft-headed fools in the Indian Bureau to get away with that any more—but we've got to break the back of the Kiowa nation. It's not just a military issue any longer—it's *political!*"

Major Cameron agreed. "I promise you, sir, that by the time snow falls, we'll have them rounded up." He rolled a map flat on the table. "I think they're way south of the Red, maybe even near the Llano Estacado country. But now we've got Tonk scouts that may be able to put us in the way of Water Turtle and his Kiowas. Those Tonks hate the Kiowas, you know. A Kiowa killed Cat, you remember—the big Tonk that used to cause us so much trouble."

And if, in the process of chasing Kiowas, Hugh Cameron should be put in the way also of Philip Rainbolt, he knew what he would do with the conniving murdering bastard. Rainbolt was, Major Cameron came to believe, the source of all his troubles.

CHAPTER NINE

Philip Rainbolt was a complicated man, more delicately wrought than Ellen had imagined. He had seemed to be the antithesis of herself: mature, dependable, phlegmatic, stable. In the passion and confusion and emotion of her relation to Hugh Cameron, Rainbolt had been a kind of rock for her to lean on. Often, after the enlisted men's reading and writing and ciphering classes, she found a pretext to ask Private Rainbolt to stay. He was her chief assistant in the class, although she was the nominal schoolma'am. But Philip Rainbolt was the real teacher, the one the eager men looked to for enlightenment.

Once, after a stormy encounter with Hugh, she had been near tears when she reached the condemned tentage set up for a schoolroom. But after the class she and Private Rainbolt talked. Although he was shy and awkward, he started to recite a stanza of Keats in response to some point:

"My heart aches, and a drowsy numbness pains
My sense, as though of hemlock I had drunk
Or emptied some dull opiate to the drains
One minute last, and Lethe-wards had sunk."

Listening, she knew a strange sense of peace, of repose. Care left her.

"White hawthorn, and the pastoral eglantine;
Fast-fading violets covered up in leaves;
  And mid-May's eldest child,
The coming musk-rose, full of dewy wine,
The murmurous haunt of flies on summer eves."

He knows all of Keats, she thought drowsily, hearing the brassy bugled tattoo and not caring.

". . . with a waist and with a side
White as Hebe's, when her zone
Slipt its golden clasp, and down
Fell her kirtle to her feet
While she held the goblet sweet."

Hugh had arrived to take her home, then, annoyed and suspicious she had stayed so long after the students left. He was very curt, too, with Private Rainbolt, though it had been her fault. But Rainbolt's eyes followed her when she left. That night Ellen dreamed of herself in a golden-clasped kirtle, drinking from a jeweled goblet. It was her first real disloyalty to her husband.

Now, a prisoner in an Indian camp, she felt strangely free and released, perversely brimming with life and spirit. Star Sister was still ill of some mysterious malady, and had gone back to her uncle's lodge; Ellen was left alone with Philip Rainbolt. In spite of his dislike of her, his gruffness, his strange ways, she sensed a rare savor in the autumn wind, and was happy and fulfilled in a completely illogical way. There was no hurry to reach Memphis and her Uncle Nestor and Aunt Alice. She trusted Rainbolt, and waited on him; he would make everything come out all right. Sunsets delighted her, clear water from the brook was sweeter than French champagne, she sang to herself as she scraped hides, made moccasins, cut firewood. But now that she was happy and fulfilled, Rainbolt was moody and mysterious, weighed down under some problem she did not understand.

At first, when she reached the Kiowa camp a captive, he had seemed an Indian himself, easy and confident in the savage dress. The Kiowas accorded him some mysterious place in their tribal hierarchy, and people deferred to him. He spoke their tongue, joked with them, played with the children. The arrow loosed from ambush that deadly afternoon might still be troubling him—apparently he had enemies in the camp—but there was, she suspected, something more. Well, being sought as a murderer was enough to make any man apprehensive. Yet in the Kiowa camp Rainbolt appeared to be as safe as any man could be. She did not think that was it, either. Pondering, she tried to remember the story that Star Sister had once tried to tell her about an itinerant trader— a comanchero—with whom Philip Rainbolt had had some unpleasant dealings. But Ellen had never been able fully to understand that. Star Sister's English was not equal to the task. She did not really know *what* was troubling him, and they were not as yet on good enough relations for her to question him. That would have been nosy, in any case. But he brooded, staring for long periods of time into space, preoccupied and silent. She was used to being answered brusquely, but Rainbolt's present curtness seemed to stem more from inattentiveness than from his old dislike of her.

Though she still did not think it proper to sleep inside his tipi, Ellen nightly laid her buffalo robe as close as she could, comforted by his deep breathing. But of late he thrashed about in the brass bedstead, muttering things she did not understand. One autumn night, concerned and frightened by the note of panic in his wild mutterings, she ran in bare feet and ragged camisole to the tent flap. By the light of the dying fire she saw him sit nakedly upright in bed.

"Is—is something the matter?" she called.

Only then did he seem to realize where he was.

"No," he muttered. "It's nothing." He seemed almost relieved to see her, as a child wakes from a nightmare and sees a familiar face. "A—a dream, that's all. Go back to bed."

Rebuffed, she continued to worry about him. She was not really concerned, she told herself, as a woman might be for an attractive man. No, her concern was entirely proper. It would withstand the finest scrutiny from even Uncle Nestor, who was an elder in the church, and Aunt Alice, who was recording secretary of the Missionary League to the Heathen. It was simply that he was her only protector in this savage camp, and what affected Philip Rainbolt adversely affected Ellen Cameron also. She was pleased at the neatness of the equation.

The summer ended in a burst of bloodshed. Attacking the hated Texans, the Kiowas, Comanches—even the Kwahadis from the Llano Estacado—all swooped down on the Red River settlements, burning, pillaging, looting. The Kiowas, leading the assault, brought back dozens of head of prime stock, more guns and ammunition, plenty of rum and whisky. They also brought back tales of increasing resistance to their raids. The settlers were fortifying their villages, settling in for a long stay, and the Red River swarmed with soldiers; their old enemy the Eighth Cavalry, and now a new threat— Negro troopers from the Ninth.

Red Sleeves, Star Sister's brother, was especially

indignant. Speaking before the council, he threw down a woolly scalp, crying, "They are good fighters, those black men! But look at this!"

The elders crowded around, passing the strange dead pelt from hand to hand.

"No good!" Red Sleeves protested. "Who wants a thing like that hanging from his coup stick? It looks like a dead mouse!"

Many of the Kiowas did not return from the last big raid of summer—Stumbling Bear, Big Eagle, Kicking Wolf, others of the onde, the Kiowa aristocracy. Red Sleeves himself was wounded in the groin and the wound still suppurated, though packed with ground sage leaves. But Red Sleeves was more concerned about Star Sister, who lay ill in Water Turtle's tent. For several days now she had complained of chills and fever, with occasional vomiting. At Water Turtle's request the shamans danced over her, sang curative songs, burned holy and powerful herbs and grasses. But there was no improvement.

At first, knowing the sensitivity of the Kiowas to any slight or reproof, Rainbolt suspected that Star Sister was merely jealous of Ellen, and chose this way to show her displeasure. But jealousy could hardly be responsible for the boneracking chills, the burning fevers. Others in the camp, too, were beginning to complain of headaches and fevers, to take to their beds. It was a worrisome time.

Water Turtle called Rainbolt to his lodge.

"Play for me," the chief instructed, pointing to the harmonium. "Sometimes the sound calms me, helps me think."

While the old man puffed moodily on his pipe, Rainbolt played scraps of melody that came to him—a *schottische* he had danced with Lily Cantrell at Nine-Mile Plantation, so long ago—the chorus from a scurrilous ballad a profligate uncle once taught him—a few lines of "Laura Lee" from the War. Behind a canvas screen rigged in a corner of the great lodge Star Sister slept fitfully; once he heard her whimper in her sleep, like a small and troubled child. Softly, picking out the tune with a forefinger, he played a lullaby his black nurse used to sing.

"I don't know," Water Turtle mused. "I don't know. The young men, they all want to fight. But there are so many soldiers." With ancient gnarled fingers he rubbed his forehead. "Sometimes I don't want to be a chief. But there it is. I was born to it. I cannot run away. It will always find me out."

For a long time he listened to the harmonium, eyes closed, the only sign of life a regular puffing of smoke from his pipe. Outside the sun hung low in the west and a chill warned of a hard frost. *Back home,* Rainbolt thought, *the chinkapins are falling, and they are getting ready to butcher hogs and make sorghum.*

"I hear," Water Turtle said, "they have a new

agent for the Kiowas. A Quaker, he is called—a good man. If we go back on the land they laid out for us, if we turn in all our guns, if we stop fighting with the Texans, they say everything will be all right. We will be happy then, they say. But I don't know about this. I need a sign. Satank and the others went in to talk to them about these things, and they killed my brother Satank. It is all right for *me* to trust the white men, maybe— but I cannot trust them for the People. If they kill me, the way they did Satank, that is all right. Sometimes a chief must die for the People. But it is hard for me to trust the white men when I know I am speaking for all the Kiowa people."

Finally, after a long spell of brooding, the old man dismissed Rainbolt. But he lingered to kneel for a while beside Star Sister. She lay on a wolf robe cushioned by bundles of sweet grass. Her brow was hot to the touch; when his awkward fingers brushed her forehead she cried out in some wild dream. In the failing light he bent over to inspect the small red blotches on her face and hands. Fleabites, probably; the Kiowas bathed regularly, and every day aired their bedding and robes, replacing old grass and boughs with fresh. But fleas were a constant problem, here no less than in the Fort Sill barracks. At Nine-Mile there had been fleas, too. There was a kind of gallows humor in it—he had come a long way in thirty years, but the fleas had followed him.

For a while he stood outside the great painted lodge, staring toward the west, where the sun was waning in a tangled swirl of red and yellow streamers. A knife-sharp freshness was in the air. Far away, a band of coyotes howled, a tremulous keening sound. Under a low-hanging pall of smoke from cooking fires, the Kiowa lodges were beginning to wink on like giant tapers. *This is home, now,* Rainbolt thought. But the camp was strangely and forebodingly silent, and apprehen-sion gripped him.

Not knowing why he felt so strange, so unsettled, he squatted beside his own fire while Ellen Cameron spooned a stew of deer meat and *pomme blanche* roots onto a wooden plate for him. He was silent, as was his wont. But Ellen seemed also under some restraint, not chattering and gossiping as she usually did of late. It was not till he had finished the stew and drunk a tin cup of scarce coffee that he looked up to see the fresh bruise on her forehead.

"What's that?" He pointed.

She made a great fuss over scraping food from soiled plates, wiping them clean with a hank of grass. "Nothing. Nothing at all."

Leaning intently forward, he took her wrist and pulled her to him. Trembling, not looking at him, she let him inspect the bruise. "I put some wet moss on it—I heard that would relieve it— but it kept falling off."

"How did it happen?"

She shook her head, trying to pull away from him. "It's nothing. I—I just—"

"Damn it," he insisted, "What happened? Tell me!"

Close to tears, she explained. "There was this sick woman in the small tipi down the way—kaan, you called them, poor people—Star Sister used to take food to this woman."

He nodded, impatient.

"She's been sick—there seem to be a lot of chills and fever and things—maybe it's some kind of a cold. Anyway, I went there to see if I could help, shake out her blankets, cook something, bring her water—oh, anything! That was the way my mother always did."

"So you wanted to help. But what—"

"Then some other women came in. They—they drove me away. They threw stones at me!" Her eyes filled with tears. "They screamed at me, and said ugly things. I didn't know what they were saying, but it almost seemed as if I were responsible for the sickness that's going around. That's silly, of course. But they—"

She broke off, staring at Rainbolt. "What's the matter?"

He was thinking of the fleabites, the apparent fleabites on Star Sister.

"What's the matter?" Ellen insisted.

He took her by the arms, looking closely at her.

"She was sick, you said. The old woman."

"Yes, but—"

"Listen to me," he said. "Did she have red splotches on her face? Her neck? Arms and hands?"

"Yes," Ellen said. "I remember that. But—"

"Chills and fever? Back pain?"

"Yes," Ellen said.

He knew now why he had had that feeling of apprehension, of approaching doom. All this time an inner knowledge had been trying to speak to him, but he had not listened.

"Smallpox," he muttered.

Ellen's eyes were wide and dark in the fire-streaked gloom of the tipi. "Smallpox?" she asked, in a small voice.

He nodded. "At Nine-Mile, once, we had it. Some of the slaves. I remember the symptoms. We—"

"Where? Nine-Mile?"

Impatiently he shook his head. "Doesn't matter where. But it's smallpox, for sure. It's bound to be smallpox!"

Frightened, she asked, "But what—what do we do now?"

Almost as if not hearing her, he went on. "In a few days some of them will begin to feel well again. But that's a mistake, a cruel mistake. The pustules come then, break out all over. I remember a Negro boy I used to play with. Caesar, they called him. His face was so swollen with those pustules I didn't recognize him. The pustules break out inside your nose and mouth, and it's hard to breathe." He took out a soiled handkerchief and wiped his forehead, reliving the experience. "Later there are boils, abscesses, all kinds of unpleasant things. Some people go blind, and most that live are horribly scarred."

"Philip," Ellen said. "Oh, Philip!" Her voice trembled. "It sounds so awful!"

"It is," he said grimly.

"Will—will a lot of the people die?"

He shrugged. "Never heard a cure for it. Some will outlast it—maybe half. They're the ones who'll have the pits and scars the rest of their lives, maybe be blind. The other half will die."

Trembling, she sought to put her hand in his. She was terribly frightened. "But what can we do?"

He did not return her grasp, only sat cross-legged beside the fire, staring into the coals.

"Maybe," she urged, "we ought to—to get away from here. Go quickly, before we catch it too."

"Run away?" He stared at her. "You mean—just light out?"

"Of course," she said. "It's the only thing to do, isn't it? You told me how—how horrible it was." Little by little her voice steadied, became practical. "I have money." Feeling in the remains of her bodice, she drew out a soiled roll of bills.

"I've hung onto these. There's enough for us both to—"

"To run away?" he asked again. He seemed to be in a kind of a daze, to be wrestling with something.

"Of course," she said. "There's nothing we can do here. You said yourself there's nothing to be done—they'll just die."

"But something could be tried," he insisted. "There are herbs and things—"

"I didn't leave my husband, just to die of the smallpox in some Indian camp!" Ellen cried. "I've always wanted lights, gay voices, champagne, dancing, the good things of life a young woman wants and needs, things I never got as a soldier's wife. And I still intend to get them!"

He shrugged, pushing away the proffered greenbacks. "Suit yourself. In the morning I'll make arrangements for you to leave for the railroad—you can go to your Nashville or wherever it is."

"It's Memphis!" She was annoyed. "I guess I've told you a hundred times! And if it is so easy to arrange it, why haven't you done it a long time ago?"

He took out his scratching stick. It was a habit he had borrowed from the Kiowas, and it annoyed her. Poking about in his long sun-bleached locks, he murmured, "Memphis. Or wherever."

Still holding the bills, she was silent for a moment. Then she said, "But you."

"Me?"

"I want you to go, too. With me."

He shook his head. "I'm going to stay here."

"Stay here? Here? With the smallpox?"

"Yes," he said. "I'm going to stay here. I doubt if I can make you understand it, but for the first time in a long time I've had a chance to take time—the luxury of time—to make up my mind about something. I'm not being just driven into something, you see, by circumstance. I thought things over, and now I've made up my mind."

"I don't—I don't understand," she faltered.

Carefully, deliberately, he put the scratching stick back in the beaded pouch at his waist. "I like these people. I respect them. They took me in when I needed help, and made me one of them. They're the first people in a long time to judge me for what I am, not for what I used to be, or for something foolish I did in the past. They're honest people, they believe in a God, and they follow the laws of that God, without pretense or hypocrisy. I've thought it over—yes, by God, I've thought it over, and now I'm going to stay here and try to help the People."

"You'll get sick, and die," she protested.

"Doesn't matter. Good riddance to bad rubbish." He looked curiously at her. "What possible difference does it make to you? You'll go on to

204

Philadelphia or New York or Boston and drink champagne and dance the german and the waltz and the rest of the new dances. You'll—"

"I don't want you to die." Staring down at the roll of notes, she repeated the words. "I don't *want* you to die!"

He grinned, an odd levity in his voice. "If it makes any difference to you, I promise. I won't die."

She put a hand on his arm. "Don't joke! I don't feel like joking. But come with me. Please."

He shook his head. "No. It's settled."

Her tone became wheedling. "Oh, Philip, please!"

"No!" Suddenly he shouted the word. Startled by his anger, she drew back. The dirty string around the bills broke, and a cascade of greenbacks swirled down. Some fell into the smoldering fire and blazed quickly.

"*Now* look what you've done!" she wailed.

He hardly seemed to notice her frantic efforts to rescue the bills. "Goddamn it, no!" he said again, almost as if talking to himself, staring into the fire and working big-knuckled hands together in a tight grip, as if fearing something would escape from them.

Suddenly Ellen knew why he slept so badly in the night, why he often called out in panic and remorse, why Philip Rainbolt seemed always stooped under the weight of some burden. She remembered what Hugh had told her—about a Captain Philip Rainbolt, at Petersburg, Captain Rainbolt of Heth's Division. *Lee was withdrawing to tighten his lines. The battery and all of the men were destroyed.*

"I won't run," Rainbolt insisted. "No, by God, I won't!" Very pale, he rocked back and forth on his haunches. His hair was cut short over the right eye in the Kiowa fashion and he brushed at it with his fingers impatiently. After a while he looked at her strangely, as if she were a stranger to whom he had accidentally blurted out a secret.

"I'll see you get away from here," he said. "In the morning, you can go away." This time his hand searched for her. "I'll miss you," he said.

But by morning everyone was fleeing. The Kiowas themselves finally recognized the deadly plague that had fastened itself on them, and the news swept the camp like a prairie fire.

In the Sett'an Calendar was an entry some thirty years back, the Winter of the Boils. That winter there had been a scourge of smallpox which decimated the Kiowas. The elders remembered; many of them still bore the telltale sprinkle of ancient pockmarks, and some were indeed blind.

The Kiowa camp was a frenzy of activity. Sick people, according to Kiowa custom, were left in the lodges where they lay, with only a small store of food to sustain them. Friends and relatives fled. Men tore down tipis and rolled them around precious lodgepoles, women loaded travois with household goods, older children snatched up younger children and ran, the well deserted the sick. Panic laid its hand on everyone. Even Water Turtle, with a battle record few men could match, said an anguished good-bye to Star Sister, his favorite niece. Then he loaded some robes and panniers of food on a packhorse, along with the sacred Tai Me dolls, and galloped away.

When Ellen awoke that morning, after a troubled sleep, she found Rainbolt standing over her. Brutus was saddled and bridled, and one of Rainbolt's savage friends sat a paint pony nearby, looking scared.

"Get up on Brutus, now!" Rainbolt ordered.

Still dazed from sleep, embarrassed to be only in her shift, she tried to rub the sleep from her eyes, uncomprehending.

"Hurry!" he snapped. "Go with the others! White Bull will take care of you. After they find a new camp, he'll see you get to the railroad."

"Memphis," she insisted drowsily. "I have an uncle there. An uncle and an aunt. Uncle Nestor and—"

"Good God, will you stop your chattering and hurry?" He seized her wrist, dragging her toward the patient Brutus.

For a moment, not understanding yet, she

stared about her, seeing the camp in wild confusion. Children, uncomprehending, laughed and screamed. Men, women, old people, young, striplings and tottering ancients ran wildly this way and that. From the pall of dust emerged whinnies, the barking of dogs, a flashing hoof or a madly arched neck as a horse reared.

"Stop it!" Suddenly remembering, she snatched away her wrist. "You're hurting me! Wait a minute!"

He put his arms around her waist and tried to lift her onto Brutus, but she fought him, scratching his face.

"Stop it!" she screamed again. "I'm not going! I don't want to go!"

Staggering back, releasing his hold on her, he felt the scratch on his cheek, half-incredulous, half-angry. "What in hell are you doing? Don't you realize it's the smallpox? Don't you realize that—"

"I'm not going," she insisted, adding coolly, "You can't make me!"

White Bull said something to Rainbolt and pointed down the valley where people were galloping away from the contaminated camp.

"I've decided to stay," Ellen said. Keeping her eyes averted, she fumbled at her torn dress, slipping it on over her head.

"Stay?"

"Yes."

Rainbolt seemed at a loss for words. Finally he asked, "Do you remember? Half of them die, yes—but if you stay, you are part of *them*. Do you understand?"

She nodded, tossing back her long red hair and tying it with a strip of rawhide. "You are staying," she said, "and you are part of *them,* are you not? And—and where you are, there will I be also. It is no use to argue."

Exasperated, he stared at her. Many emotions crossed his face. Finally he said, "You are under no obligation to them. I am."

"I have obligations, too," she said crisply. "But I do not care to discuss them now. There is work to be done, I understand."

Shaking his head, he dropped Brutus' reins and motioned to White Bull. "Go into my lodge," he said, "and stay there. In all this confusion, you might get hurt. Later, I will come to you."

Running through the dusty sunlight, blowing his own eagle-bone whistle, Rainbolt managed to round up most of the Sun People. They, too, were running from the Sickness. But the wild look in his eye, the eloquence of his pleas, stayed many, even as they had pack ponies loaded and were ready to join the long file of fleeing Kiowas.

"But we will all get sick and die!" Tsoli howled, casting an agonized glance at his wife and three children on their ponies, frantically gesturing to him.

"Die!" Rainbolt snorted. "Since when is a Kiowa afraid to die?"

"I am not afraid to *die,*" Tsoli protested. "But a man cannot count coup on the Sickness! What kind of a fight is that?"

Rainbolt was a spectral figure, eyes burning, long hair blowing about his face, one finger upraised in prophecy. The sun shone dustily down on him; he seemed like an apparition growing from the earth.

"It is the best kind of a fight!" he cried. "It is the kind of fight that makes Sun Boy's eye glad and his heart cheerful! Sun Boy is proud of his warriors when they fight a fight like this—to save the People—Sun Boy's own People!"

Tsoli blinked, he rubbed his eyes, a beading of sweat broke out on his forehead.

"I don't know," he muttered.

Remembering the Kiowa gesture, Rainbolt laid his hand flat on Tsoli's chest. *To see if there is any scare.* That first night in Water Turtle's lodge, after they had captured him, the Kiowas had done that to their white captive. *To see if there is any scare.*

Angry and perplexed, Tsoli knocked Rainbolt's hand away. Before Rainbolt's challenging eyes he dropped his own, and a moccasined toe scuffed uncertainly at the dirt. When an excited cur yapped at his heels, Tsoli picked the animal up by the loose skin of the neck and dropped it in a pannier of one of the loaded pack animals, where a little girl immediately hugged it to her breast.

Still Tsoli hesitated, looking at his pleading wife and then at Rainbolt. Finally he heaved a great sigh.

"Go!" he ordered his family.

The wife looked at him, uncomprehending.

"Go!" Tsoli shouted. "Do you need a beating, woman, to do what I tell you?"

Until his family, too, was lost in the haze of dust, Tsoli watched them go. Then he turned to Rainbolt, hefting his Sun People shield in one hand, carbine in the other.

"In this fight," he explained, "I guess I will not need these things. But I want to carry them anyway."

In like manner Rainbolt persuaded Crow Bonnet, Two Time Talk, Bird Bow, Bull Tail, most of the other Sun People who had not already fled. Brave men all, they were seared with panic, but Rainbolt prevailed.

"What?" he demanded. "Will you run away, like mice, and let your own people die, all alone? Is that the way a Kiowa does? Why, even a coyote fights for his mate, his cubs!"

Torn by emotion, they hesitated. They rubbed the oiled stocks of their guns, fidgeted with their shields, looking longingly at the departing column, now dwindling as the last of the People, the well People, left the camp behind.

"That is all right for you," Bull Tail complained to Rainbolt. "You are Sun Boy, I think. Yes, you are Sun Boy himself, come down to us. And the gods protect you. But"—he looked around, gesturing despairingly at the rest—"who is to protect us?"

For a long time Rainbolt had carried in his belt pouch the green bottle of calomel pills he took from the settlers' cabin—the dark death-smelling cabin where the man and the woman and the tow-headed boy lay as in sleep. He held it high; the glass sparkled green in the sun.

"This is great medicine," he chanted. "This is the Sun's own medicine." Prying open the cork with his thumb, he held up a pink pill. "With this medicine," he sang, "the Sickness cannot harm a man!"

Anxiously they crowded around him while he doled out the pills, one to each man. *I am a liar,* he thought, *but in a good cause.* Watching them chew the bitter pills, grimacing and wiping their mouths with the backs of their hands, he felt a queer elation. For better or worse, he was for the first time in a long time in control of his own destiny.

"*Hopo!*" he cried. "Let's go!"

CHAPTER TEN

Rainbolt and Ellen, aided by the Sun People, made a quick survey of the situation. In the abandoned camp were over forty sick Kiowas—men, women, children, babies—in various stages of the Sickness. Some had only the chills and fever characteristic of the early stages of the disease; others had progressed to the eruptive stage, skin of face and hands marred by tiny yellowish pustules; still others, with their dreaded illness probably known to themselves or others, yet kept secret from fear of being banished from the camp, already displayed the boils and abscesses marking the terrible third phase.

The task was staggering, yet somehow Rainbolt managed to force a rude kind of order on their efforts. That first day, two or three of the Kiowas died, and were immediately buried; their tipis and their belongings were burned. The still living were transferred to Water Turtle's great lodge, made for the time into a kind of hospital. There was not enough room for all the sick, so skins were robbed from other tipis to make a warren of supplementary shelters, clustered around the central lodge in lean-to fashion.

They had no medicine beyond Rainbolt's green

bottle of calomel pills. But he found some odd-looking plants near the camp that he told Ellen were a species of *chrysothamus*, and on his orders she boiled the stems and leaves to make an evil-smelling tea which he remembered once reading about as a cure for the smallpox. Though late in the season, with cold winds and occasional snow, the Sun People managed to find a few wild onions still growing. These, cooked to mush and made into poultices, relieved much of the itching and discomfort. Night and day, white sage leaves were crumbled and thrown on the fire to disinfect the air. When all else failed, when one of the Kiowas was near death, fevered, breathing heavily, covered with the vile pus-filled boils, it was time for a calomel pill. Rainbolt's calomel, the Kiowas believed, was great magic. The pills were only a purgative, but he knew something about what the doctors called placebos, the harmless sugar pills which sometimes cure because the patient believes they will cure. Though some of the Kiowas died, most still clung tenaciously to life, trusting in Pai Talyi— Sun Boy—and his powerful medicine.

For weeks they labored with the sick, hardly knowing whether it was day or night. Rainbolt and Ellen Cameron were always on call, nor did the Sun People know any rest. It was a dirty and difficult business—emptying slops, cooking for sick people from the scanty store of meat and

214

beans and flour and coffee left behind, preparing wild-onion poultices, hunting for the scarce chrysothamus, bathing babies, comforting the dying. In their haste Water Turtle and the rest of his people left the brush corral almost full of prime stock, good horses and cattle, and the Sun People had to herd them out to pasture, too—feed and water them, somehow take care of almost two hundred head grown thin and wild from neglect. Over and above this backbreaking toil hovered the knowledge that at any time any one of them—possibly Crow Bonnet, maybe Two Time Talk, perhaps Tsoli or Bull Tail, conceivably even Ellen Cameron or Rainbolt himself—might fall ill, com-plain of back pains, chill, fever, might fall under the onslaught of the blotchy skin, the apparent fleabites that heralded the coming of the Sickness.

More people died, but less——many less—than Rainbolt expected. One night, while he was dozing for a few minutes on a buffalo robe, under the stars and away from the fetid evil-smelling hospital tipi, Two Time Talk shook Rainbolt gently awake.

"Twisted Horn is dying," he said. "He wants to talk to you first, before he goes."

Almost automatically, Rainbolt reached for the green glass bottle, now with only a few of the calomel pills rattling around in the bottom.

"I—I think," Two Time Talk stammered, "that

it is—it is too late for that medicine. But he wants to talk to you anyway."

Wondering, Rainbolt knuckled his red swollen eyes and staggered to his feet.

"He is over here," Two Time Talk said, guiding Rainbolt to one of the crude lean-tos.

In spite of the sage leaves smoldering on the fire, the shelter stank. On a pile of blankets— there were plenty of blankets, since the fleeing Kiowas had abandoned much of their household goods—lay a tall and powerfully built young man, now wasted with disease. There was, Rainbolt suspected, more than one kind of the smallpox rampant in the camp. Physicians had identified several strains of the disease; Twisted Horn, he believed, suffered from the "black smallpox," a variation in which fatal hemorrhages occurred in the body.

"Brother," Rainbolt said, kneeling beside the young man.

"I cannot hear you very well," Twisted Horn muttered. "There is a ringing in my ears, and voices come to me very faint, far away, like a child crying in the forest."

Rainbolt upended the bottle, taking out one of the precious calomel pills. But Twisted Horn pushed it away.

"That is good medicine," he said. "That is powerful medicine. But it is not strong enough to cure me. Save it for the others, the ones who

216

have a chance to live. Because, brother, I am going to die. I know it. So I want to get ready."

For a long time the young man was silent, staring upward at the smoke-blackened poles near the apex of the tipi. Rainbolt thought Twisted Horn had died, but when he made a small move-ment, thinking to close the staring eyes, Twisted Horn blinked and started to talk.

"I want to get ready," he said. "When I get up there, when I see the Great One Above with my own eyes, I want to tell him there is no bad in my heart. I want to tell him I am friend to all men. So now I have to tell you something."

With great effort he rolled his head toward Rainbolt. Blood dampened his lips; Rainbolt sponged away the pinkish froth with a rag.

"Stone Teeth," Twisted Horn said, "was my cousin. When I was a little boy he used to carry me on his back. I always wanted to be like him. When you killed Stone Teeth, it was as if my own father died."

"You are very weak," Rainbolt said. "Do not try to talk. Everything is all right."

But Twisted Horn pushed away his hand. "Let me alone, now. I am going to die, so I have to say these things." Pausing as if to gather strength, he went on. "We smoked together, the men of Stone Teeth's family, and decided you were a bad man. We decided you were bringing bad luck to the People. I drew the short stick, and that was how I came to try to kill you, that afternoon when you sat on the wagon tongue talking to the white woman with the fire-colored hair." Twisted Horn closed his eyes in shame. "I missed with my arrow. When you moved your head, I missed. But now I am glad I missed." For a moment he seemed to run out of breath. He struggled for air as more of the pink froth bubbled from his lips. But when Rainbolt wiped it gently away, the youth summoned his strength for one more effort.

"You are a good man. I do not know if you are really Pai Talyi, but it could be. Anyway, I am glad I missed." For a moment he trembled and shook under the blanket, and Rainbolt thought it was the death throe. But Twisted Horn was only trying to raise himself on an elbow. "My hand," he said. "Here, friend—take my hand."

A few moments later the young man died, holding Philip Rainbolt's hand tightly, as if Rainbolt himself were accompanying him to the land of the Great One Above.

Of perhaps forty sick people, a dozen had died, and were buried in pits the Sun People dug behind the camp. The ground was hard and nearly frozen, and the snow-dusted pines sang a weird lament as the wind sighed through their branches. There was, of course, an elaborate Kiowa cere- mony for the dead, but now was no time for niceties. The infected corpses had to be disposed of, and promptly. But Ellen Cameron found a tattered Bible in the pile of old bureaus, churns, string beds, and rusted wagon wheels. She, like Philip Rainbolt, was tired and worn, dirty, great circles under her violet eyes. But she insisted on reading the Twenty-third Psalm over each body. "For," she told Rainbolt, "I don't think He will send to hell anyone whose only sin was being born a heathen, and so not knowing the true God."

Never having known this side of her, he looked up in surprise, and thoughtfully leaned on his shovel. The Sun People were puzzled, too. But the whole calamity of the Sickness had brought out in each of them new and unsuspected virtues and strengths.

"Amen," Rainbolt said finally, and thought the word strange though comforting on his lips.

Eventually, of course, others died. Tsoli perished, crying for the wife and children he had sent away, and a few others. Star Sister lived, though nearly blind, and scarred with great pits over her gentle melancholy face. Somehow, the effort Rainbolt organized had beaten back the Sickness. It took a while to realize what had happened.

Ellen was boiling tea water over a small fire in Rainbolt's lodge when he came in, standing for a while in the doorway, holding the door flap back, a dark figure silhouetted against the brilliance of a fall day.

She did not look up. "I know it's you," she murmured. When he did not answer, she went on. "Your moccasins," she explained. "They play a certain tune, different from the others. It's your music, Philip—your very own music."

He dropped the flap and squatted beside her at the fire, accepting the tin cup, gazing absently into the fire in a bemused way as she put a pinch of precious sugar into his tea.

"Why, whatever is the matter?" she asked, seeing the look on his face.

He sipped the tea, staring at her over the rim. His hair had grown long and straggly, the high cheekbones seemed almost to poke through the skin, the bush of beard showed red lights from long confinement inside, away from the bleaching sun.

"Do you realize—" His voice broke, and he made a great deal of noise blowing at his tea to cover his discomfiture. Finally he started again, his voice still shaking with emotion. "Do you realize we've passed the crisis?" He put down the cup, and ticked off on his fingers the status of their patients: Owl Eyes, Kicking Horse, the wife of Stumbling Bear, the three small children of Dangerous Eagle—he went on and on, describing the condition of each.

"They'll live!" he wondered. "They're all past the worst, now. Some will have scars—White Wolf's daughter has some pretty bad ones—all of them are weak—but they're going to live! *They're all going to live!*"

For a long moment she only squatted on her legs, feeling faint, not comprehending. For so long they had drudged, suffered, toiled, presided at deathbeds, bathed stinking bodies, and carried out pail after pail of night soil that she could not believe he was serious. It had gotten to be a way of life. She was like a newly freed slave, doubting freedom.

"They're going to live!" Rainbolt marveled. Exultantly he grabbed her and drew her up, holding her close. "By God, we've done it!" he shouted. "You, me, the Sun People! We've prevailed, Ellen! We've prevailed!"

Attracted by his shouts, Two Time Talk and some of the rest crowded around Rainbolt's tipi, peering fearfully within.

Still holding Ellen Cameron to him, Rainbolt shouted at them, "We've won!" In his exultation he spoke in a jumble of Kiowa and English, and threw in a few hand signs. "We've beaten the Sickness! Everyone is getting better!"

They understood. And seeing him holding the red-hair woman so tightly, they understood something else too. Delicately they smiled, waved at the couple, and withdrew. Pai Talyi's magic had won; it was only right that he claim a prize. Of course, they themselves did not see any beauty in her, but that was really Pai Talyi's business.

Although it was full day outside, Rainbolt and Ellen Cameron lay for a long time in the big brass bed. For a while one of them would sleep, cradled in the arms of the other. Then he would wake, or she, and they would again love each other. It was an outpouring of love long denied to each of them, but finally bursting its bonds and carrying all before it. The moon came out, a yellow harvest moon low in the sky, threading its way through the tangled black skein of pine branches. Night birds called, a long way off a solitary wolf howled. But the sound did not frighten Ellen Cameron. It was almost like an affirmation of her safety in his love as she lay replete and drowsy in Rainbolt's arms.

"Philip?" she whispered.

"Yes?"

"Do you love me?"

He laughed. It was the first time in a long time she had heard him laugh, and she delighted in the sound.

"I mean it!" she insisted. "Do you love me?"

He stroked her breast with a finger, lingering delicately on its contours. "What more do I have to do to prove it?"

"Say it!" she insisted. "Say you love me!"

"I love you."

"Did you—then? I mean—at the post? In the garden, and places like that?"

His voice was gently amused. "You made me

furious, but I guess that's one of the first signs of love."

Satisfied, she nestled against his breast; they slept again. It was dawn when she awoke. Philip was still sleeping, and she blew the fire into life and added some twigs. Waiting for the fire to catch, she stood naked at the foot of the brass bed, looking down at him. In spite of his height, in spite of the unkempt beard and the face and hands and shoulders and neck burned dark by the sun, he looked curiously like a child, a child dreaming a peaceful dream.

She was standing so, entranced, when sunlight streamed into the lodge. Old Water Turtle poked his head about, blinking in the darkness. "Is anybody here?" he asked. He stumbled across the threshold and held out his hands to the fire. It had been a cold night. "Where is the white man?"

Ellen Cameron snatched up a blanket to cover her nakedness. Embarrassed, she cowered behind a painted cowhide trunk, not knowing what to say. But Rainbolt woke and rolled to the edge of the bed, yawning and scratching his armpit.

"Good morning, father," he said, blinking in a shaft of sunlight. "I am glad to see you."

"And I you, my son," the old man said.

Wearing a bearskin robe against the wind, a fur cap pulled down over the red turban, Water Turtle squatted beside the fire and accepted the cup of tea Rainbolt handed him. After a while,

Rainbolt respectfully silent, the old man looked down into the grounds at the bottom of the cup. "It has been a long time since I saw you."

"Yes."

"Star Sister is well," Water Turtle said. "She has lived. There are scars, and she can see very little, but my niece is well. While you were asleep, you and"—Water Turtle nodded his head toward the painted trunk—"while you were asleep, I came to the camp. It was still dark, and the moon shone. But I had to come, to see my girl, to see my people who were in the shadow of the Sickness."

Rainbolt was silent.

"I waited," Water Turtle explained. "I waited till the sun came up. It was very cold, but I waited. I—well, I was afraid! Everyone knows there are ghosts at night—evil things. The Sickness, too, is stronger at night. But when the sun came up and warmed me a little, I heard Star Sister's voice. I heard her laugh." The old man turned his wrinkled face toward Rainbolt. "I thought she was *dead!* But Star Sister was laughing—she was playing a game of *do a* with another girl! I ran from one lodge to another, and found a lot of people well! Oh, they are weak—some have scars, some do not see very good. But you fought the Sickness, my son, and saved many of the People. I am their chief, but I was afraid and ran away. You—you stayed, and fought to save them!"

Rainbolt was uncomfortable. "We all helped," he said. "Two Time Talk, Tsoli, the red-hair woman —we all worked together. The gods, too, helped us. It must have been that way, because the Sickness was very strong, yet we won. The gods showed us certain plants to use, certain herbs—"

Water Turtle waved the stem of his pipe. "Yes, yes! All that is so! Yet it took one man to show the way!" When Rainbolt tried to speak, the old man gestured him to silence. "You are forgetting I am much older than you, and you should listen to me! After all, I do not have much more time in this world, and have to hurry!"

Abashed, Rainbolt sat silent, and took the blanket Ellen shyly brought him.

"For a long time," Water Turtle went on, "I have been in doubt. I did not know what to do. I did not know what was best for the People. I told you—I did not know whether to fight the soldiers or make peace. I did not know whether to trade with the comancheros or send them away. I did not know whether to stay here, or to go away someplace"—he gestured westward— "someplace out there, where the white men will leave us alone. I was looking all that time for a sign—for a message from the gods."

The old man let Ellen fill his pipe again. White man's tobacco was long gone, and she tamped the bowl with scrapings of red willow bark.

He puffed for several minutes, staring somberly at the rings of smoke he blew.

"Now," he said, "I have a sign."

In spite of himself, Rainbolt asked, "A sign?"

Water Turtle nodded vigorously.

"A sign that is true. A true message that comes straight down from the Great One Above."

"What sign?" Rainbolt asked, puzzled.

Ruefully, Water Turtle shook his head. "I was very foolish not to see it from the start. But in times like these, the real gods often go away, and false gods come around. Anyway, a man came to us. A man with pale hair and eyes, as the gods said. He conquered a great warrior—Cat, the Tonkawa. He lived among us, this man. When the Sickness came, he with his god's strength was the only one strong enough to stand and fight the Sickness." The chief stared at Rainbolt with sharp button eyes. "What better sign than that? What better sign—that the gods are talking to us?"

Rainbolt shook his head.

"I am not a god. I am not—"

Water Turtle's face was pained. "Do not make this so hard for me!" he shouted. "I was very foolish, yes! I did not listen to you! I did not want to believe! But now I know! I know you speak the truth of the gods! You have come down to guide us!"

Embarrassed, Rainbolt looked helplessly at Ellen Cameron, but she only looked back at him with a quiet steady gaze that made him more uneasy. Finally he sighed, and muttered, "Whatever my father says. I am a god."

"Good," Water Turtle said. "I will go back and tell the onde and the *ondegupa* and the rest of the People that the Sickness is killed! But first"—he rose, pulling at Rainbolt's blanket—"it is only right to give something away for the favors done the People by the gods."

Drawing Rainbolt after him, he went out into the sunlight. The Sun People, curious, and some of the patients who felt better straggled after him. Ellen Cameron followed, too, having had time to pull on a deerskin skirt and moccasins. The little group trailed Water Turtle and Rainbolt into the meadow, toward the big brush corral.

"What is happening?" the wife of Stumbling Bear asked Ellen. "Where are they going?"

With her little Kiowa, Ellen understood, but only shook her head as she hurried along, fastening a rawhide thong about her waist to support the skirt.

For a November day the sun was hot, though low in the south. The sky was eye-achingly blue and cloudless, and a few late bees bumbled among the faded remnants of summer bloom. In the corral the stock milled about restlessly. On scant rations for several weeks, they were lean and hungry, sending up a chorus of whinnies and bellows as the group approached.

Water Turtle went to the gate of saplings and walked in a wide quarter circle, dragging the gate. "Hi!" he shouted at the wide-eyed horses. "Hoo! Hoo!" he yelled at the steers, the cows, the yearling calves. A small indomitable figure, he ran among them, slapping with his blanket, howling and prancing.

At first the animals pressed back against the brush walls, frightened and uncertain. Still shouting, Water Turtle dashed among them, waving his blanket. So deeply did he venture that for a time all they could see was an occasional flash of his red turban, or the fringed hem of the blanket tossed high.

"Hi!" he shouted. "Hoo! Hi!"

Suddenly a mare near the gate stepped through the open gate, sniffing the air of freedom with flaring nostrils.

"Hi!" Water Turtle shouted. "Hi! Hoo! Hi!"

A colt trotted after the mare, trembling and afraid. Then a wall-eyed steer stumbled after the pair. Others came.

Water Turtle appeared again, dancing and waving the blanket.

"Hi! Hoo!"

Suddenly it was as if a dam had broken. The animals poured through the gate in a flood, stampeding toward freedom. Cattle bawled, horses neighed and tossed their manes. Water Turtle was borne along like a chip on a flood until

Rainbolt, anxious for his safety, grabbed the blanket and pulled the old man out of the way.

"Look at them!" the old man exulted. "Look at them go! It is good to be free! Animals like to be free just as men do!"

Hoofs pounded, clouds of dust rose into the air and boiled like storm clouds. Ellen Cameron put her fingers in her ears and looked faint. The Kiowas chattered among themselves; one pulled at her, trying to say something in her ear, but she did not understand.

Water Turtle was still shouting "Hoo! Hi!" but finally the tide of animals slackened. Only a few remained, milling dazedly about in the corral. Dangerous Eagle's smallest boy, caught up in the excitement, ran into the corral with a switch and chased the last of the animals away.

Rainbolt felt exhausted. After the peril and emotion, the deadly toil of the last few weeks, he felt drained, hollow, lifeless. The flight of the animals seemed almost unreal. Dazed, uncomprehending, he stared at Water Turtle.

"A gift!" Water Turtle howled. "A gift to the gods! Oh, what a great gift! People will talk about it for a long time!"

"But—"

"No more," Water Turtle explained, "no more do we soil ourselves with comancheros! No more do we raid on the Red River! No more do we trade stolen guns and horses for bad whisky and cheap blankets! No, we have stopped all that! Now, as the gods want, we leave our home here, in the canyon that sheltered us so long. We leave this place, and go west, out there—" He gestured. "We do not fight the white man any longer. There are too many of them, as Pai Talyi has told us!"

Rainbolt still felt dazed; the pounding of hoofs, the shrill whinnies, the lowing of cattle were still in his ears. He did not feel like a god. He felt very tired.

"We will go west to join our brothers, the Cheyennes, and make a new life for the People," Water Turtle said. "The People do not like to run away from a good fight, but Pai Talyi brings us the true advice of the gods! So we leave the white men and go west." Forgetting for a moment Philip Rainbolt's divinity, Water Turtle clapped him on the shoulder. "As soon as everyone is well enough to travel," he said, "we will go! It has taken a long time to find the right path, the true path for the People, but now we know, and we obey the gods!"

It was not quite so simple, however. All the warrior societies had to be convinced—the Biters, the Black Boys, the Pulling Up People, the Big Shields, the rest. There were divisions, too, among the social strata of the Kiowas—the onde, the aristocracy; the ondegupa, the second rank of warriors, medicine men, and the rich; the kaan, poor people; even among the *dapom*, the grab bag of lazy, shiftless, and no-account.

One faction, proud and warlike, insisted on staying in the canyon and redoubling their raids on the Red River, believing they could thus drive away the white men. Others pointed out that Water Turtle's Kiowas were safe in their great canyon, and should not leave such a shelter for an uncertain journey to join the Cheyennes. Others, while fearing the growing strength of the soldiers, called attention to the fact that it was now almost winter. A band of Kiowas on the move in such weather would be easy prey for the horse soldiers.

Water Turtle, however, was persuasive.

"Everybody knows," he scoffed, "that the horse soldiers are afraid of the cold! In winter they go about in bearskin coats and fur boots. They stay in their camp and get drunk and play cards and are afraid to go outside!"

"What does Pai Talyi say, now that he has heard these arguments?" the head of the Biters Society asked Rainbolt. "We want Pai Talyi to speak!"

The wrangling had gone on for weeks; the camp simmered with opinion. Rainbolt knew a word from him would suffice to turn the tide in Water Turtle's favor. But still he hesitated. It was one thing to speak as a renegade white man, a glib deserter, a fugitive dependent on Kiowa hospitality. It was another thing to speak as Pai Talyi, the representative of Kiowa gods. Most of the People were now convinced of his divinity; in addition, he had been made a Koitsenko in place of the dead Stone Teeth, and wore the impressive sash of black elkskin. People fell back in awe at the mere sight of his zebat, his medicine lance, ornamented with many trophies signifying his powers. Now from the very top of the zebat dangled the green medicine bottle, empty of the magic pills, but recalling to everyone his triumph over the Sickness.

His fame had begun to spread. Wandering bands of Kiowas and Comanches, many of them on their way back to the fort in response to the general's orders, paused at Water Turtle's camp to exchange views and get the latest news. The miraculous defeat of the Sickness was on everybody's tongue, and legends began to spread about the great and powerful Pai Talyi, come down from the heavens to lead Water Turtle's Kiowas to a new destiny in the West.

Of course, that was all very well for Water Turtle and his People; they had Pai Talyi as tribal property. The other tribes, however, were not so certain of divine intervention, and so went unwilling off to the fort. Winter was a lean time, anyway; government *wohaws* delivered to them twice a week and shelter in huts with glass windows and a stove sounded better than any other course. Anyway, spring would soon come again; they would flee the reservation and go back to their raiding along the river. That was life, that was the way it was lived. They could not conceive of any permanent change in their ways.

Before Pai Talyi spoke, however, there was a commotion in the camp. Old Ike Coogan arrived to observe the stock herd collected for the comancheros, prepared to gloat over its size and reflect that it was his, all his in exchange for a few rifles and some pistols, along with a barrel or two of white lightning. By now, Coogan reasoned, that rascal Rainbolt should have old Water Turtle's Kiowas well under his thumb. He and Rainbolt would divide the spoils. Seventy-thirty, that would be about right. No, seventy did not sound adequate to his own part in the scheme. After all, the whole idea had been his, Ike Coogan's. Eighty-twenty, that was more like it. Or even ninety—

When he saw the empty corral his mouth fell open. He sat his horse for a long time, staring at the abandoned enclosure, rich with recent droppings, the gate of sapling hanging twisted and askew. What had happened? Had Rainbolt double-crossed him, somehow gotten the herd of prime stock for himself, and fled? But in response to Coogan's volley of profanity, a frightened Kiowa boy fled with the news of the arrival. In a few minutes they were all around him—Water Turtle himself in his red turban, arms crossed, staring at him as if he were a stranger, the Biters, the Black Boys, and the onde. Although it took the frustrated and angry Coogan a while to identify him, there was Rainbolt himself, decked out in Koitsenko gear, looking as if butter wouldn't melt in his mouth.

"What the hell's going on here?" Coogan demanded. His voice rose shrilly; the paint, startled, capered about while he sawed at the reins. He swept his arm toward the empty corral. "Where in hell are all the horses was promised me—the stock—the goddamned prime steers and oxen and the rest? Where are they, eh?"

Rainbolt himself spoke; the others drew back in a gesture of respect that made Coogan furious.

"Hello, Ike," Rainbolt said.

"Don't 'Hello, Ike' me!" Coogan squalled. He held the quirt so tightly in his fist that his ancient knuckles whitened. "Give an account of yourself, you two-timing bastard! *What happened to that stock?*"

Rainbolt seemed very calm. He nodded toward Water Turtle, saying, "He turned them all loose."

"Loose?" Coogan wailed. "But why? You and me—we was gonna—"

"He turned them loose," Rainbolt went on, "because he wanted to give a present to the gods. You see, Ike, there was an epidemic of smallpox here this fall. One of the gods came down, so the story goes, and drove away the Sickness. In order to be properly grateful, Water Turtle opened the corral and let the animals out. There must have been two or three hundred—maybe more."

Ike gnawed balefully on the butt of the quirt.

"A god, eh? You?"

Rainbolt did not need to answer. The reverent and respectful eyes of the Kiowas, their deference to Philip Rainbolt, told Coogan all he needed to know. But it was still hard to believe.

"You?" His voice thick and strangled, incredulous. "A goddamned deserting yellow leg?"

Rainbolt nodded. "Strange as it may seem, Ike —that's what happened. I didn't plan it that way—I really didn't. I'm not even sure, now, that I wanted it to happen that way. But that's how it is."

For a long moment the comanchero stared, the cords in his neck standing out as if under tension. Suddenly, almost as if something in him had broken under the strain, Coogan flailed with the quirt, wheeling the big paint.

"Ike!" Rainbolt called. "Wait a minute! I—I—"

The paint, frightened, gathered its powerful haunches and sprang into a gallop. Screaming imprecations, Coogan dashed madly away, the quirt rising and falling in a furious rhythm. A moment later he disappeared over a snow-dusted rise, but the wide-eyed Kiowas could still hear the sound of his cries. Even Ellen Cameron, peering fearfully through the flap of Rainbolt's tipi, heard, and was afraid.

CHAPTER ELEVEN

Fort Sill lay under a thin blanket of snow, softening the outlines of the raw-wood barracks, the stables, the comfortable verandaed house recently built for the commanding officer. Blurred in a haze of snow, the general's blue wagon stood before the CO quarters. The corporal driver wrapped himself in a blanket and cursed the old man's garrulousness. In another ten minutes, the corporal judged, he would freeze to death. Not that it was so cold—only forty degrees on the Fahrenheit scale—but the wind was strong, straight from the north, with a bite to it that might mean a blizzard.

In Major Cameron's parlor the general leaned back in his chair and lit a cigar. "By God," he said, puffing hard and looking at the glowing coal of fine Havana, "I'd give a box of *claros* to know the whereabouts of that old rascal!"

"Water Turtle?" Hugh Cameron asked.

"Who else? Who else has been on my mind for months, and made me lose my proper sleep at nights?" Expertly the general balanced the growing ash of the claro. He believed a cigar grew tasteless once the fine first ash fell. "As a matter of fact, I'd give a great deal more, including a certain portion of my privates!" He laughed, but there was no mirth in it.

Most of the troublemaking tribes had been gathered in on the reservation for the winter, and were peaceful enough in the shacks the Indian Bureau built for them. But Water Turtle and his Kiowas were still outside the pale. During the summer the old man's braves had terrorized the Red River country; well into autumn, bitter at the death of Satank at the Army's hands, the Kiowas raided, burned, killed, and drove off huge numbers of settlers' cattle and horses. Water Turtle was probably holed up in some winter camp on the Llano Estacado, cozy and warm, waiting for spring to resume his raids. If only the general knew *where* the old man was!

"I don't see," the new Indian agent protested, "what difference it makes, really." He was a Quaker named Tate, and he peered reprovingly over the steel rims of his spectacles. "Most of the hostiles are on the reservation now. Why do a few stragglers matter so much?"

The general sighed; Mr. Tate was only one more cross to bear. "That's the trouble with you missionary johnnies! You don't know these blood-thirsty bastards the way Hugh and I do. Come next spring and the grass greens and the sun shines, the reservation Indians are going to get mighty restless. When they see old Water Turtle and his bucks out sniffing the breeze and getting ready to raise hell, it's Katy bar the door! The whole Army hasn't got enough soldiers to keep them from busting out of the reservation and going to join Water Turtle!"

"Oh, I don't think so!" Mr. Tate objected. "After all, even an Indian is bound to come to realize the odds after a while, and give up! There's this business of Pai Talyi, too, or whatever his name is. My Caddoes tell me that he's practically running the Kiowa camp now. He's trying to get them to stop bothering the Red River people."

The general had good sources of information; he had already heard about the mysterious Pai Talyi from Comanche turncoats in his pay. Pai Talyi was only another of the white renegades he had so often dealt with, and probably as mean and treacherous.

"That's a lot of balderdash, Tate!" he snorted. "There never was a one of these so-called prophets yet that didn't stir the Indians up and cause trouble! A white man doesn't leave civilization and go to live in an Indian camp unless he hates white men—doesn't that stand to reason?"

The major's striker brought in a tray with beans, fried sidemeat, and a plate of burned-hard biscuits. The general glumly ate beans and side-meat. Hugh Cameron, brooding, said he was not hungry. Mr. Tate tried to break open one of the biscuits with his knife. He succeeded only in fracturing the bone handle, and had to fish the fragments from his beans.

"Christ!" the general snorted. "I remember how Ellen used to cook! She could do wonders with commissary beef and a few onions!" He coughed, and wiped his mouth with the back of his sleeve. "Sorry I brought the subject up, Hugh. It was thoughtless of me."

"That's all right, sir," Major Cameron murmured. "I—I don't think of it much any more, except in—in—"

"In revenge?" The general looked at him with fox-bright eyes. "That's what you mean, isn't it?" Carefully he peeled the wrapper from a fresh claro. "Carry the rest of that slop out to my driver," he ordered the striker, "and tell him I'll be along directly."

Lighting the cigar, he peered at Hugh Cameron through clouds of fragrant smoke. "Revenge!" he repeated. "Yes, I'd hate to be in that fellow's shoes if you ever caught him! Raintree, wasn't that his name? Or Rainwater?"

Hugh Cameron flushed. "Rainbolt," he said. "Philip Rainbolt."

The general picked a fleck of tobacco from his lip. "I remember. Heth's Division—at Petersburg, wasn't it?"

"Yes," the major said. "Abandoned his command."

"Well—" The general rose, painfully stretching

his game leg. "Been good to see you again, Hugh. What with the bad roads and snow and all, I may not come again till good weather. But there's always the military telegraph. Keep me informed."

"Certainly, sir," Major Cameron said, trying to keep an edge of bitterness from his voice. There was always the telegraph. Somehow or other, the old man always knew more about his command than he did.

The new Indian agent shook hands with the general too, saying, "I hope, sir, you won't take any ill-considered action against that handful of Kiowas. When it gets cold enough, old Water Turtle will come in for government beef—you'll see."

Hugh finally got the general swathed in his muffler, his gum-rubber boots, and his blue greatcoat. But as the old man was bidding them a last farewell, someone knocked at the door. The striker answered, and came to whisper to Major Cameron.

"Eh?" Hugh Cameron asked, annoyed. "Coogan? You mean that old drunk—the comanchero?"

"Yes, sir. He wants to talk to you. Says it's important."

"What's that?" the general demanded. "Coogan? That rascal?" He hesitated, pinching his lower lip between his fingers. Then he said, "Better bring him in, Hugh. He's a scoundrel, and ought to be behind bars. But he knows what's going on in the Territory. Can't ever tell what he'll put you onto."

Cameron swore to himself at the general's nosiness, but nodded to the striker. "Show with him."

Coogan's face was blue with cold. His nose was peeling from frostbite, his beard a snow-dusted wilderness. He wore a blanket with a hole cut in it to resemble a poncho, and his boots were wrapped in rags against the cold. But his ancient eyes shone beadily.

"What do you want?" the major demanded.

The comanchero looked from Cameron to the general, and back again.

"Only a few minutes of your time," he said. "And fifty dollars of the Army's money. That's the prize for a deserter, ain't it?"

"What deserter?" the major asked.

Coogan licked his lips. "Rainbolt. Philip Rainbolt."

Major Cameron was startled. "Rainbolt?"

"One and the same," Coogan chuckled. "The rascal that busted out of jail and took Stone Teeth and the rest of Satank's Kiowas with him last spring."

Cameron was speechless, but the general pressed forward and took the comanchero by the arm.

"Rainbolt? The one that killed poor Huckabee—

Huckabee was with me at Manassas—and broke out of the guardhouse?"

"The same," Coogan repeated.

Major Cameron was pale. He struggled to keep his voice composed. "But where is he? Rainbolt?"

"With Water Turtle and his Kiowas, of course." Coogan grinned. Hacking and coughing, he peeled off some of his rags and asked, "Can't I have a little drink to warm me? I rode a long ways to do my duty as a citizen and inform the Army where Philip Rainbolt could be found. Seems to me you ought to be gracious enough to give an old man a swallow of brandy or some sort of a revivifier!"

Cameron nodded to the striker, who brought a bottle of rye whisky. The general eyed Coogan sourly as the old man tossed down half a water glass of the stuff, and then held out the empty glass for another.

"Giving you a drink, you old bastard," the general muttered, "is pouring good liquor down a sewer."

Coogan smacked his lips and belched. "Nevertheless, I know where Philip Rainbolt is."

"You told us that," Major Cameron said in a tight voice. "He's with Water Turtle and his damned Kiowas. But where in hell are *they?*"

Coogan turned suddenly shrewd. "Goddamn *me!*" he chuckled. "I never saw it in the right light before! All I was interested in was the fifty dollars—things ain't been very prosperous lately —but I almost passed up a good proposition!"

"What do you mean, you old fool?" the major blurted.

The general put a restraining hand on his arm. "Take it easy, Hugh. Don't get excited—let me handle this." He poured himself two fingers of Oneida Genuine Rye—The Honest Whisky— and a larger drink for Coogan. "Now," he said, taking off his greatcoat and muffler and sitting amiably across from Coogan, "what's this all about, eh?"

"Well," the comanchero said, looking brightly from the general to Cameron and back again, "you, Major, want Philip Rainbolt. You, General, want Water Turtle's Kiowas. Only thing is— neither of you knows where to look, ain't that right?" He stared at them with button-bright eyes. "Guess I stumbled onto something to make up for the double-cross Rainbolt did me!"

"Go on," the general encouraged.

The liquor and the warmth of the room were making Ike Coogan's tongue thick. But he remained wary, choosing words with care. He told them how he had come across Philip Rainbolt in the Kiowa camp, how Rainbolt managed to gull the poor savages, how the deserter finally pretended to be Pai Talyi—Sun Boy himself.

"This soldier—Rainbolt—is Pai Talyi?" Mr. Tate asked in astonishment.

"Sure is." Coogan belched painfully, and beat himself on the chest with a clenched fist to settle his gas. "Him and I," he explained, "we had a deal to freeze out the other comancheros—George Washington and Nigger Nate and the rest—and divvy up the take between us. Oh, it was a fine plan! It would have made us both rich! But Rainbolt double-crossed me. He jawed old Water Turtle into turning loose all that fine stock—" Coogan's eyes misted with tears. "Gimme another drink, will you!"

The general himself poured the drink, an ample one. "So Rainbolt is Pai Talyi, eh?"

"Sun Boy," Coogan howled. "Sun Boy hisself! I tell you, he's a slick one! He's got those Kiowas in the palm of his hand, and no telling what mischief he's planning now!"

Mr. Tate, polishing his eyeglasses with a clean white handkerchief, coughed. "Well, I really don't think—"

"Tell us," the general said soothingly. "Tell us, Mr. Coogan, where we can find Water Turtle, and we'll make everything come out all right. You'll have your fifty dollars, Major Cameron here will have his deserter back, and I'll round up old Water Turtle and his Kiowas. Won't that be fine, Coogan? Everything will be fine!"

But Coogan shook his grizzled head. "Oh,

no!" he protested. "Oh, no! It's worth a hell of a lot more than fifty dollars, ain't it?" He wiped his streaming nose with a corner of the blanket. "Seems to me we're talking about *big* money!"

"Fifty dollars," the general said, "is the fee for turning in a deserter. That's regulation."

Major Cameron interrupted, lips pale and the skin drawn taut over his cheekbones. "How much do you want, Coogan?"

The comanchero's words were very slow, as if savoring them. "A—a thousand dollars," he said finally.

The general was astonished. "Now you're talking foolishness! Who's got that much money?"

"Wait a minute," Hugh Cameron interrupted. "Sir, I've got money saved up from selling a piece of property in San Francisco. I can—"

"Be quiet, Hugh," the general said. "I'm handling this! What about—say—two hundred, Coogan? That's a very generous offer, I think."

"This is all very irregular!" Mr. Tate protested. "On a matter like this, General, the Indian Bureau will want to be consulted! After all, those Kiowas are presently bothering no one. It's the policy of the bureau, administered by me, that force and violence is to be avoided wherever possible. Not one cent of accountable Indian Bureau funds can be spent on such an unholy deal! If you just leave those poor savages alone they'll get good and cold and come in peaceably enough! After all, the Indian Bureau is—"

"Screw the Indian Bureau!" the general growled. "There's only one way to deal with a tribe that defies the government and makes fools of the U. S. Army! Teach them a lesson, that's what!"

Major Cameron agreed. "In winter," he pointed out, "they'll be tied down by their stores of food and supplies. If we can only find them, we can wipe them out."

"And teach the reservation Indians a lesson," the general added. "That's important!" He turned again to Coogan. "Three hundred? After all, the comanchero business has gone bust. Isn't three hundred a fair offer?"

"Seven-fifty!" Coogan insisted. "After all, think of the thousands of dollars in Army appropriations saved if you capture old Water Turtle! Think about next spring, when the weather gets fine! Think of the lives spared—the stock! Think of the settlers along the Red River! They're writing nasty letters to their congressmen, I hear, saying the Army ain't properly protecting them!"

He had hit the general in a vulnerable spot.

"All right," the general sighed. "I've got a private source of nonappropriated funds put away. No one but me knows how to get at it. There's five hundred dollars in it, not a cent more, and that's my last offer. It's *got* to be. Five hundred dollars?"

"Done!" Coogan put out a dirty hand to clinch the deal, but the general was not yet satisfied.

"Now wait a minute! How do we know you're telling the truth? After all, maybe you don't even know where Water Turtle and Rainbolt are. Maybe it's only a drunken tale!"

The comanchero was hurt. "I tell you I was *there!* I know that camp of theirs, back in the rocks, better 'n anybody! Ain't I rondyvooed with the Kiowas a dozen times? Ain't I traded them more guns and liquor than anyone in the business? Didn't I palaver with old Water Turtle, and with Rainbolt, too, not a week past?"

The general spat the tip of a fresh cigar into the cuspidor. "Where are they?"

The major brought a map, and Coogan put his finger on the place, the protected rocky gorge two hundred miles to the southwest. "It ain't going to be easy!" he explained. "But with a couple of twelve-pounder cannon and those new Gatling guns, you can flush 'em out."

The general sucked wetly on his cigar. "Hell!" he protested, "that's not even *in* the Department of the Missouri! That's another command."

"That's true," Major Cameron said quickly. "But look at it this way, sir. Water Turtle and his Kiowas are your responsibility. They started their depredations here, in your command. Rainbolt broke out of my guardhouse, right here at Fort Sill. And next spring, where will the Kiowas

247

come to raise hell again? Right here!" He pointed to a sinuous line on the map. "Back to the Red River again—right in the middle of the Department of the Missouri!"

The general stared at the map, thumb scratching his grizzled beard. "That's right," he admitted. "Well put, Hugh! Not only that, Water Turtle's breaking the Medicine Lodge treaty he signed four years ago, and the treaty talks were held in my department. I guess that makes it a pretty good case."

Mr. Tate angrily polished his eyeglasses and clipped them on his nose. His voice quavered with anger:

"I won't have a thing to do with it! I'll report the whole thing to the Indian Bureau! You're motivated by viciousness and revenge, all of you!"

The general did not seem to hear. He went to the window and stared out. Though it was only three in the afternoon, the approaching storm made it appear almost full dark. Yellow pinpricks of light began to glow in the soft downpour: barracks, stables, regimental head-quarters. *A winter campaign—unseasonable snow—a long march—a rocky canyon.* It was quite an assign-ment. But there was only one answer.

"Ordinarily," the general said, turning back to the comanchero, "I don't care to have truck with a rascal like you, Coogan. When all this is over, when Hugh here and I get old Water Turtle and his Kiowas safely back on the reservation, I want you to light a shuck out of the Department of the Missouri and never come back. Is that clear?"

Coogan growled. "What if I don't?"

"Because," the general said, "if you don't, I can have your rascally conniving ass in federal prison quicker 'n an alligator can chew a puppy! And this time you won't have money to pay a jackleg lawyer to get you out! It's the end of the line for you and George Washington and Nigger Nate and the rest of the comancheros that trade guns and whisky to my Indians for stolen stock!" Grudgingly he held out his hand. "It's a deal, then—five hundred dollars?"

Coogan swore, but there was no way out. "It's a deal," he said.

"Good!" The general turned back to the map. "Now, Hugh, let's look at the terrain, shall we?"

Mr. Tate, the Quaker agent, stalked out, slamming the door in protest against their scheming. Deep in plans for a conclusive winter campaign against the last vestige of Indian power in the Department of the Missouri, the trio did not even hear him go.

The Kiowas did not move immediately from their ancient winter home. There were many tedious preparations to be made. Supplies had to be put in sacks and rawhide boxes, travois made from buffalo hides and long saplings, household goods picked over and only the essentials retained. Corn and beans traded from the Caddoes had to be packed, along with bales of dried buffalo meat and cans of fruit and vegetables plundered from the Red River settlers. The Kiowas had captured many bags of a mysterious white grainy stuff which Rainbolt told them was "rice." Nobody cared for it much, but it was edible and nourishing. They took it with them to supplement the dried pomme blanche roots and mesquite bean cakes which they preferred, but which were running short.

Water Turtle's precious harmonium, wrapped in a fine blanket, lay in the bed of a splay-wheeled wagon put together from wheels and tongue and an ancient oaken bed from the junk pile of settlers' effects. The wagon also held the Sett'an Calendar and the Tai Me dolls. Because of its sacred and precious burden, the wagon would head the procession. Additional delay was caused by the old man who kept the Sett'an Calendar; it was nearing the end of the year, and he had not yet finished bringing the calendar up to date. Finally, grumbling at the haste demanded, he completed the year's spiral, entering the important events. This was *The Year Pai Talyi Came Down to the People.*

There were other sources of delay, too. Water Turtle despaired of ever getting the Kiowas started on the journey. In spite of Rainbolt's ministrations, some of the invalids were slow in recovering their strength, and litters had to be made for them. There were not enough horses, and the stronger Kiowas would have to walk. Star Sister, scarred and nearly blind, would travel with Ellen Cameron in an ancient buckboard. Ellen insisted on walking, but Rainbolt convinced her she should stay with Star Sister. Ellen was now pregnant with his child; though she declared she felt strong and well, he persuaded her to ride in the buckboard.

There were also those who, in spite of Water Turtle's orders, would simply not leave the rocky canyon. It had been home to them for a long time. Most were old men and women who might die anyway on the trail, so it was decided to leave them behind, with food to sustain them till spring. After that—no one knew.

Many of the Kiowas were anxious to go but pointed out the dangers of a winter journey. Most were persuaded when Rainbolt said, "If we wait here, I think the soldiers may decide to come against us soon. I do not trust them to stay in their fort all winter, as they have done before. They are so angry at the Kiowas that they may come after us here, in this rocky place, with big guns that shoot many miles and knock down big boulders on us. No, I think it is better to go now and join our Cheyenne brothers, before something happens. I cannot tell you why I feel this, but it is very strong in me." And since he was Pai Talyi, they bowed to his wish.

The weather had been cold and leaden, with occasional sprinkles of snow. But when the appointed day came, the Great One Above smiled on the venture. Though there had been a heavy frost the night before, the sun now shone brilliantly in a sky of cloudless blue. The *akasitas* —camp police—ran this way and that, calling people to their proper places. The Sun People, tootling their eagle-bone whistles, organized the column and kept order. The boys in the various junior societies—the Young Sheep, the Rabbits, and the rest—had been pressed into service as messengers. Someone started singing the ancient guadagya song and the rest took it up until the entire column was bright with melody. Everyone understood, of course, that this was not a war party. But it was an exciting journey toward a land of new hope and promise, and so they all sang the guadagya song, laughing and waving to friends and neighbors in the lengthy procession.

Water Turtle rode at the head, very old but sitting proud and straight on his fine t'a kon— the black-eared horse so prized by the Kiowas. Next to him Rainbolt sat Brutus, holding his zebat, his medicine lance, high. On it dangled and whipped in the wind the trophies of his prowess: relics of Cat, the Tonk warrior, Stone Teeth's beaded bag, the green calomel bottle, colored pennants, ritual bits of fur and hide, bear claws, and beaver teeth. But in spite of the excitement of the moment, in spite of the good spirits of the People, in spite of his pride in the neat and businesslike organization of the march, he felt a lonely apprehension.

Water Turtle's Kiowas added up to almost four hundred lodges. This meant about three hundred braves, and perhaps nine hundred women, children, and old people. All of these people trusted Philip Rainbolt. And while Water Turtle was their nominal leader, Pai Talyi was the source of divine guidance. Water Turtle commanded them to do only what the gods recommended. In spite of the warmth of his buckskin shirt, his fine leggings, and the red blanket thrown around his shoulders, Rainbolt felt suddenly cold; his stomach tightened into a hard knot. For a moment he was not aware Water Turtle was speaking to him.

"Yes, father?" he finally murmured, embarrassed at his rudeness.

"I said—this is the time!"

Rainbolt looked back. The column seemed endless in the sunshine, a long sinuous creature of which he was perhaps the brain—certainly the heart. He bowed his head.

"When you are ready, father."

They rode out on the prairie, where the sun had already melted the frost and ice that lay heavy on the grass. Small animals fled before them, birds lumbered into the air and squawked, a startled coyote bounced from his daytime lair among some rocks and ran parallel to the column, staring with what seemed incredulity. According to plan, mounted scouts ranged far before, others rode the flanks several miles to right and left, scanning the country. Behind, now out of sight, a picked band under Crow Bonnet formed a swift and disciplined rear guard. The Kiowas had been indifferent to such measures, but Rainbolt, remembering his *Manual of Military Tactics*, insisted on them.

It would, he estimated, take the crawling column better than a month to reach the Cheyenne camp at the uppermost headwaters of the Red River, 150 miles to the northwest. There were still a lot of buffalo there—the Kiowas were encour-aged by the increasing droppings—and they would be among Cheyenne friends, distant from Army posts and angry settlers. But as the weather continued fine—cold and clear—he hopefully revised his estimate. Perhaps three weeks would do it. In three weeks they would be safe among friends and allies, and he would be free of the leaden apprehension that gripped him.

In spite of the rigors of the trail, everyone was

good-natured. Some old people died, and were buried. But that would probably have happened even if they had remained in the granite canyon, now a hundred miles behind them. A small boy was bitten by a rattlesnake, dying in spite of Rainbolt's efforts. But several women gave birth, and their numbers actually increased by a small amount.

Food was meager but enough to sustain them, when supplemented by game killed along the way. Though there was little water, there was plenty of coarse grass for the animals. Instead of the barren alkaline soil surrounding their old home, the earth now seemed more fertile, arable because of the gypsum it contained, and supported a greater variety of vegetation. They were gradually rising in altitude, too. From his memory of military maps Rainbolt guessed the elevation to be now on the order of two thousand feet. It was correspondingly colder, with flurries of snow. But the air was so bright and bracing they hurried on, cheerful and laughing, looking forward to the early completion of the hegira.

Ellen Cameron, in spite of his protests, had turned over her place in the buckboard to an old man and his wife, and cheerfully led the team of fractious Kiowa paints, unaccustomed to the makeshift harness that had been fashioned for them. She took loving and tender care of Star Sister, finding time during rest stops and in the evenings to play the *do a* game with her patient. At night Ellen shared Rainbolt's buffalo robe. They lay together and looked up at the winter stars, recalling other times, other places, though none had been so happy as this time and this place.

For a long time Rainbolt had wished for socks, even a pair of the coarse ill-fitting woolen socks the Army was pleased to issue its soldiers. Like the rest of the Kiowas, he wore only moccasins, occasionally wrapping his feet with strips of cloth against unusually chill weather. But one night in what must have been December, though he had lost track of the white man's calendar, Ellen lay quietly beside him for a long time, head in the hollow of his neck and shoulder, not saying anything. After a while, he asked curiously, "What are you thinking?"

She looked at the sky, at a bright star in the east.

"Philip, do you know what day this is?"

He pondered, deliciously content and relaxed with her warm body next to his.

"Monday? Tuesday? I don't know. Who cares?"

"I mean—what date?"

He stroked his beard, thoughtful, and finally admitted, "I don't know."

She wriggled upright in the buffalo robe, sitting on her knees in the moonlight and smiling

"It's December the twenty-fourth, as nearly

as I can figure it out," she said. "It's Christmas Eve."

He pulled her down to him then, feeling somehow sad and happy at the same time. Together, very softly so as not to disturb Star Sister, who was asleep wrapped in a blanket on the seat of the nearby buckboard, they sang as many Christmas songs as they could remember. In the morning, wrapped in a scrap of brown paper tied with a ribbon, a pair of socks was tied to his saddlehorn.

"I don't understand," he marveled. "Socks! And they fit me!" He pulled her close and bussed her hard, while the Kiowas looked on and grinned. "Where does a new pair of socks come from in the middle of the Llano Estacado?"

She had painstakingly unraveled a worn-out blanket, and at her instructions the old man in the buckboard had whittled a pair of knitting needles. While Rainbolt was at the head of the column with Water Turtle, she made the socks.

"Merry Christmas!" She laughed, and clung to him, laughing and perhaps weeping, until he had to plead the necessity of riding forward again.

If that had been the twenty-fifth of December, it was New Year's Day, 1872, when a troublesome report reached Rainbolt's ears. One of the flanker scouts rode in at evening, chilled from his long vigil, to report he had seen, during the afternoon, a lone mounted Caddo sitting a rise to the northeast of the Kiowa column. The Caddo did not venture closer, but paralleled their route for an hour or more, then turned back toward the southeast, the direction of the granite gorge they had recently left.

The Kiowas and the Caddoes were not friends. Perhaps the rider had been only a wandering hunter, anxious to avoid the route of enemies in force. But why did he tarry so long, watching them? Rainbolt was uneasy. The Army had Caddo scouts, he knew. But they had Tonkawas and Arapahoes, too. And at this time of the year, the Army was probably sitting near a red-hot Sibley stove, drinking coffee and playing coon-can or monte. Still, the intruder worried him.

The news was kept among Water Turtle, Rainbolt, and the scouts, so as not to alarm the People. Next day, however, they hurried the march. No further reports of interlopers came in. By now they were no more than fifty miles, Rainbolt estimated, from the Cheyenne camp and safety. A holiday spirit prevailed in the column. It was the Moon When the Owl Calls; the Rabbit Society boys decorated themselves with feathers and ran about the camp, hooting, flapping imaginary wings, finally dancing the traditional Owl Dance in the firelight before their elders.

The next day they crossed an ancient trail, now in disuse but showing plainly old wheel ruts and a path worn smooth by men and horses. It was, Rainbolt figured, the trail made by the Santa Fe Expedition over twenty years before. They could not be far from their destination. Sitting high in the saddle, craning his neck to extend his gaze,

he looked about him. Ahead, the Kiowa column descended a grassy slope. The point already wound its way into a sheltered bottomland along one of the tributaries of the Red, where they would camp for the night. To the north, a long ledge of limestone sheltered them from the wind; under its outcropping jut they would be comfort-able. There was plenty of wood, water, and grass for the animals. To the rear, in the slanting rays of the winter sun, the rest of the column inched nearer. In another hour the Kiowas would be lighting campfires, broiling meat, going about the homely tasks of living. It was a peaceful, well-ordered scene. Rainbolt thought suddenly of an old painting at Nine-Mile Plantation, a faded dun-colored representation of peasants in the fields of twilight, pausing a moment to listen to the village church bell ring the Angelus.

Hearing the distant shot, he started. A moment later he saw a dot grow rapidly larger—horse and rider, pounding hard. In a few minutes the scout sent by Crow Bonnet galloped up, pony dusty and flecked with foam. The youth pointed back, toward the end of the column, saying simply, "Soldiers! Many soldiers! Wagons! Guns!" The pony, excited, pranced and sidled, and the young man jerked hard at the nose rope. "For soldiers," he gasped, "with all those wagons and guns and things, they are coming very fast! Crow Bonnet wants to know what to do!"

Rainbolt knew the origin of the feeling that had been plaguing him. His head had denied it, but his tight stomach always knew. The Army had caught up with them. Unbelievable as it was, the unbelievable had happened. The Kiowas were caught—caught on the open prairie, burdened with women and children and old people. Iktomi, the jester god, had made a fool of Philip Rainbolt, and now his People would suffer. Pai Talyi had betrayed them.

CHAPTER TWELVE

On a gloomy rain-swept day they sat in the general's tent drinking Bourbon—Mr. Jared Bennett, the reporter from the Philadelphia *Press* who was writing articles on the Indian Wars, Ike Coogan, and the general himself. Gusts of wind flapped the canvas, the wooden floor smelled dank and moldy, the general's claro was wet and refused to burn.

"I don't like this kind of an action," the general complained. "I like maneuver, clever tactics, a little dash and sweep to a campaign! But if I have to stay here and grind the red bastards down like Grant did the Rebs, I'm going to do it! Can't have old Water Turtle and his Kiowas thumbing their nose at the Department of the Missouri!"

The expedition started off in fine style—three companies of Eighth Cavalry, two companies of Colonel Grierson's Negro Ninth borrowed for the occasion, and a long train of mule-team-drawn supply wagons and pack animals. There was plenty of hardtack, bacon, and coffee, and the men all had the new .45-caliber Springfield carbines. The band played them out with "Susan Jane"; everyone was filled with spirit and determination. The finding of the granite gorge empty of Kiowas, except for a few old people, did not dampen their enthusiasm. They had flushed the bird, the game was on the wing. The general promised a bottle of Duggan's Delight Scotch Whisky to the first man to sight the fleeing Kiowas. He had abandoned his wagon and rode with an embossed and decorated English fowling piece across his saddle, anxious to wing a few birds himself.

But the venture so bravely undertaken had turned into a slogging dreary operation that made it hard to keep up the spirits of the men. The crisp winter weather changed to rain, cold pelting rain. The Kiowas, trapped in the river bottom, took shelter under an overhanging cliff of limestone, and would not be dislodged. Napoleons and Gatling guns were of little use against them; because of the ledge, it was impossible to get a decent field of fire. Too, the Kiowas seemed to have plenty of food and ammunition. Water was no problem for them either, the river running adjacent to the troublesome ledge.

In the last few days, it had been apparent too that someone with a keen military mind was directing the actions of the beleagured Kiowas. Small mounted parties of warriors slipped out of the jumbled rocks at night, conducting an effective guerrilla campaign against the general's sprawling command. Mules were stampeded, sentries found with throats cut. Once—before the damnable rain began—a prowling Kiowa band set fire to a group of wagons. That was bad enough, but somehow or other the rascals stumbled on the ammunition train. Half the command's supply of black powder went up in a tremendous explosion that lit the sleeping camp like the summer sun.

"Rainbolt!" Hugh Cameron had said between tight lips. Unbelieving, he stood beside the general in hastily pulled-on breeches, staring at the smoke and fire rolling into the night sky. "It was Rainbolt—it must have been! Those Kiowas would never think of anything like that themselves!"

While the general was annoyed with Major Cameron's habit of blaming everything on the deserter Rainbolt, it was probably true. The Caddo scouts reported seeing a white man riding along the river bottoms before they could take action. Pai Talyi, the Caddoes said, and seemed unnerved by their close brush with such powerful medicine.

"I beg pardon," Mr. Bennett said, clearing his throat. He was a gangling, diffident young man, always with a small notebook and pencil at the ready, and made the general nervous. Abandoning the hopeless cigar, the general poured himself another drink.

"Well?"

Mr. Bennett coughed again. "Sir, as I understand it, you and Mr. Coogan believe Water Turtle and his people are heading for a junction with the

Cheyennes. What I don't understand is why the Army is pursuing them."

"Why—why we're *pursuing* them? Mr. Bennett, what in hell do you think the U. S. Army is *for?*"

"I—I didn't mean that, exactly," Mr. Bennett stammered, determined to make a point. "What I meant to say—if they want to join the Cheyennes, why not let them?"

Ike Coogan covertly poured several fingers of whisky into a tin cup, but the general was too astounded and angry to snatch the bottle away.

"*Let* them? Let them join up with the Cheyennes?"

"Yes, sir," Mr. Bennett insisted. "After all, I understand there are only a few hundred of them, and a lot are women and children. The Cheyennes are presently giving the Indian Bureau no trouble, so what difference does it make if the old man takes his people there? Why fight a pitched battle when the Kiowas are by now practically out of your department anyhow?"

This last was a sensitive spot with the general. Perhaps he *was* slightly exceeding his authority. He suspected that Mr. Bennett's articles in the *Press*, dispatched via special rider and thence by military telegraph, were not helping his case. Bennett was from Philadelphia, probably another of those soft-headed Quakers like old Tate, the agent at Fort Sill. Too, the meddlers at the Indian Bureau in Washington would be sure to cause trouble for the general unless he finished off the campaign quickly—smashed the Kiowas for once and for all. But he was saved from the necessity for reply when Major Cameron pulled aside the tent flap.

"Well, Hugh!" the general greeted him. "Pour yourself a drink, if Coogan has left any! There's tea in the pot on the stove, too—whatever you'd like. Anyway, what's the latest?"

The major's lean face was jubilant. Rainwater sparkled in his heavy eyebrows and beard, dripped from his nose. Carefully he spread a damp sketch on the table before the general, lighting a lamp so the map could be better seen.

"I know how we can get at them!" he said. "Look here, sir!" His long finger traced a sinuous pencil line. "This is the river, and right above is the limestone cliff, as you know. We're strung out along here"—he pointed—"here—and here. Just to orient you, the wagons are here. Grierson's brunettes are—" He frowned, then said, "Here! Right here!"

"I know," the general snapped. "But what—"

Cameron's finger stabbed wetly at the map. "Right here, on this elevation, we put one Napoleon! Two hundred yards down the stream, we put the other one!"

"That's no good!" the general objected. "The Kiowas are behind the overhang of that damned limestone cliff!"

Forgetting the deference due rank, Cameron gripped him by the arm. "That's just the point! We can fire *at* the cliff, with short fuses. The shells will ricochet down right on top of them! General, the Kiowas can't get away! They're trapped in that place! We can destroy them at will!"

Coogan came over to look at the map. Mr. Bennett made notes in his book. "Ain't a half-bad idea," Coogan admitted. "At least it's better 'n sitting here in a damned wet tent till we grow mold all over us like a spoiled piece of pork!"

The general stroked his beard. He closed his eyes, thinking of azimuth, elevation, angles of incidence, fuse lengths. For a while, right out of the Point, Hugh Cameron had been an artillery officer. Perhaps the major knew what he was talking about. Favoring the game leg, which pained him in wet weather, the general hobbled about the tent, hands clasped behind his back.

"It *will* work!" Hugh Cameron blurted, daring to interrupt the old man's thoughts. "Sir, it's *bound* to work!" He gestured with an imaginary cue. "Like a carom shot at billiards!"

The general pulled aside the flap of the tent nd peered out. In the gathering dusk a few campfires, rigged under shelter halves, winked and sputtered. Men sprawled dejectedly on sodden blankets, a wagon was stuck hub-deep in the mud while a teamster flailed the mules with his whip. From somewhere came the melancholy strains of a mouth organ. The general recognized the tune; it was "The Regular Army, O!" He remembered one verse:

We went to old Red River
For to fight the Injuns there;
Came near to being made bald-headed
But they never got our hair.

Another verse complained:

We lay among the ditches
In the dirty mucking mud,
And never saw an onion
Nor a turnip or a spud.

It was true enough. After a month on the trail, his men were showing the lack of fresh vegetables. The bacon had turned yellow and malodorous; the beans were moldy. Malingerers were lining up at sick call, complaining of loose bowels, fevers, itching rashes. The surgeon had run out of Blue Mass pills, and was reduced to quinine and castor oil. The general closed the flap and limped back to the yellow stain of light on the table, the sodden map. Major Cameron looked at him expectantly. His face was lean and eager, a spark of flame from the lamp reflected in his dark eyes.

"All right, Hugh," the general sighed. "At first light in the morning set up your guns and we'll see what happens." Then, with a touch of asperity, he added, "I want Philip Rainbolt as bad as you and Coogan do, Hugh. But remember we're soldiers, not vigilantes!"

At first Rainbolt thought his Kiowas were hopelessly trapped in the river bottom. There was no way out but surrender or extermination. However, the situation was better than it first seemed. They were protected from cannon fire by the great limestone ledge. Though food had to be rationed carefully there was perhaps enough for two or three weeks. Plenty of water was in the shallow river, and the spirits of the People were high.

Both he and Water Turtle realized, however, that defense was not enough. The old man did not understand a strategy of digging in, forcing the enemy to come to you. Kiowas attacked—hit hard and quickly, then faded away before counter-attack could be organized. From his own military background, Rainbolt also knew the danger of burrowing under the cliff, awaiting the enemy's pleasure. At a lengthy council he argued for action, and found opinion favorable. The People, having tried hard to avoid conflict with the Army, were angry at being attacked while on their way to a peaceful junction with

Cheyenne friends. Quickly, with Water Turtle's approval, Rainbolt organized what, according to Philip St. George Cook's *Tactics*, were really light cavalry patrols. At night they slipped out of their refuge and harried the wet and fearful sentries. The raid on the ammunition train, led by Philip Rainbolt himself, was their greatest success.

Two Time Talk, wriggling near the Army outposts on a dark and moonless night, returned to report the soldiers were sick and disaffected. Grierson's Negroes fired off useless vollies at "red spooks." Major Cameron's Eighth shot up their own camp one night when a foraging fox overturned a cooking pot in the mess tent; three troopers were wounded, one later dying.

Though too old to go with the patrols, Water Turtle insisted on stationing himself at the clef in the tumbled limestone boulders where they rode out. He staked himself to the ground each night with an arrow through his black elkskin sash—the sash of the Koitsenko—vowing not to leave till the raiders safely returned.

"No," Water Turtle objected, "it is *not* an even fight! The People are better fighters. They are fighting for life, for their way of living. The soldiers are fighting just because Two Star Chief orders them to."

The People were crowded tightly together under the overhang of the great cliff—animals, mothers, children, old people pressed almost shoulder to shoulder. But they were cheerful and tolerant of each other. Cooking, sewing, watering and feeding the animals all went on as in their old home. Pai Talyi was with them, Pai Talyi would get them out of this predicament. They trusted and respected Water Turtle but they revered Pai Talyi.

Rainbolt lay at night with Ellen Cameron in a hollow in the rocks she had lined with a buffalo robe and some blankets. Nearby smoldered a tiny fire where she made coffee for him, and warmed one of the scarce mesquite-bean cakes.

Wolfing it down, he felt suddenly uneasy. Mouth half-filled with the oily powder, he stammered, "But—but you! What did you eat?"

She shook her head. In the dying firelight her red hair glinted. She was thin, too thin. The high cheekbones cast her face in planes of shadow.

"I wasn't hungry," she murmured. "Besides, you are very tired. You need strength more than I."

"You should eat," he reproved her. "You are going to have a baby, and must stay well."

Hands clasped behind her head, she lay in the furry depths of the robe, looking up at him with joy and delight.

"You are all I need," she said. "You are my food. Just to see you makes me content." She pulled him down, pressing her lips tightly against his cheek. "To feel you here, tight against me, is almost more happiness than I can bear."

He was very tired, and lay quietly in her arms. Tonight Crow Bonnet was leading the raiding parties. Rainbolt could sleep till dawn, or at least until some alarm. Drowsily he stared at the smoke-blackened ledge over their heads. Ancient people must once have used this cavern as a shelter, too. All around the People were preparing for the night. There was the sleepy whimper of a baby, a dog yawning and snuffling as he turned in circles before lying down, the distant call of a sentry, one of the many guarding their refuge. Smoke, cooking smoke, the rich sharp smell of smoke— at Nine-Mile Plantation Rainbolt remembered winter mornings, the tang of wood smoke from the kitchen range as Della, the black cook, fried bacon, baked biscuits, boiled coffee. How far away that seemed, how long ago!

"Philip?"

"Yes," he said.

"I was just thinking. It's so funny. I mean— right now my father and mother are sitting in the parlor! Imagine! My father is reading the *Chronicle*, and mother is knitting something—a muffler, maybe, for papa. It gets cold, in San Francisco, in the wintertime."

"We are both," he said, "a long way from home."

She raised quickly on her elbow. "But I would not have it any other way." Her hand sought his; she placed it on her stomach. "Do you feel any-thing there? Is it getting bigger?"

He laughed. "It's too soon!"

"Nevertheless," she said. "Nevertheless." She lay back down, thoughtful. "Sometimes I feel something there. Movement. Life. It's beginning."

Exhausted, bone-weary, he still could not sleep. Instead, he fell into a series of catnaps—waking with a start, listening, waiting, then drifting again into a kind of catalepsy that was not sleep, did not refresh. After a while a gray light filtered into the cavern; it was dawn.

Rolling over on his side, he peered down into the mass of slumbering people. A few were awake. An old woman blew coals into flame and set a blackened tin coffeepot over the fire, a gray-beard shuffled his way toward the latrine area Rainbolt had laid out. From the cottonwoods along the river a crow squawked, flapping heavily into the leaden sky.

He was pondering the crow, what had so frightened it, when the first shell hit the granite ledge. The orange flower of the blast drove him down to sprawl across Ellen's body. Showers of splintered rock fell from the roof of the cave, a cloud of dust boiled up, choking and suffocating. Dazed, he lay for a moment across her. In his shock and surprise, all he could think of was the baby.

"Did—did I hurt you?" he gasped.

272

She clung to him in terror. "What was it? Philip, what happened?"

Moans and shrieks rose from below. Rainbolt staggered to his feet and looked down from the rocky nest where they had lain. It was a scene from Dante's *Inferno*. As the gray rock dust settled, he could see people running this way and that, wailing and screaming. Some had been crushed under falling rock, and begged for help. Others lay bleeding from wounds. The old woman who had tended the fire still crouched beside it, but half her face had been torn away. For a moment her body remained upright, then fell forward into the fire.

"What is it?" a teenage girl whimpered, pulling at Rainbolt's sleeve. Her face was smeared with blood and dirt, eyes round with shock. "Pai Talyi, what is happening?"

"The cannon!" he shouted. "The cannon! They've—they've—"

A second shell hit the ledge, exploding directly below in a mass of struggling bodies. It blew the Kiowas away from the center of concussion; they lay in windrows, pointing outward like the petals of a flower—a red and hideous flower.

The cavern—the sheltering cavern—had been transformed into a slaughterhouse. Like the tolling of a monstrous bell, each few seconds the cannon boomed. Great slabs of rock dropped, people were caught and twisted and torn open like sacks of grain, vital contents spilling out in tangled webs. Clambering over the rocks, Rainbolt found Water Turtle sitting propped against a boulder, still staked to the ground with his Koitsenko sash. His red turban was askew, and blood seeped through the fingers held flat over his stomach. But he still clutched his rifle tightly.

"What are they doing?" he asked Rainbolt in a voice that was not frightened, only surprised. "What is going on?"

Rainbolt squatted beside him, gently pulling away the clawlike hand. Under it, through the jagged wound, he could see bluish loops of intestine.

"They have found a way to turn their cannon on us," he explained. "I did not think it was possible. But I was wrong."

As he spoke Water Turtle sighed, very gently. When Rainbolt took away his supporting hand, the old man's head sank on his chest and he died, still tightly holding the rifle.

Carrying his lance, Rainbolt ran to the improvised corral and caught Brutus, now wild-eyed and trembling. "Steady," he muttered. "Steady, boy!" On the ground nearby, in a welter of torn bodies, he found a white rag, tying it high on his zebat. Clapping his heels to Brutus' ribs, he galloped through the rubble, out into the river bottoms, through the groves of bare-branched cottonwoods. In ironic display, the clouds had parted. The morning sun now shone blindingly in his face. Shading his eyes, he looked across the river. Someplace in the brush must be those cannon. He had to find them, stop them.

Splashing through the shallows, he drove Brutus across the grassy plain. As he galloped he could see the panorama of conflict spread before him like a topographical map. To the left lay the main body of the Army troops, a jumble of wagons and picket lines, tents and brush huts. To the right, far down the river, sun glinted on gun barrels and sabers that belonged to the Negro cavalrymen blocking their exit. Between lay the cottonwood-bordered stream, the bottom lands; above the long gray rampart of the ledge that had protected them. It was clever of the Army; they had found a way to carom Napoleon shells off the ledge and into the cavern.

The grass was tall and wet, hampering Brutus' strides. Once the horse stumbled and fell; Rainbolt was flung headlong into a patch of brush. Dazed and panting, he staggered to his feet. Brutus stood patiently, sides heaving. He pulled himself onto the sweat-damp back again, urging the winded horse forward.

For a moment he caught sight of the guns. They were drawn up on a shallow elevation, a knot of cannoneers around each, ramming, firing, swabbing like small mechanical toys. He screamed, waving the white flag, but at that distance they did not hear him, probably did not even see him. Plunging through horse-high brush, he felt his thighs torn and ripped by cat's claw and devil-thorn.

"Stop!" he screamed. "Stop shooting!"

When he broke out onto the dishlike top of the hill, they finally noticed him. A slug tore past his ear; a moment later he heard the faint flat *pop*. Waving the white flag, he galloped toward them. A figure thrust aside a raised rifle barrel as he flung himself into their midst, waving the white flag.

"Stop shooting!" he pleaded. "Stop the cannon!" He recognized the general, brassbound telescope under his arm and a smoldering cigar between his teeth. He slipped off Brutus, leaning for a moment against the heaving flanks for support. He was very tired.

"My name," he said "is Philip Rainbolt. I'm a deserter from F Company, Eighth Cavalry. I have come to ask you to stop the shooting. It is all over now. It is all over."

CHAPTER THIRTEEN

For January, the weather was good. The sun shone from a hard blue sky and wind snapped the starred flag before the general's tent. The mercury thermometer registered in the fifties, the needle of the Army surgeon's barometer inched higher. Putting on his best tunic, the general carefully brushed out a few wrinkles around the shoulders, thinking that even at sixty-three he cut a dashing figure. All that remained now was the formal conference with Pai Talyi and the beaten Kiowas, the ultimatum to return to the reservation, the breaking of camp, and the escorting of the savages on the long road back to Fort Sill.

"Respectfully, sir, I think this is all a charade!" Major Cameron protested. "We should have put the rascal in chains then and there, and had an end to it! Demanding a parley! Why, that was a damned impertinence!"

Lifting his grizzled chin, the general fastened the top button of the tunic. "Hugh, you're trying my patience! We can afford to be a little generous, and listen to them before we herd them back to the post. After all, these Kiowas are people, with complicated customs which are very important to them. Let them blow off a little steam! After all, there is no place for them to go—they are beaten, and trapped."

"I think it's an unnecessary delay," Cameron said angrily. "I mean—what is there to discuss? They have lost—we've got Rainbolt—"

"Pai Talyi," the general corrected. "We've got to be very careful about this. Now that Water Turtle is dead—I respected the old man for the fighter he was—Rainbolt is their leader. Indians, you know, are easily offended, so these things should be carried off with a certain style. His name is Pai Talyi, and I want everyone to so refer to him."

Major Cameron flushed, and gnawed at his mustaches. The general had lately been worried about Cameron; there was something feverish and brittle in the way the major acted. When the deserter Rainbolt had galloped up to their Napoleon positions with his white flag, asking for a truce, the general himself had to knock up the major's carbine. The fool would have killed Pai Talyi then and there, causing some very serious consequences, had the general not interfered.

If Cameron was not enough of a cross for him to bear, there was always Mr. Jared Bennett of the *Press* with his notebook, his increasingly critical dispatches. The general did not want any nosy reporter on his strike against the fleeing Kiowas, but Mr. Bennett had arrived with a letter from the Secretary of War; there was no choice.

With a final fluffing of his beard, the general turned back to the can of peaches he had been eating.

"Have some, Hugh?"

"No, sir."

The general drained the can of syrup, saying, "You really ought to eat more. Since we left the post, you haven't eaten enough to keep a bird alive. Stomach bothering you?"

Mr. Bennett came in then, dusty and dirty, a tear in the knee of his trousers where he had been clambering over fallen rocks. He sat down in a chair and put his head in his hands.

"Well," the general asked, "how did it go, Bennett?"

He was unprepared for the outburst.

"I'll tell you how it went!" the reporter cried. "It went damned bad! That's a charnel house down there, an absolute stinking abattoir! There are dead and dying all around, and some of the bodies are beginning to smell. There are women and children—there are—there are—" He broke off, staring down at his knuckles, white and bloodless where his hands gripped together.

"I've done everything I could," the general snapped. "I sent the surgeon and his orderlies down with all the medical supplies we have! These things happen in war, you know." More kindly he added, "You're young, Bennett. You haven't yet seen much of war. Why, at Shiloh we—"

"Damn Shiloh!" Mr. Bennett said. "These are women and children we're talking about!"

Major Cameron rose and stalked angrily about. "Bennett," he said, "what do you news-paper people know about fighting Indians? They had to be taught a lesson! Every dead Kiowa is one less to burn and loot and kill along the Red River. That's our job—the Army's job—to keep peace out here. I must say, though, that it's a thankless job, with busybodies like you looking over our shoulder, meddlers that never give the Army a good word!"

"Be quiet, Hugh," the general ordered. Bennett and the newspapers were a fact, a powerful fact, and had to be gotten along with somehow. A general always had to think of appropriations time on the Hill. "We regret," he explained, "the killing of women and children. But there was no way to separate them from the fighting men. You could explain to your readers that we Army are human beings too—family men, many of us, who are only doing a job."

At about ten in the morning the Kiowas arrived to parley. There were about a dozen, dressed in their best buckskin shirts, moccasins with the long trailing flaps that tinkled as they moved, lean bodies ornamented with jewelry—necklaces of shells and bright beads, breastplates of pipestone, pendants on leather thongs, fetishes and amulets and silver disks attached to dusky braids. Many bore mute evidence of the fighting—a broken arm splinted with a whittled branch and wrapped with rawhide thongs, a bloodstained bandage around a head, a wounded leg assisted by a makeshift cane. But they were all proud, defiant in appearance. The general wondered if he were going to have more trouble with them.

Rainbolt—Pai Talyi—was dressed more simply than the rest. With no suggestion of defeat, the deserter strode proudly at the head of the party. The general felt a twinge of annoyance at the way his Caddo and Tonkawa scouts shrank back, averting their eyes as Pai Talyi passed by. There was little doubt of the power and influence of this long-maned and lanky ex-cavalryman.

It was a colorful scene, however. With approbation the general noticed that Mr. Bennett, apparently recovered from his disapproval of the Napoleon operations, was taking voluminous notes to describe it: the orderly rows of tents pitched on the newly green grass, the Kiowa band squatting in the middle of the throng of soldiers, himself in a commanding position sitting on a scrubbed-white canvas chair on a little rise where the Indians would have to look upward toward him. Cameron and the rest of his officers were in dress uniforms and sabers behind him. The cavalry—his cavalry—traveled prepared for anything. It was only good planning.

"Well!" he commenced briskly. "No need for an interpreter, is there?" He gestured toward old Ike Coogan, the comanchero.

Rainbolt, arms crossed over his chest, shook his head.

"Then," the general said, "we'd best get right to the business at hand." Pleasantly he leaned forward, gesturing. "You and your people are fairly caught, that's a fact. Nowhere you can go. That's hard lines for you, I suppose, but I intend to be fair. The point's been made—I don't think your Kiowas will cause the Army any more trouble. So we'll just sashay you all back to the post. There's a new agent there, a Mr. Tate, a Quaker. Your people will get along just fine with him. He'll teach you to farm, to plant seeds, you know, and harvest, to put up food so you won't starve the way Indians often do in winter. You'll find it a good life after a while."

"No," Rainbolt said.

"Eh?" Startled, the general cupped a hand to his ear.

"I said no. I speak for my People." Rainbolt flung wide his arm. "They say no! I say no! We are not farmers. We are hunters. No one can make farmers out of us."

Behind him Hugh Cameron made an angry

sound, but the general raised his hand, still speaking calmly in spite of the provocation.

"Now this really isn't the point at issue, sir. You and your Kiowas have been defeated. I am trying to make it easy on you. After all, we are reasonable people. But you must do what I say. There is no choice."

"Listen," Rainbolt said. "Listen to me." He rose, very tall, almost awkward in appearance, red blanket thrown over his naked shoulders and chest. Among the silent savages his presence seemed strange, almost bizarre, with the winter sun shining on his long hair. "We have not been defeated," he said. "A Kiowa is never defeated." He spoke slowly and deliberately, at the same time signing his words to the impassive warriors at his feet. "We do not come here as a defeated people. We come here to talk with you, to make a bargain."

The general was annoyed at the cheek of the scoundrel. Behind him Major Cameron stirred, saying in his ear, "Remember, sir—this man is a deserter, and wanted for murder, too! He's not a fit spokesman for anyone!"

"I know that, you fool!" the general muttered. "He's also Pai Talyi, or whatever the Kiowas call him!" Striving to suppress his annoyance, he said to Rainbolt, "I do not really see any grounds for bargaining."

"Listen to me," Rainbolt said again. He held up

two fingers. "You give us no choice, you say. All right. But we give you choices—two choices. The People want to be reasonable too."

The general feared that in spite of himself his face was beginning to get red.

"Choices?" he demanded. "What possible choices?"

"First," Rainbolt explained, tapping one long finger with the tip of the other, "you can let the People go. They want only to travel to their Cheyenne friends, out of the way of the white men. They only want to hunt buffalo again, to dance their dances, to sing their songs, the way they did before the white men came into the Red River country and pushed them off their lands."

The general wished that Bennett would stop scribbling so.

"Why, that's ridiculous!" he cried. "If I let the rest of you go on to the Cheyennes, why—what will happen? You'll just stir them up, too, and General Chapman will have an Indian war on *his* hands!"

Rainbolt tapped the other finger. "There is a second choice."

The general's bad leg suddenly began to pain him. He stretched it stiffly out, saying nothing.

"If you try to make us go back to your reservation, we will stay down there in those rocks and keep on fighting until the last man is dead. Yes, the last woman, too, the last child big enough to lift a gun and pull a trigger. It will take a long time and a lot of killing to get the rest of us out of those rocks. There are caves back under that ledge, and we will fight you forever!"

The general shook his head. "That would be very foolish."

Rainbolt shrugged. "It is a matter of viewpoint."

"The Army is only trying to be fair!" the general protested. "We do not want any more blodshed. You ought to try to convince your people of that!"

Rainbolt seemed not to have heard. He closed his eyes, seeming almost in a mystic spell.

"The People," he said, "those that are left—cannot escape. They know that. They are prepared to die there, in the rocks."

The general was uncomfortable. He had a vague feeling he was about to lose an important piece in an intricate chess game.

"What good would that do?" he asked.

Rainbolt opened his eyes. "At night," he said, "under cover of darkness, it would be possible for a small group of my People—perhaps only one man—to slip through your lines and reach the Cheyennes." Suddenly he raised clenched fists above his head in a prophetic gesture. "I will be that man!" he cried. The red blanket fell from his shoulders, the sun lit the fine golden hairs on his chest, bathed his long locks in radiance. "I am Pai Talyi!" he shouted. "Your Caddoes and

Tonkawas know me, and are afraid! I came down to save the People, and I will do so! I will go to the Cheyenne brothers and preach war against the whites—all whites!"

Excited, the Kiowas jumped up and surrounded Pai Talyi, eager to touch his medicine, yet awed and respectful. Some brandished weapons, and Major Cameron gave a low order to the detachment of riflemen behind him. But the general held up a placating hand, and gradually the commotion quieted. At Rainbolt's urging the Kiowa braves squatted sullenly on their blankets and were still. There was silence, an eerie silence, the only sound the riffling of the wind in the long grasses, the call of a crow wheeling overhead, a mule's bray from the picket line.

Thinking, the general rubbed his sore leg. By God, the madman would probably do it, probably *could* do it! One man—a determined man—could slip through and cause no end of trouble. In his pursuit of the damned Kiowas the general knew he had already strayed into Chapman's department. The fire-eating Chapman would have an apoplectic fit if anyone tampered with his Cheyennes.

Not only that, but Mr. Bennett of the *Press* was looking at the general very oddly, with a kind of reportorial wariness in his spectacled eyes. The *Press* had a large circulation in the East, and was regularly read in Washington. The *Press* had made quite a hooraw about the unfortunate death of old Satank last summer. Not only that, but the general suddenly remembered old Tate, the Quaker agent at the post, wattles quivering with indignation at the handsome expedition mounted against the fleeing Kiowas. *I won't have a thing to do with it! I'll report the whole thing to the Indian Bureau! You're motivated by viciousness and revenge, all of you.*

It was hard to be a general, surrounded as he was by damned Indian-lovers. He swore to himself, and stood up, putting most of his weight on his good leg. To match Rainbolt's deliberateness he chewed the end from a fresh cheroot and spat it out.

"I have heard your words," he admitted.

Someone proffered a match. He sucked at the cigar, watching the flame come and go as he puffed.

"You offer me a bargain," he said slowly. "That's damned insolent of you, you know. But somehow I respect what you say." He drew hard at the cigar, savoring the rich tobacco. Now that the weather had cleared, his cigars had dried out; this one was burning well. "The only thing," he went on, "is this. It seems to me that the bargaining is damned one-sided! You have given me certain assurances. But how do I know that your damned Kiowas won't give the Army more trouble if I let them go?"

"You have my word," Rainbolt said defiantly. "You see the power I have over them. They will die down there in the rocks if I tell them to. They will go away to the Cheyennes and live peaceably if I tell them to. They will do what I say!"

The general shook his head, tolerantly.

"Maybe you are Pai Talyi to them. But to me, you are an Eighth Cavalry deserter, first in trouble for insubordination, then under charges of murdering Sergeant Huckabee. After that, you broke out of the guardhouse, which is a third offense. I daresay there are still other crimes, but I'll settle for those." He shook his head, blowing a perfectly formed smoke ring that spun and shimmered its way upward in the sun. "No, just your *word* isn't enough for me."

Under the vestiges of summer tan, Rainbolt's face was pale. *He knows what I'm about to say,* the general thought with sly satisfaction, *and for the first time he is afraid.*

"No," the general went on, "your word isn't enough to bind the bargain." He stabbed the butt of the cigar toward Rainbolt. "What I want is *you!* I want Pai Talyi himself! I want Pai Talyi as a pledge for the good conduct of the Kiowas."

Rainbolt was silent, motionless. After a while, wondering, the squatting Kiowas looked up at him. One spoke to him in low, puzzled tones.

The deserter swallowed; the general could see the big Adam's apple move up and down. Then, hesitantly, Rainbolt started to gesture, to sign the general's words to them.

"Look out!" Major Cameron said sharply. He tugged at his holster. "There's going to be trouble!"

The Kiowas were indeed upset. As they grasped the import of Pai Talyi's words they sprang to their feet again, whooping and brandishing weapons. They ringed Rainbolt in defense, and one man snatched the deserter's hand and held it to his heart in sign of fealty.

"Don't be a fool, Hugh," the general warned. "Put away that damned gun! There's not going to be any trouble!" He had seen Rainbolt's face, and knew the answer.

"After all," he said to Rainbolt, "your heart bleeds for them, doesn't it? So it's little enough to ask—Pai Talyi for the freedom of his People." He chewed wetly on the cigar, relishing his cleverness. After all, two could bargain—and he needed some kind of trophy to bring back after the long hunt.

"Well?"

The Kiowas were still. They looked at Rainbolt with a kind of desperation. To give up Pai Talyi was like giving up Sun, Moon, Thunder, Rock, the Tai Me themselves. It was giving up deity.

Rainbolt swallowed hard again. His face was

pale, almost white. The long arms hung limply at his sides. "I—I—" He stammered something, then broke off.

I've got the poor devil, the general thought. Almost, he felt sorry for Philip Rainbolt.

"Well," he asked again, "what is your answer?"

Rainbolt's heavy locks hung over one eye in the Kiowa style, and he tossed his head back, looking at the general for a long time. But he did not seem to see the general, the officers in their dress blues, fourragères, medals, and ribbons. He did not seem to notice the waiting riflemen, the tents, even hear the snapping and cracking of the starred flag on its staff. He seemed to be looking far beyond all these—far distant in space, certainly, but perhaps distant in time also, back to a long-ago time.

"I must have your answer," the general insisted. "Otherwise, the truce is ended, and your people must prepare to fight again."

Rainbolt took a deep shuddering breath. The general could hear the sound of it making its way deep into the chest, then slowly expelled.

"All right," Rainbolt said in a low voice. "It—it is agreed."

Perhaps the Kiowas did not understand the words but they knew the meaning of the sigh, the half-inaudible response. A low cry burst from them. They clustered around Pai Talyi, grief-stricken, touching him awkwardly as though their groping hands could somehow strengthen him, restore him.

"Fine!" the general said. "I think it's a reasonable solution to the problem."

He did not have time to be impressed by the devotion and grief of the Kiowas as they mourned Pai Talyi. After all, it was high time to break off this exercise and get back to department head-quarters. His desk was probably stacked with urgent papers demanding action. Too, he had robbed Fort Sill of most of its effectives; it was time to return them and get back to business. He turned to Major Cameron.

"Take him into custody, Hugh. Put him in a wagon, and use manacles. Don't want any slip-ups."

Major Cameron's eyes gleamed. "Yes, sir."

"One thing!" the general warned. He looked hard at Cameron. "If anything untoward happens to the prisoner, I'll hold you directly responsible."

Major Cameron flushed. "Of course."

"This man—Pai Talyi or whatever he is called—is important to the Army. A symbol, you might say testimony, to this department's humane policy toward the Indians. And Hugh—"

"Sir?"

The general spoke very softly.

"If anything happened to him—why, Hugh, *I'd have your skin!*"

Rainbolt, wrapped in his red blanket, walked

slowly toward the general. "There is one more thing," he said. "I—I will need a little time."

"Time?" the general asked, impatient of delay. "Time for what?"

"Many things," Rainbolt said. "For one, to say good-bye to the People. For another"—he nodded toward Major Cameron—"I have a message for the major."

"Well, give it to him then!"

The deserter shook his head. "He—he will have to come with me." Rainbolt gestured toward the great limestone ledge. "Down there. The message is there."

The general's black brows drew warily together. "What kind of trickery is this?"

Rainbolt shook his head. "No trick. The major will not be harmed. And I will return in the morning, at sunrise, to keep my promise. I will go then, in the wagon, back to Fort Sill—and not until then."

"Can't wait that long!" the general said brusquely. He waved his hand toward the tents, the wagons, the Napoleon batteries, and the tethered horses and mules. "We've got to get moving!"

Rainbolt shook his head. "No," he said. "At sunrise I will be back."

Exasperated, the general threw his cigar into the grass and stamped on it. "All right, then goddamn it! But if you're not here when the sun comes up over that ridge"—he pointed toward the east—"we'll come and get you!" To Major Cameron he said, "Hugh, take a few men with you when you go—just in case."

Major Cameron stared at Rainbolt. "I'm not afraid of anything he can do," he said. "Go ahead, Rainbolt—I'll follow."

They went away then—Pai Talyi, the cavalry officer who had so long pursued him, the file of silent Kiowas—down the slope into the river bottom, through the lacy shade of the naked cottonwoods, finally into the near blackness of the tumbled rocks where the smell of death was all around them.

"Hello, Jerry," Major Cameron called to the surgeon, who had set up a hospital in a sandy clearing among the rocks. "How's it going?"

The young lieutenant wiped his forehead with the back of a hand. It was cold among the giant boulders where the sun did not penetrate, but he was sweating. His hands were filled with shiny surgical instruments and there was a spattering of fresh blood on his apron.

"Bad," he said, "very bad," and turned back to his work.

Rainbolt led Cameron up a staircase of fallen slabs. They stopped at a cup-shaped depression atop a giant boulder the size of a house. The depression was lined with blankets and buffalo robes, and a small fire smoldered near, an orange eye winking in the gloom. When she saw them a woman got up, hand over her mouth in a half-frightened gesture. But her eyes were wide and steady as she looked at Hugh Cameron.

"It was her idea," Rainbolt explained in a tired voice. "I didn't want it that way, but she had to talk to you once more."

"Hello, Hugh," Ellen Cameron whispered. Her voice shook, but she managed a hesitant smile. "How—oh, how are you?"

Major Cameron's dark face turned ashen. He looked at her unbelievingly, face working in emotion. One hand groped at his bearded chin in an effort to compose himself.

"Ellen!" he said in a choked voice. "Ellen!" He closed his eyes in disbelief, then opened them again; the fingers still worked near his mouth. "You were—we thought you were—they said—"

He took a wondering step toward her, but she drew back. He stopped, uncertain.

"Dead," she murmured. "Yes, I suppose you all thought I was dead. But things happened in a very strange way, Hugh. I—"

Angrily he pointed at Rainbolt. "You ran away —with *him!*"

"No!" she cried. "No! That was not the way of it at all, Hugh! I don't wonder you thought so. But I ran away to go to Memphis—to my Uncle Nestor and Aunt Alice Beecher. I was lonely— and you were so jealous."

"With good cause, I think," Major Cameron said.

She raised her eyes, looking at him squarely. "With no cause at all. I was a foolish young girl then—I am a little older, and not so foolish now. But I was faithful to you, Hugh. You will have to believe that." When he said nothing, only staring at her in that unbelieving way, she went on. "I ran away. But the teamster that took me became ill and died, the Mexican boys left, the prairie caught fire—" Remembering, she shuddered. "Philip passed by with his Kiowas, and they rescued me. Since then"—she looked at Philip Rainbolt—"I have been living with him."

Major Cameron made a gesture that seemed an attempt to wipe something away, to blot out a memory. "Come back with me!" he pleaded. "Ellen, I loved you! No matter what has happened, I still—"

"No," Ellen said. "We can't go back again, Hugh. That's all over." Gravely she touched her stomach. "I am carrying his child, you see. It is his child—and mine. I would not have it any other way."

Wildly, unbelievingly, he looked at her. "I don't believe it! Ellen, it's not true! Come with me, please! I've—I've got to have you!"

She shook her head. "No, Hugh," she said gently. "That's all over. You must go away now, and forget."

For a moment he stared at her. His hands

trembled as if he wanted to reach out, to touch her, to do anything to dispel the awful moment of reckoning. But when she did not move, only looked at him with that quiet and forgiving smile, it was too much. He blundered past Rainbolt, pushing him aside, and half-climbed, half-fell down the tumbled slabs of rock.

Watching together, they saw him walk swiftly past the surgeon, looking neither to right nor left, and disappear in the pale wilderness of the cottonwoods.

There were not many to say farewell to. Star Sister was dead, Crow Bonnet, Water Turtle, Heap of Bears and his wife, many others—too many others.

Each year when autumn approached the Kiowas performed a dance that bade farewell to summer with its good hunting, the warmth and happy times of the season. Now, resigned to Pai Talyi's going, they danced that dance and pounded their drums below the big rock where Ellen and Philip Rainbolt lay. They stamped and shuffled in dogged rhythm, a dancer occasionally calling out a lament. Finally, the Kiowas departed, quietly, one by one. A single drummer kept the beat. Finally he, too, picked up his drum and vanished into the night.

"It was wrong," Ellen murmured. "I—I should have not asked to see him again." She lay quietly in his arms. The camp was still, though from a long way off they could hear boisterous merriment from the cavalry bivouacs. "I so wanted to see Hugh one more time. I—I loved him once, you see, and I—I wanted to explain to him how it was."

He buried his face in her hair, letting the womanly scent bathe him in richness. He would want to remember that, when he was gone.

"Your uncle," he said, "and your aunt. They—"

"No!" she said, very firmly. "I will not go to them now. I will stay here, with your People, and wait for you."

"It may be a long wait," he said, a hollow feeling within him. When she did not speak, only pressed tighter against him, he said, "I—perhaps I will not come back."

She shook her head. "You will come back. I know it. And I will be waiting." Again, gravely, she touched her stomach. "*We* will be waiting. The People will be waiting. And my place is with them, until you come again."

Sometime during the night, she stirred. "What was that noise?"

"Nothing," he said. "I heard nothing."

"Nevertheless," she said drowsily. "Nevertheless, I heard something. Was it a shot?"

He pulled her warmer, tighter, against him. He was growing cold. "I don't know. Perhaps." Hearing the noise from the bivouac area, he said,

"Some of the soldiers are probably getting drunk. It has been a long campaign, and they are anxious to get home."

Early in the morning, a gray cold light seeping into the great cavern, he rose quietly. He picked up his zebat, and looked down at her. Perhaps it was better this way, to let her sleep. But as he left she woke, calling to him.

"I thought," he explained, coming back to bend over her, "I would leave without waking you. I didn't want to say good-bye."

She did not look at him, only lay quietly, staring at the smoke-blackened roof of the cavern.

"We have said our good-byes," she murmured. "Now, go away, Philip. I—I will hear the sound of your moccasins for a little while. Then the music will grow fainter, and fainter. Finally it will disappear, and I will know—I will know—"

Not looking back, he walked away, went down through the sleeping Kiowa camp. An old man, wounded in the head and arm, lay on a pallet of twigs and watched him go, raising a withered hand in salute as Pai Talyi passed by.

He was sitting in the wagon, manacled, when the sun came up to warm the dew-wet canvas of the top. All around were the sounds of the Eighth and the Ninth getting ready for the march to Fort Sill. In one hand Rainbolt still held the zebat; they had allowed him to keep that. From time to time he looked at it, drawing comfort from the decorations, the pennons, the signs of triumph—the scalps once taken by Cat, the Tonkawa, Stone Teeth's beaded corn pouch, the green calomel bottle, now empty. He was lost in thought, remembering the times, the places, when Ike Coogan came to the opening and looked in. The comanchero seemed uneasy.

"Hello, Ike," Rainbolt said.

Ike rubbed his grizzled chin, and spat.

"What did you say to him?" he asked.

Rainbolt was puzzled. "To who? What do you mean?"

"You ain't heard?"

Rainbolt shook his head. "I don't have the faintest idea of what you're talking about."

The old comanchero looked at him queerly. "Major Cameron killed hisself last night."

Rainbolt drew in a quick breath. "Killed—himself? Cameron?"

Ike nodded. He had a small chamois bag in his hand, and began to pick at the knot that closed it.

"In his tent. Right through the head with his revolver. Upset everyone some, I can tell you!"

Rainbolt remembered Ellen waking during the night at the noise she had dreamed. Or *had* she dreamed it?

"I'm sorry, Ike," he said. "I—I don't like for any man to end like that."

Ike stared hard at him. "You said something to him, or did something—I dunno what. But he came back here yesterday, they say, like a man that's seen the gates of hell! Stayed in his tent, wouldn't come out, finally shot hisself." Ike shook his head. "The general was shorely upset." His fingers worked at the knot of the chamois bag. "But it ain't any of my business," he concluded.

From somewhere came the sounds of "Boots and Saddles," brassy and strident in the rising sun. The trooper told to guard Pai Talyi climbed into the wagon, nodding curtly, and sat down, holding the carbine in the crook of his arm. Rainbolt thought back to a summer morning long before, when they tried to put Satank into a wagon, to carry him off to Jacksboro for trial. The old Kiowa would not go into captivity; he had wrested away the guard's gun, and been killed.

The guard, nervous, must have been thinking the same thing. He shifted his weight on the seat, moving farther away from Philip Rainbolt, tightening his grasp on the stock of the carbine.

"Look," Ike said, "goddamn it, I'm sorry! I never meant no harm—no real harm, anyway. I hated your guts, I did, but I didn't mean to have old Water Turtle and his folks slaughtered the way they was. I thought they'd just give up, see, when the general and all those troops came at 'em. I thought they'd just give you up, and go along peaceable, and that would be the end of it." He looked thoughtfully at Rainbolt. "You remember—a long time ago I said something to you? It was when I first seen you in Water Turtle's camp, after you busted out of the guardhouse. I said maybe I seen some good in you no one else seen. I was kinda jokin' at the time, but it looks like I spoke truth, don't it?"

The driver climbed on the seat of the wagon. Rainbolt could feel the vehicle tip slightly, creak a little on the springs, as the trooper settled his weight and picked up the whip.

"So," Ike said, "take this money, huh? The general give it to me for leadin' him to Water Turtle and the Kiowas and you. Just take it, will you, and remember I didn't mean no harm?"

Rainbolt shook his head. It was blood money.

"Goddamn it," Ike pleaded, *take* it! It's burning a hole in my goddamned hand!" His face was stricken, his ancient paw trembled as he held out the chamois bag. "Look—you'll need money! When you get to Fort Sill, you can hire you a lawyer, the way I always did. I can put you in touch with a lot of smart lawyers— they'll get a federal writ and spring you just like they always did me!"

Rainbolt felt a twinge of pity. Ike Coogan must have seen the compassion in his face.

"Hell," Ike cried, pushing the bag into Rainbolt's

hand, "you got a good chance to beat 'em! You never killed old Huckabee, I know that! They ain't got no proof! Old Tate will speak up for you, I bet, and that nosy reporter from the *Press* is on your side, too!"

Seeing Rainbolt's hand close uncertainly over the bag, he became almost gleeful.

"Christ, you're too important a man now for them to convict you in no drumhead kangaroo court-martial! Why, you're a symbol, like the general said. Why, you might even—"

His words were lost in the growing noises— the grinding of wheels, the shouts of teamsters, the crack of whips. Rainbolt waved to him. The wagon lurched forward, bouncing and swaying in the long grass. Ike Coogan finally stopped on a little hillock, shading his eyes with his hand, watching the vanishing wagon.

Beyond the comanchero Rainbolt saw the Kiowas, his Kiowas. They had come to see Pai Talyi leave; they stood silently, dozens of them, the remnants of Water Turtle's band, now *his* band, his people. From that distance he could not make out individual faces. Perhaps somewhere among the silent People was Ellen Cameron—he did not know. But he closed his eyes and could see her in his mind's eye. That was enough. He felt strangely content. Someday he would come back to the People—and to her. For now, that was enough.

BIBLIOGRAPHY

1. Battey, Thomas C. *The Life and Adventures of a Quaker Among the Indians*. Boston: 1876.
2. Dodge, Colonel Richard Irving. *The Plains of the Great West*. New York: Archer House, 1876.
3. Foster-Harris, William. *Look of the Old West*. New York: Viking Press, 1955.
4. Leckie, William H. *The Buffalo Soldiers*. Norman: University of Oklahoma Press, 1967.
5. ——. *The Military Conquest of the Southern Plains*. Norman: University of Oklahoma Press, 1963.
6. Mayhall, Mildred P. *The Kiowas*. Norman: University of Oklahoma Press, 1962.
7. Nye, Wilbur Sturtevant. *Carbine and Lance: The Story of Old Fort Sill*. Norman: University of Oklahoma Press, 1962.
8. *Pioneer Atlas of the American West*. San Francisco: Rand McNally & Company, 1956.
9. Rickey, Don, Jr. *Forty Miles a Day on Beans and Hay*. Norman: University of Oklahoma Press, 1963.

Center Point Large Print
600 Brooks Road / PO Box 1
Thorndike, ME 04986-0001 USA

(207) 568-3717

US & Canada:
1 800 929-9108
www.centerpointlargeprint.com